Dear Reader,

Home, family, community and love. These are the values we cherish most in our lives—the ideals that ground us, comfort us, move us. They certainly provide the perfect inspiration around which to build a romance collection that will touch the heart.

And so we are thrilled to offer you the Harlequin Heartwarming series. Each of these special stories is a wholesome, heartfelt romance imbued with the traditional values so important to you. They are books you can share proudly with friends and family. And the authors featured in this collection are some of the most talented storytellers writing today, including favorites such as Tara Taylor Quinn, Janice Kay Johnson, Jillian Hart and Shelley Galloway. We've selected these stories especially for you based on their overriding qualities of emotion and tenderness, and they center around your favorite themes—children, weddings, second chances, the reunion of families, the quest to find a true home and, of course, sweet romance.

So curl up in your favorite chair, relax and prepare for a heartwarming reading experience!

Sincerely,

The Editors

LYNNETTE KENT

lives on a farm in southeastern North Carolina with her five horses and five dogs. When she isn't busy riding, driving or feeding animals, she loves to tend her gardens and read and write books.

HARLEQUIN HEARTWARMING

Lynnette Kent

A Song for Kate

HARLEQUIN®
entertain, enrich, inspire™

Recycling programs
for this product may
not exist in your area.

ISBN-13: 978-0-373-36568-5

A SONG FOR KATE

Copyright © 2012 by Cheryl B. Bacon

Originally published as THE BALLAD OF DIXON BELL
Copyright © 2003 by Cheryl B. Bacon

www.Harlequin.com

Printed in U.S.A.

A Song for Kate

To the Southern Gentlemen I know best:
Frank, Barry and Ed.
And, as always, for Martin.
Love you, guys.

CHAPTER ONE

March
Boswell, Colorado

"YOU MAKING TIME with your sweetheart again, Dixie?"

"That ain't his sweetheart. That's his baby girl. Right, Dixie?"

Dixon Bell just grinned at the cowboys' teasing and kept walking at a slow, easy pace toward the three unbroken horses poised along one curve of the corral. The buckskin and the pinto danced away as he got close. The black quarterhorse mare knew him, though, and had come to trust him a little. Ears twitching, tail flicking, she watched him approach. She was nervous, sure. But willing to give him a chance.

"Hey, there, gorgeous," he crooned, coming to a stop by her shoulder. He put a hand on the smooth, warm skin of her neck. "Thanks for waiting for me. How's it going?"

She turned her head toward him, nosed his arm and chest, then jerked away as the buckskin came near again. Ears drawn flat against her head, eyes wide, the mare warned the other horse off.

"No need to be jealous, sweetheart." Dixon chuckled as he stroked his palm along her back. "I've only got eyes for you."

Talking quietly, he ran his hands over her ribs, her flanks, her chest, combed his fingers through her jet-black mane. As she calmed, he bent to stroke her legs, lifting each foot in turn, all the time praising her for standing still, for letting him have his way.

Then he straightened up and allowed the halter he'd hooked over his shoulder to drop down to his hand. "Remember this?" He held it under her nose, watched her sniff. "We got this on yesterday. Let's try again."

She wasn't happy about it, but did finally let him slip the soft halter over her nose and ears. Left to run wild in the Colorado hills since her birth two years ago, she hadn't been trained to accept human restraints. Though she balked when he hooked the lead rope to the halter, the mare eventually consented to be led around the corral without too much fuss…as long as the buckskin kept her distance. This quarter horse wasn't interested in sharing her man with anybody else.

"She'll make a good mount," the ranch foreman commented when Dixon left the corral. "You're sure taking your time, though. There's easier, quicker ways to break a horse."

"I'm not interested in easier and quicker," Dixon told him. "Usually that means some kind of pain for the animal. I'm content to take things slow, exercise a little patience."

"Next thing we know, you'll be hugging trees." The foreman gave him a friendly punch in the arm as they parted ways. Dixon returned the halter to the barn and headed to the bunkhouse to wash up for dinner. The aroma of grilled meat hung in the dry mountain air, teasing him with visions of steak and potatoes. He'd been up at dawn, heading out to round up cows and calves, and the only food he'd managed all day was a quick sandwich at lunch. *Hungry* wasn't a big enough word for the emptiness inside him tonight.

A stop at the mailbox on his way in rewarded him with a letter from home. Dixon delayed the pleasure until he'd changed into a clean shirt and jeans and washed his hands. Then he sat on his bunk to read what his grandmother, Miss Daisy Crawford, had to say.

She wrote, on lavender-scented paper in an old-fashioned, flowing script, of her friends, her neighbors, the civic meetings she went to, the goings-on at church. One of her cats had been sick, some kind of kidney problem, but the vet prescribed a new diet which seemed to be work-

ing. The weather had been strange this year—
variably cold and hot—so she never knew what
to wear when she went out.

Finally, I thought you might want to know
that we've had something of a scandal here
recently. L. T. LaRue—whom I would des-
ignate a scalawag, if there were still such a
thing—up and left his family a few weeks
ago. Moved out of their house and into a
love nest with his office secretary, declar-
ing to the world his intention to get a divorce
and marry this girl young enough to be his
daughter. I taught her in Sunday School just
a few years ago; I can't imagine what could
have happened to bring her to such a state.
This domestic tragedy leaves Kate LaRue—
she was Kate Bowdrey, as I'm sure you recall—alone to take care of two teenagers.
Poor Kate, she's struggled to put up with that
man these ten years, even adopted his children, and look what he's gone and done to
her. Some men just are not to be relied upon.

Dixon read those next-to-last paragraphs several times, then sat staring at his grandmother's
pale-blue stationery without seeing the words
written there. His brain had latched onto one important point—Kate Bowdrey LaRue was getting

a divorce. That meant she wouldn't be married anymore. As in single. Unattached. Available.

And that meant the time had come for him to go home.

July
New Skye, North Carolina

WITH A CLAP OF THUNDER, the sky broke open. Raindrops pelted the pavement and windows like bullets. Caught unprotected as she locked her car door, Kate LaRue shrieked and dashed for the nearest cover, which happened to be the green-and-white striped awning of Drew's Coffee Shop.

She was drenched when she got there, of course, her thin linen top completely soaked, her skirt hanging heavy around her waist. Water squished between her sandals and the soles of her feet.

"What a mess," she muttered. Around her, the smell of wet pavement blended with the pungent scent of coffee brewing inside the café. "I'll have to go back home and change."

"Beautiful day, don't you think?" The voice, strangely familiar, came from behind. "There's nothing like a southern rainstorm to clear the dust out of the air."

Kate turned to look at the tall, lean man standing with a shoulder propped against the brick wall that framed Drew's window. "You're joking, right?"

He had a wide, white grin in a tanned face. "Not at all. After a few years of eating dirt in the west Texas oil fields, I appreciate a good rain."

"You don't sound like you're from Texas." In fact, he sounded as if he'd lived right here in New Skye, North Carolina, his whole life. She should know him, Kate was sure. But good manners forbade that she just out and ask him what his name was.

"That's good. I'd hate to be identified by my twang." He straightened up to his full, lanky height. "Would you like to step inside and get a drink? Something to warm you up?"

Holding out his hand, he directed her to the entrance of Drew's, where she was certain he would open the door for her. Suddenly, just from the way he looked at her, she was equally certain he knew exactly who she was. She studied him for a long moment, searching for a clue in the rich, brown waves of his hair, the glint in his dark eyes, the tilt of his head. When the answer swam up from the depths of her memory, she caught her breath at the impossible rightness of it. "Dixon? Dixon Bell?"

His grin widened. "Took you long enough." He put his hands on her shoulders and leaned in to kiss her cheek. "I was beginning to think I'd have to show you my driver's license. How are you, Kate?"

Without thinking, she threw her arms around his neck and hugged him tight. "You've been gone so long. Welcome home!"

She felt his warm hands through the wet cloth on her back. His shoulders were wide and strong. He smelled of starch and soap. And man.

Another bolt of lightning struck, this one inside Kate.

"Oh, my." Drawing a shaky breath, she dropped back on her heels, letting her arms slide from his shoulders as she stepped away. "I still can't believe it's you. How long have you been home?" She pushed her hair off her face, registered how wet it was and knew what a mess she must look.

"Just a few days. I got here at the beginning of the week." Dixon slipped his hands into the pockets of his slacks and glanced at the shops and businesses around them. "Seems like there have been some pretty big changes. Downtown looks great."

"It does, doesn't it? We're not finished, of course. But I think the restoration and renovation projects are going really well, with no small thanks due to your grandmother. I haven't seen her for several weeks. How is she?"

"Hard to handle, as always. She mentioned that she's worked you to death on some of her committees."

Kate chuckled. "Miss Daisy's a pistol, that's for sure. I hope I have half her energy when I'm her age. I think we celebrated her eighty-fourth birthday at the women's club last month, didn't we?"

"That's right. And as far as I can tell, she keeps a cat for each year. I can't find a chair in the whole house that isn't occupied by at least one feline." He hunched his shoulders. "I'm not crazy about cats."

"She didn't have so many when you lived with her?" Dixon's parents had died when he was very young, so he'd grown up in his grandmother's house.

"One or two at a time—not a whole herd. I guess when I wasn't here, she collected cats to keep her company."

"So where have you been all these years? We haven't seen you since the summer after graduation."

He shook his head. "To get that story, Ms. Bowdrey, you have to let me buy you coffee."

She pretended to sigh in resignation, even as she smiled. "If I have to." But as she crossed the threshold, Kate realized she'd better set things straight. "By the way, it's LaRue."

His forehead wrinkled as he stood holding the door open. "I beg your pardon?"

"I'm married." She walked into the shop ahead of him. "My last name is LaRue."

Thunder pealed again and Dixon sucked in his breath. Kate's declaration hit him like a punch to the ribs. Miss Daisy had definitely mentioned a divorce in her letter. They hadn't talked about Kate since he'd been home—he wasn't prepared to let anybody in on his plans yet, not even the lady herself. But surely he hadn't misunderstood. Miss Daisy had said that L. T. LaRue wanted a divorce. Was Kate contesting? Did she intend to stay married to the jerk?

He couldn't ask her outright, of course. Not a mere fifteen minutes after they'd met for the first time in thirteen years.

Not even though he'd thought of Kate Bowdrey *LaRue* every single day since their high school graduation.

But today, at last, he could do more than just think about her. He followed her into the shop, taking great pleasure in the sight of her slim figure. Her long, coffee-dark hair lay heavy on her shoulders with almost too much weight, it seemed, for her graceful neck to support. She appeared fragile, in need of protection. And yet she'd held her family together in the face of her husband's desertion. His Kate was much stronger than she looked. The thought gave Dixon tremendous satisfaction.

As they sat down at one of the tiny tables with ice-cream-parlor chairs, he glanced around and took in their surroundings. "Drew's Coffee Shop is a real change from the newspaper and cigarette stand holding this space when I left. New Skye must be getting seriously upscale."

"We like to think we're coming into our own," Kate said earnestly, her hazel eyes wide and serious. With her face washed by the rain and her rich curls springing to life around her face, she looked very young, as young as his memories of her. But she was even lovelier than he remembered, which seemed almost impossible. "This hasn't ever really been the hick town it looked like. We're trying to adjust the image to reality."

"I don't know...I recall going to class with some real yokel types. Remember that guy Elmer? He wore overalls and plaid shirts and bright-yellow work boots to school every day?"

"Elmer Halliday." Kate nodded. "He sold his daddy's tobacco farm about ten years ago and bought a chain of convenience stores. He's one of the richest men in town these days."

"But does he still wear yellow work boots?"

"No, he wears Italian-knit shirts and custom leather loafers and spends a lot of time on the golf course at the country club."

Mouth agape, Dixon dropped back against his chair. "They let Elmer into the country club?"

"Well, his family can trace their roots in the area to the War Between the States. And all that money…" She shrugged. "There's a lot of new blood coming into town. Nobody can afford to be a snob these days."

"Hey, Kate, how are you?" As if to prove the truth of her words, a woman with blue, buzz-cut hair and a row of silver rings curling around the rim of each ear stood beside them. "Nasty storm, isn't it? What can I get you two?"

"Hi, Daphne." Kate tucked the laminated menu into its metal holder. "I'll have a mocha latte with whipped cream and cinnamon."

The waitress didn't have to switch her attention to Dixon—she'd been staring at him since she arrived at the table. "And for you, gorgeous?"

Dixon grinned and gave her a wink. "How about a double regular coffee?"

"I knew you were the strong silent type. Coming up."

When Daphne was out of earshot, he turned to Kate. "Definitely new blood."

Smiling, she shook her head. "So what have you been doing all this time, Mr. Bell? Where did you go when you left home?"

"Well, let's see…I hitched a ride out of town on an empty livestock truck and spent the first night on a picnic table in a state park in Greensboro."

Her jaw dropped. "You're not serious."

"The second day, I rode to Knoxville on an oil truck."

"And where did you sleep that night?" When he hesitated, she gave him a stern look. "I don't want the censored version."

"Yes, ma'am." He sketched a salute, though he was a little surprised at her forthrightness. The Kate Bowdrey he remembered had been vitally concerned with appearances and propriety. "A very nice woman took pity on me as I stood on a downtown corner in the pouring rain and she let me sleep on the couch in her apartment."

"'A very nice woman'?"

"She owned an all-you-can-eat pizza joint."

"You must have been so excited."

Dixon gave a hoot of laughter. "How would you know that?"

"I have a teenage son. I can imagine how he and his friends would react to all of that pizza." She grinned. "How long did you stay in Knoxville?"

"A few months. I got a job playing guitar in a bar, but the bar changed management, and music styles. Then I decided to move on. At least this time I had a car, so I headed west on I–40 toward Nashville."

Daphne brought their drinks. She stood close enough that her hip brushed Dixon's shoulder as she set down the mugs. "Anything else?" There was no mistaking the message underlying her simple question.

"Don't think so," Dixon said without emphasis. Daphne pouted all the way back to the serving counter.

Kate's eyes twinkled as she sipped her latte. "That was quite adept of you."

Dixon shrugged. "She's nice enough, but my hair's longer than hers. I couldn't handle it."

"So what happened in Nashville?"

He took a long draw from his coffee. "Didn't get there. At least, not right away."

"Why not?"

"Well, this was a used car, see, and I was a dumb kid. 'Bout as soon as I got it up to seventy miles an hour on the interstate, parts started popping off. I left a fender in Knoxville and a couple of springs in Dobbin, about eight miles west. The muffler dropped off in Timothyville."

Kate shielded her face with her hand. Her shoulders were shaking.

"Things got loud then, but I was bound and determined to make Nashville. When the transmission dropped, though, I knew I was done for."

"Oh." She gasped with laughter. "I imagine you might. What did you do?"

"I walked to the nearest town—'bout five miles, I guess. The first gas station I came to had a Help Wanted sign in the window. I didn't have much money and I had this seriously broken automobile. So—"

"Kate LaRue, I haven't seen you in weeks!" A willowy blonde wove through the tables, approaching like a ship at full sail. "Where have you been keeping yourself?"

Kate got to her feet to return an enthusiastic hug. "The kids and I spent some time at the beach after Mary Rose's wedding. How are you, Jessica?"

"I'm just fine, except for being a bit damp." Her glance took in Kate's wrinkled clothes. "You must have gotten caught in the downpour, too." Dixon thought her smile looked a little spiteful. Then her gaze turned to him and all the spite smoothed away into frank interest. "Hello there. I don't think we've met."

"Oh, but you have." Kate put a hand on the blonde's arm. "Jessica, this is Dixon Bell. Dixon, you remember Jessica Allen? She married Jimmy Hyde, who's now the district attorney."

Dixon put out his hand. "Sure, I remember. Good to see you again, Jessica."

"Dixon Bell?" Her voice went high with surprise, and then she was clutching him around the neck—not nearly the enjoyable experience Kate's hug had been. Though she was a lovely lady, he felt absolutely no desire to hold Jessica Hyde in return, and he drew back as soon as possible.

"Dixon Bell." Jessica shook her head, resting her hands on his chest. "I would never have believed it. We wondered about you for simply years. You sit right down and tell me where you've been all this time." She grabbed his wrist with one hand and turned a chair from a nearby table around with the other, then sat down, forcing him to sit, too. As an afterthought, she looked up at Kate. "Sit with us, Kate. I know you must be dying to hear about what Dixon's been doing."

Kate stayed standing, and Dixon knew he was doomed. "I most certainly am. But I have a couple of errands I can't put off any longer. So I'll let you two talk and I'll catch up later."

As she pulled the strap of her purse over her shoulder, Dixon rose to his feet again and moved so that he blocked Kate's exit. He put a hand on her elbow. "It was great to run into you." Leaning close, he brushed her soft cheek with his lips and got a whiff of the rose and spice scent that was her perfume. "I'm going to call you," he promised in a whisper. "Soon."

When he straightened up, she was staring at him like a startled rabbit. "I—I…" She took a deep breath. "Thank you for the coffee." As soon as he stepped out of her way, she hurried past him to the door of the shop. Dixon watched through the window as she braved the rain to unlock the door of the green Volvo she'd arrived in. In another second, she was gone.

He took a deep breath of his own and prepared

to face the ordeal ahead. "So, Jessica, you and Jimmy are married. Kids?"

She put a hand on his arm as he sat down. "Well, of course. Three boys, all of them playing ball just like you and Jimmy did. But I'm not the one who disappeared for so long. Where have you been?"

"Here and there." The story lost a lot of its pizzazz with the wrong audience. "Spent some time in Texas…"

KATE SHIVERED in her wet clothes as she came into the air-conditioned house from the steamy warmth outside. The absolute quiet reminded her that she only had an hour before she had to pick Kelsey and Trace up at summer school. In that hour she needed to get to the dry cleaner's and the hardware and grocery stores. She gasped as she realized she'd completely forgotten to collect the historical society programs from the printer's next door to Drew's Coffee Shop, which was why she'd gone downtown to begin with. What had happened to her mind? At two o'clock this afternoon, she'd been sure of completing all her errands on time.

And then Dixon Bell had stepped back into her life.

She couldn't quite believe he'd reappeared so suddenly, after thirteen years away. But he'd left with the same abruptness. Just a few days after graduation, while the members of their class were still celebrating by staying up late and sleeping until noon, Dixon had stopped showing up for the parties, picnics and get-togethers they'd thrown that summer before college.

No one in town had mentioned him since, not even his grandmother. Kate couldn't remember anyone who was particularly upset by his absence—he hadn't dated, had come to the prom by himself, she recalled. If he had been good friends with one or more of the boys, she didn't know who it would have been. Dixon was just... Dixon. A little weird, a lot unfocused, apt to go off by himself with the guitar he'd always carried to make music only he really listened to.

And now he was back, not at all the vague, blurred teenager she remembered, but a vital and incredibly attractive man. That moment when he'd held her against him still sang in her veins.

She caught sight of her reflection in the black door of the microwave—hair flat and tangled, makeup washed off by the rain, clothes still damp—and groaned. Not exactly the picture to inspire a man to romance.

Embarrassed and, to be honest, disappointed, she hurried up to her bedroom to repair the damage. Chances were slim she would encounter Dixon Bell again today, or ever again, but she did try to look her best when she went out. People tended to think better of you when you presented yourself well.

As she smoothed her damp hair into a ponytail, the phone rang. She should have let the machine answer it—she wasn't going to get to the cleaner's or the hardware and grocery stores at this rate—but she never could let a phone ring if she was there to answer.

"Hello?"

"You believed me when I said I'd call, right?"

Heart pounding, she sat on the side of the bed. "Dixon?"

"I just escaped from Jessica. I wish you hadn't let her run you off. She always did want to be the center of attention."

Kate smiled, because he was so right. "I—I didn't run off. I do have things to do."

"I'm sure of that. Can I see you when you get them all finished?"

"See me?"

"Yeah. Dinner, maybe?"

Her heart slammed to a stop, then started pounding again. "That sounds like...a date."

"It does, doesn't it?"

"But, Dixon..."

"Mmm?"

"I told you that I'm married."

"Well, according to Jessica, that's kind of a

technicality. I understand you're well and truly separated and on the way to a divorce." Kate drew a deep breath, embarrassed all over again at the idea of being talked about. "And before you get too upset, I didn't ask. Didn't mention your name. She volunteered the information. Better be careful what you tell Jessica Hyde."

"I am." But the separation and pending divorce were pretty common knowledge, she supposed. "Still, I don't think I should be dating."

"Okay. We won't call it a date. Just dinner for old friends."

He made her want to laugh. "It's not that simple. I have two teenagers to think about."

"Oh, yeah." That actually seemed to slow him down. "I'd say bring 'em along. But I kinda hoped to have you all to myself, the first time, anyway. How about tomorrow night? You could make arrangements for them and then we could get together."

Oh, how tempting. Kate blinked back tears as she realized how much she would love to have dinner with Dixon, just the two of them. "It sounds wonderful. But…" She drew a deep breath. "I can't."

"That's too bad. I was looking forward to catching up." He didn't sound angry, or even particularly disappointed. "You take care of yourself, okay? I'll talk to you again soon." Almost before she could say goodbye, he'd hung up on his end. That quickness gave her little hope that he'd cared one way or the other that she'd turned him down. But really, why should he?

Kate glanced at the clock and realized she had missed the window of opportunity to get groceries before picking up the kids. That would mean taking them along, with the resulting sulks and sighs. As children, they'd loved to join her in the adventure of shopping. These days, they seemed to expect the food to appear on the shelf or on the table, ready for consumption. Providing for them was part of her role as parent, Kate realized, a role she cherished with all her heart. Sometimes, though, she wished the decisions and responsibilities could rest with somebody else. Or at least be shared. But her ex-husband-to-be didn't feel much like sharing anything with her these days. Least of all responsibilities.

Waiting in the school parking lot a few minutes later, Kate tried to balance her checkbook in an attempt to keep her mind off Dixon Bell. Not a very successful effort, she had to admit. Instead of focusing on the numbers in her register, she kept staring off into space, thinking about his smile, picturing him sleeping on a picnic table one warm summer night so long ago. What courage it must have taken to strike out on his own. She couldn't imagine being completely free of other people's expectations and regulations.

So deep in reverie was she that she didn't realize Kelsey had come out of the school building until the car door swung open.

"Hey." Her daughter dropped into the front seat of the Volvo, her blond hair gleaming in the sunlight, her brown eyes and heart-shaped face enhanced by makeup as perfect as only a teenage girl's could be at this hour of the day. She'd obviously just renewed her cologne, and the latest fashion scent filled the car.

Kate smiled in greeting. "Hey, yourself. Where's your brother?"

"He'll be here in a minute. He had to get a book out of the library for his homework."

"How was class today?"

Kelsey rolled her eyes. "Booorrring. As usual." A genius when it came to putting together the right clothes, she wasn't a terribly focused student.

Without warning, Trace appeared in the passenger-side window and opened the door his older sister was leaning against. "You get the back seat. You had the front this morning."

Kelsey gave an unfeminine snort. "Like I'm going to get out and get in again?"

"Yeah, you are." Trace was a replica of his father, with the same athletic build, the same handsome face, the same dark-blond hair and bright-blue eyes. When he got angry, as now, the resemblance was even more striking.

"No, I'm not." In an instant, their voices were strained, their faces heated. "You can have the front seat both ways tomorrow."

"Oh, sure, that'll happen. Get out, Kelsey." He reached in and took hold of her arm, trying to pull her out of the car. Where once brother and sister had been staunch allies, in the last few months they had become adversaries, if not downright enemies.

But Kate drew the line at physical conflict. "Trace, that's enough."

He didn't seem to hear her as Kelsey kicked out with a foot aimed at his knee. "Get lost."

"You get lost." The brawl intensified, with more pushing and shoving. A pair of kids crossing the parking lot had stopped to watch, and an approaching teacher stood gazing, openmouthed, as Kelsey and Trace pummeled each other.

Kate didn't try to be heard over the yelling. Gritting her teeth, she planted the heel of her hand on the car horn and pressed down. Hard.

Trace jerked back at the blare of sound, which gave Kelsey a chance to get in the last blow. The boy staggered back against the car parked next to them, arms clutched over his stomach. "I'll get you for that," he panted.

Kelsey swung her legs into the car and closed the door without deigning to answer. After a minute, Trace fumbled his way into the back seat, where he curled into a ball, his head on his knees.

They rode home without speaking. Once inside the house, Kate didn't have to tell the kids to go to their rooms—isolation was intentional and immediate on both their parts. She sank into a chair at the kitchen table and put her head down on her arms, too numb to think about how to deal with Kelsey and Trace.

And she still didn't have anything in the house to cook for dinner.

THE ONLY PHONE CONNECTION in all the fifteen rooms of Magnolia Cottage was in the front hall, which didn't allow for much private conversation. Miss Daisy came down the stairs just as Dixon hung up from his call to Kate.

She paused on the last step. "I gather from the frown on your handsome face that your dinner plans fell through."

"Yes, ma'am, they did." He tried to erase the frown. "That's okay—there'll be another night."

At the mirror beside the front door, his grandmother checked the smooth sweep of her silver hair, always worn in a knot on the crown of her head, then dabbed a little powder over her fine skin and checked the set of her lavender suit jacket. Convinced she was perfect—as, indeed, Dixon thought she was—she turned and put a hand on his arm.

"Why don't you come with us, then? We'd love to have a good-looking male at our table to pass the time with. LuAnne Taylor just loves to flirt with younger men."

Dixon lifted her hand and kissed the cool fingers, feeling them tremble just a bit in his hold. She smelled like his childhood—lavender water and talc and Dove soap. "You're sweet, Miss Daisy. But I think I'll let you go on without me. I might not be the best of company tonight." He wanted to treat Kate's refusal lightly, but the disappointment harkened back to the old days, when getting turned down by Kate Bowdrey had changed the course of his life. At seventeen, a boy was permitted to take love so seriously. By the time he'd reached thirty, he really ought to have gained a little perspective.

"If you say so, dear." Miss Daisy patted his cheek with her free hand. "I'm just grateful to have you home again." Outside, a car horn beeped. "Don't wait up—sometimes we go to LuAnne's and play bridge until the wee hours."

Dixon opened the front door. "Miss Daisy, you're a wild child."

She flashed him the smile that had captivated most of the men in New Skye at one time or another. "Of course. At my age, what else do I have left to do?"

Chuckling, Dixon escorted her down the house steps so she wouldn't have to depend on the rickety railing, and held her arm as they went toward the twenty-year-old Cadillac waiting at the end of the walk. The crumbling brick pavers made the footing shaky, at best, but the grass on either side was too high and too weed-grown to walk through. He was surprised one of the older ladies who visited his grandmother hadn't fallen and hurt herself before now.

As Miss Daisy settled herself in the Caddy, Dixon spoke with Miss Taylor. "Don't y'all get too rowdy tonight. I want to be able to hold my head up in town tomorrow."

"The very idea." Miss Taylor pretended to be embarrassed. "Just four old friends having dinner together. What could be more refined?"

Dixon shook his head. "Four wild women is more like it, I'd say."

"LuAnne, Alice is waiting for us," Miss Daisy commented. "And you know how she fusses when she has to wait."

With the ladies inside and the windows rolled up against the humid evening, the Caddy followed the curve of the driveway and headed down the quarter-mile gravel lane toward the street. Dixon turned toward the front porch, hands in his pockets, wondering what he would do for dinner.

But then he caught sight of the house, gleaming white in the twilight, and forgot his train of thought. An antebellum relic built by his many-times great-grandfather, Magnolia Cottage had been a plantation house before a bad economy and an ugly war stripped away most of the land, leaving only a few acres of gardens around the main building. The Crawfords and Bells had never been very lucky with money, so the gardens had eventually fallen into a state of disrepair, followed soon enough by the house itself. Growing up, Dixon hadn't recognized the problems, but after so long away, he was appalled at the conditions in which his grandmother continued to live.

Not dirty, no…Miss Daisy had a woman in twice a week to keep the place clean. But the plaster walls and ceilings were crumbling as badly as the brick walk. Floorboards were loose all over the house. Miss Daisy had learned to avoid certain steps and particular danger spots, but Dixon had banged a shin with an exploding board in the bedroom floor on his first night at home, leaving him with a deep bruise.

There was no central air-conditioning, of course, only window units in the rooms Miss Daisy used. The kitchen was old, the appliances barely functional, the bathrooms—two of them for the whole house—archaic. Magnolia Cottage needed a serious renovation before it could serve as a home to raise a family in. Which he hoped to do, if only Kate Bowdrey LaRue would cooperate.

While he was pondering the possibilities, enjoying the way the humid air held the scent of leaves and grass and pine, a dark-blue SUV pulled around the curve of the driveway and stopped in front of the house. Dixon didn't recognize the man who got out and came to join him.

The stranger nodded toward the house. "A wreck, ain't it?"

Dixon ignored a flare of temper provoked by the insult to his home. The guy was a clod, but that was no reason to get mad. "Needs some work, definitely."

"You Dixon Bell?" He wore mirrored sunglasses and a pink knit shirt and had "let's make a deal" written all over him.

"I am."

"Well, you're just the man I'm looking for, then." Turning, he stuck out his hand. "I'm L. T. LaRue. And I'll pay you three hundred thousand cash to let me take this disaster off your hands."

CHAPTER TWO

DIXON KEPT HIS FISTS in his pockets. "Thanks, but no thanks." This was the jerk who had left Kate—and his own kids—to be with another woman. No way was he going to dignify the man's existence with a handshake.

LaRue waited a few seconds, then let his arm drop. The grin stayed on his face, considerably stiffer than before. "We can deal on the price. I just wanted you to know I'm interested."

"No, we won't deal. I'm not selling."

"Aw, come on, Dixon. The place is falling down around your ears. Your grandmother needs a decent place to live out her old age. Let me build you a new house and get you out from under this white elephant."

Dixon imagined the pleasure of planting his knuckles directly under the bridge of those shiny shades, but decided not to start a brawl on his own front lawn, weedy though it might be. "Like I said, Mr. LaRue, I'm not selling. Have a good evening." He headed up the walk, leaving LaRue behind.

But Kate's husband did not, apparently, get the message. "I'll give you four hundred grand," he called as Dixon climbed the semicircular steps that had been built with bricks made on the property more than one hundred fifty years ago.

"No, thanks."

"Four-fifty's my top offer!"

Gritting his teeth, Dixon shut the hand-carved mahogany front door between himself and L. T. LaRue. He would have liked to punch a wall, but there were enough holes in the plaster already. Out in Colorado, he could have saddled up and galloped his horse through the sagebrush until they were both tired enough to sleep.

But he'd left his horses—Brady, the bay gelding, and Cristal, the quarter horse mare he had yet to break to saddle—at the ranch until he could find the right place to board them in North Carolina.

Meanwhile, the evening was wearing on and he hadn't had his dinner. Maybe some good food would take the edge off his temper, mitigate his urge to murder L. T. LaRue. And since he doubted Miss Daisy's cats would be willing to cook for him, Dixon grabbed the keys to his truck and headed for the one place in town he could be sure of getting a decent meal and friendly company.

If he couldn't be with Kate, the folks at Charlie's Carolina Diner were the next best thing.

KATE FELL ASLEEP at the kitchen table and woke to find Kelsey staring down at her. "What are you doing?"

She sat up, wincing at the stiffness in her back. "I'm not sure. What time is it?"

"Almost eight."

"It's not!" But, of course, it was. Kate braced her palms against the table and pushed herself to her feet. "Um…let me see what I can find to make for dinner." Standing at the door to the pantry, with her mind still fogged by the wisps of a dream, she couldn't seem to find much inspiration. "We're down to the bare bones here. Mushroom soup, anyone?" Kelsey stuck her tongue out. "Refried beans?"

"We could have burritos."

"Except there's no cheese, no salsa and no tortillas. Just beans."

Trace came into the kitchen. "Gross."

Kate agreed. "No eggs, no butter, no pasta or sauce."

Kelsey crossed her arms. "So let's go out somewhere."

For once, Trace agreed with his sister. "Sounds good."

Kate shook her head. "I don't have enough cash for fast food." And she really didn't like eating out of a paper bag.

"So we can go someplace that takes plastic."

"Possibly." She looked at her kids. Trace wore the oversize T-shirt and hugely sagging pants that comprised the required uniform among his friends. Both pieces had been ironed at the beginning of the day, for all the good it had done. Kelsey's shorts were just that—barely conforming to the dress code that required them to reach her fingertips. Once home, she had changed the relatively modest shirt she'd worn to school for a tank top.

As for herself…well, she was decent, in shorts and a T-shirt, but not really dressed. "Where could we go at this hour, without changing clothes?"

Kelsey snapped her fingers. "I saw a sign at the diner. Charlie takes plastic now."

"Really? I haven't eaten there in years." Kate wasn't sure why, but the suggestion seemed like the perfect solution for her dilemma tonight. "So, here's the deal. Kelsey, you put some kind of shirt over that tank top."

"Why?"

Kate ignored the question. "And the two of you agree not to fight, not even to insult each other for the next two hours. If you get into an argument while we're eating in public, I will drag you out by your ears and you'll be grounded for the rest of the summer. And that's a promise."

The two teenagers glanced at each other out of the corners of their eyes, a kind of mutual commitment. Kelsey looked at Kate again. "Do I really have to wear a shirt?"

"Only if you want to drive the car."

Fifteen minutes later, Kelsey stopped the Volvo in front of the diner. Kate let out a long, relieved breath. "That was good. You're getting to be a very smooth driver."

The girl's increasing confidence did not, however, serve to ease Kate's anxiety about being responsible for teaching her daughter to drive. And in just two years, she would have to start all over with Trace.

He walked a step behind as she and Kelsey crossed the parking lot, past a couple of pickups parked next to each other near the front door. "Next time, Kelse, maybe you could park in a regular space."

Kelsey turned and stuck her tongue out at him. "There aren't any spaces, you jerk. It's all gravel."

"But people usually line up at the same angle, in a row, more or less. You aren't anywhere close to these trucks. Talk about dumb."

Kate gave him a quelling glance. "Talk about this anymore and we're going home without dinner."

Since Trace ate almost constantly, in order to support his still-growing frame, the threat worked beautifully. The three of them got inside the diner without another cross word being exchanged.

The bell on the door jingled as they came through, drawing the attention of the four people talking at the counter. Kate was aware of Abby Brannon and her dad, Charlie, the owners of the diner, and Adam DeVries, one of her classmates from high school...familiar faces she might have expected to find here any night she chose to come. But the fourth person was, again, totally unexpected.

"Dixon?" She whispered his name, feeling as if she'd conjured him up from her dream in the kitchen.

But he heard her and got to his feet, looking just as good as he had this afternoon—tall and cool in khaki slacks and a light-blue dress shirt with the sleeves rolled back. "Hey, Kate. Two accidental meetings in one day—I'd say I've got a lot of good luck going for me. And it's not raining this time."

"No...no, it's not." Thankfully she had combed her hair and put on some lipstick before she left the house. "It's a lovely evening." She recovered her manners and pulled away from his deep-brown gaze. "Hi, Abby. How are you?"

"Just fine." The other woman came around the counter. Hands on Kate's shoulders, Abby kissed her on both cheeks. "I'm so glad you're here. The kids come in all the time, of course, but I only get to see you out in the car, waiting to take them home. Have a seat." She led them to a booth on the wall. "What can I get y'all to drink?"

The kids ordered soft drinks and Kate asked for iced tea. Abby whisked away…and then two tall, handsome men pulled a freestanding table and a couple of chairs over to extend the booth. Adam sat down on Kate's side of the table and Dixon sat across from him.

"It'll be easier on Abby this way," Dixon explained when Kate looked at him. "If you don't mind?" His grin was apologetic and yet confident, inviting her to share a private joke.

"Of course not." And she didn't, except that seeing him again had seriously disrupted her ability to think. Her heart was pounding under her ribs, her breath had caught in her lungs. She didn't think she could actually eat in this state.

Kelsey and Trace were staring at Dixon, confusion and even a little suspicion on their faces. Recalled to her responsibility, Kate made the introductions. "Dixon, these are my children. Kelsey and Trace, this is Dixon Bell. You've met Miss Daisy Crawford—he's her grandson. He went to school with Abby and me, but he's been gone for a long time and just came home. You know Mr. DeVries, of course." She only hoped they wouldn't comment on the fact that DeVries Construction competed with their dad's company for business around town. "How are you, Adam?"

Adam nodded toward the kids, then gently shook the hand she extended. "J-just f-fine, Kate. I t-trust you're the s-s-same. All r-recovered f-f-from the w-wed-ding?" Courtly in manner, tall, with dark hair and a construction worker's muscles, Adam should have been anybody's dream husband. Kate had never understood why he was still single.

Dixon leaned forward. "Somebody's just married?"

Kate met his gaze. She could feel herself blushing, though there was no reason to be embarrassed. "Pete Mitchell and my sister, Mary Rose, got married a few weeks ago."

"That's terrific. I haven't had a chance to call Pete since I've been home. I'll be sure to look him up and offer my congratulations."

"He p-p-plays b-basketball on S-Saturday mornings," Adam commented. "With Tommy C-Crawford, Rob Warren and m-m-me. F-find one m-more player and w-we could g-go three o-o-on three."

Trace looked over at the suggestion, then quickly went back to staring out the window into the growing twilight. But Kate saw that Dixon had noted his interest.

"I'll see what I can do," he said just as Abby

came back with their drinks. Then he turned toward Kelsey, on his right. "I noticed you got out on the driver's side. You're working on getting your license?"

"Uh-huh." Kelsey darted a glance in Dixon's direction, but didn't meet him eye to eye.

"I learned to drive in my grandmother's New Yorker—this big yellow boat of a car, 'bout thirty-some years old now but it only has fifty thousand miles on it because she never goes more than a few miles outside the county line. I never did learn to parallel park that monster—the officer who gave me the test was a second cousin once removed, or something like that. He let me slide."

"Parking is the worst," Kelsey agreed. "Backing up is almost as bad."

Dixon nodded. "It's always hard to know which way to turn the wheel."

Trace snorted, but Kelsey was captivated. She and Dixon embarked on a discussion about driving that lasted through most of dinner. Listening to their easy dialogue, Kate wondered where Dixon's inordinate charm had come from. When had the awkward, inappropriate boy become such a lady's man? Miss Daisy possessed more than her fair share of social skills, of course, but Kate didn't remember a single hint in the young Dixon Bell of the charismatic skill he was using to draw Kelsey out of herself.

And then she wondered if he'd used that same skill on *her* this afternoon, if the flattering interest she'd basked in was just a tool Dixon plied on any woman within talking distance. Her soon-to-be ex-husband had been a very smooth operator fifteen years ago when she'd first known him. Still was, if his success with various younger women around town was all that rumor reported. Recently, so she'd heard, he'd settled down with just one of those young women and was planning to marry her. Despite his image as a man about town, L.T. was a conventional soul at heart. Perhaps he'd just needed to find the right person...

A person who wasn't *her*. The knowledge that L.T.'s real problem with their marriage had been as simple as falling out of love with his own wife struck Kate with the force of a felled tree. Devastated all over again, she stared down at her chicken casserole and knew with complete certainty that she couldn't possibly manage another bite.

DIXON SAW a stricken look take over Kate's beautiful face, but couldn't figure out what might have caused it. He and Kelsey were getting along just fine—he'd exerted himself to reach out to her, wanting to make sure Kate knew that her kids were no barrier, as far as he was concerned. The boy would be harder to get to know. Trace had a hunger about him that Dixon had seen in runaways and abandoned teenagers, a hunger for attention, for guidance, which Dixon had no trouble at all attributing to the boy's father. L. T. LaRue had left his son at a vulnerable point in the boy's young life, with an emptiness that only a father could fill. Dixon understood that void, having grown up without his dad. At least he'd had Miss Daisy. And Trace had Kate. But even the most loving mother couldn't completely take a father's place.

"So what's everybody having for dessert?" Abby Brannon stood at his shoulder, surveying the remains of their meal. "Kate, honey, you've hardly touched your food. Is something wrong?" Kate shook her head and Abby didn't press for an answer. She moved around the table clearing plates, a woman of ample curves and ample concern for everyone she encountered. He remembered her as a shy girl, coping with her mother's terminal illness even as she got ready to leave high school and start her own adult life. While he had struck off on his own, ranging far and wide in an effort to discover who he was, Abby had stayed at home. Was she satisfied with what she knew about herself? About the rest of the world?

Then again, Dixon wasn't sure he was satisfied, after everywhere he'd been and everything he'd done. And look at Kate—valedictorian of the graduating class, voted Most Likely to Succeed, the one student among them whom everybody was sure would launch a brilliant career and make her mark on the world. As he recalled, she'd planned to be a lawyer like her dad. Thirteen years later, she was a spurned wife in the same little town she'd grown up in. Yet another of life's ironies.

She certainly didn't seem happy, didn't radiate the kind of confidence and joy he remembered adoring in her all those years ago. She was still breathtaking, with her dark hair, her pale, perfect skin and her slender figure, but muted, as if a shadow hung over her life. The shadow of L. T. LaRue.

"Who are you planning to kill?" Abby leaned over to take his plate and slide the knife out of his clenched fist. "And what do you want for dessert? Lemon meringue pie? Chocolate cake and ice cream?"

Dixon deliberately relaxed. "If I told you, I'd have to kill you, too. And just coffee, thanks. I'll save dessert for tomorrow."

"All you disciplined people." Abby sighed. "Why do I spend my time making pies for people who won't eat them?" Shaking her head, she headed toward the kitchen with a trayful of used plates and glasses balanced on one arm.

"I don't know how she does it." Kate, too, was

shaking her head. "Always smiling, always ready to serve, and she works harder than anybody I know."

"A-Abby's a w-wonder." Adam leaned back in his chair. "Charlie s-s-still comes t-to w-work, but s-since his heart attack, he m-mostly v-visits with the c-customers. Abby's d-d-definitely the p-prime mover around here."

The bell on the diner's front door jingled, announcing new arrivals. Dixon glanced over out of curiosity, only to have his gut tighten with a combination of irritation and dread when a young woman wearing a mind-bending red dress stepped inside, followed by L. T. LaRue.

Beside Dixon, Kelsey gasped and stiffened. On the other side of the table, Kate and Trace and Adam couldn't see, without turning around, what was going on. But all Kate needed was her daughter's face. As she stared at Kelsey, reading the girl's reaction, what little color she had left in her cheeks drained away. She pressed her lips together for a few seconds and took a deep breath.

"Well, this has been fun." Her voice shook slightly. "But Kelsey and Trace have homework, so I think we should be getting home. Adam, if you'll excuse us—"

DeVries had taken a quick glance over his shoulder to gauge the situation. "Of c-course." He got to his feet to let Kate slide out of the booth.

Dixon did the same for Kelsey, all the while keeping an eye on LaRue. Abby, bless her heart, had herded L.T. and his girlfriend to the other side of the diner. For a minute, Dixon thought disaster had been avoided.

But LaRue let his companion sit down and then strutted across the room to stand directly in Kate's path of escape.

"Well, look here. What an interesting group this is." He put his hands in the pockets of his slacks and rocked back on his heels. "Hey, Trace, Kelsey. I was looking forward to seeing y'all on Saturday for breakfast. How's school going?" He sounded genial enough, if a little distracted. And he didn't wait for an answer from the kids. "You're keeping strange company these days, Kate. Selling secrets to my biggest rival?" LaRue's laugh set Dixon's teeth on edge.

Kate shook her head. "Simply visiting with old friends, L.T. Have you met Dixon Bell? He went to school with Adam and me, and has just come home after a long time away."

"I have, in fact." LaRue nodded at Dixon. "Which is why I'm really interested to see him talking with the head of DeVries Construction. Thought you'd get a better offer, did you, Dixon? I'm telling you that's not likely."

"And I'm telling you I don't care what the offer is, LaRue. Magnolia Cottage is not for sale."

Dixon strived for the same calm Kate had demonstrated. LaRue had already made him mad once tonight. He didn't intend to repeat the experience. That would give the man too much importance.

"Y-you m-must have a p-p-persecution complex, LaRue." Adam shook his head and gathered up the checks Abby had left on the table. "I-I've got a-a-all the w-work I c-can handle. I d-d-don't n-need to go h-harassing p-p-people to s-sell me their a-ancestral homes." He turned to Kate, put a hand on her shoulder and leaned in to kiss her cheek. "I enjoyed s-seeing you again. Y'all, t-too," he said with a glance at Kelsey and Trace. "I'll t-take care of the b-bill."

"Oh, Adam, you don't have to do that."

He gave her a wink. "I—I know. Call me, Dixon."

"Will do."

In the silence Adam left behind, LaRue narrowed his focus to Kate. "Kinda late for my kids to be out, isn't it? Don't they have homework? Not to mention a curfew, after all that trouble they caused last spring?"

"Yes, and yes, and yes." Kate put the strap of her purse on her shoulder. "So we'll say goodbye and let you get to your dinner." She took a step that brought her within inches of LaRue, who grinned but didn't move. "You're in my way, L.T. Please let me go by."

Her husband—ex-husband?—held her in place until Dixon started around the table. Then LaRue retreated. "See you bright and early Saturday, kids. Don't be late."

Like mice caught out in the kitchen when the light was turned on at night, Trace, Kelsey and Kate scurried out of the diner while L.T. had his back turned toward them on the way to his table. Dixon stood for a minute, considering the possibility of a showdown, here and now, but decided Abby and Charlie didn't need the hassle. The time would come, though. No doubt about that. So, with a wave toward Abby behind the counter, he headed for the door.

Outside in the hot July night, Trace and Kelsey were arguing about something as they unlocked the Volvo. "Come on, Kate," Kelsey called. "Let's go."

But Kate had stopped just beside the front of Dixon's truck, as if her legs wouldn't take her any farther. When he put a hand under her elbow, he could feel her whole body tremble.

"Are you okay?"

She turned sightless eyes upon him. "Um…I don't think so. I need a minute. Which is silly, isn't it? Nothing happened. There's no reason to be so upset." She put her hand over her eyes. The deep breath she drew shook with the sound of tears.

Aware of the lighted windows behind them, Dixon pulled her around until the body of the truck stood between Kate and the diner. Then he opened the truck door, put his hands around her narrow waist and lifted her onto the passenger seat. He made himself let go quickly. She didn't need another predator stalking her tonight.

But as she sat there, elbows on her knees and head in her hands, he wrestled with the powerful urge to close his arms around her and never let go. He wanted to put himself between Kate Bowdrey and the rest of the world, make sure nothing and nobody ever hurt her again. His heart ached with the need she had always inspired in him. And he couldn't let one bit of what he was feeling show.

Someday, he would be free to tell her how much she mattered to him. Surely, someday.

But not yet. So he stood stiff and silent while Kate struggled alone with her despair.

Kate knew she was being weak, knew she shouldn't give in to the anguish L.T. provoked in her these days. When she knew she would see him, she could prepare herself and get through the encounter pretty well. But accidental meetings like this just swept under her defenses, gave her no chance to control her reaction. And so here she was, quivering like a beached jellyfish.

With Dixon Bell standing there watching.

At the realization, she jerked herself upright.

She'd accepted his help, let him practically hide her from the world, then forgotten he was there. "I'm so sorry," she gasped as her cheeks heated up. "What you must be thinking…" She couldn't meet his gaze, and she couldn't get out of the truck because he was standing right in front of her.

His fingertips brushed across her cheek. "I'm thinking you'll be well rid of that jerk. And that I'm really glad I got to have dinner with you tonight after all."

Something in his rich voice encouraged her to look up. She found no pity in his eyes, only a depth of understanding she would never have expected.

"Me, too," she admitted, under the spell of his smile. And discovered that she actually felt free to smile back.

But darkness had fallen while she huddled in Dixon's truck. Loud rock music blared across the parking lot from the Volvo where Trace and Kelsey waited. Kate sighed, sat up straighter. "I'd better go."

She thought he would step back and let her hop down from the high truck seat. Instead, he placed his hands on her waist and swung her around and down, setting her gently on her feet. She felt a little dizzy, a little breathless as she stared up at him.

"Thank you. For everything."

Again, he stroked his fingers over her cheek. "My pleasure. Good night."

She lifted her hand, backed up a couple of steps and then, reluctantly, turned toward the Volvo. With great resolve, she managed not to look around again until she had the car door closed and her seat belt fastened. Dixon was still standing by his truck, watching, with his hands in his pockets and one foot crossed over the other. When she waved, he waved back. Then Kelsey turned the car onto the highway, and they left the diner behind.

Back to the real and dreary world, Kate told herself. When she thought of the expression in Dixon's eyes, however, the gentleness in his voice, his touch, she couldn't repress a surge of hope.

Or maybe not.

L.T. PRETENDED TO READ the menu, though he pretty much always ordered the same dinner when he came to Charlie's. He pretended to listen as Melanie chattered on about her mother's new boyfriend and her sister's old boyfriend and...whatever. As long as he said something every once in a while, she was happy just to keep talking and believe he heard everything she said.

"That so?" he said when she paused.

She gave him her little-girl smile and started up again.

Charlie Brannon limped over to their table, blocking L.T.'s view of Kate and the kids as they left the diner. "What can I get y'all tonight?" The old man had been a marine drill sergeant and acted as if he still had that kind of authority.

Melanie ordered a salad plate. L.T. went for the usual. "Fried chicken, white and dark, mashed potatoes, green beans, biscuits."

Charlie nodded. "Be right back."

With Brannon out of the way, L.T. stared out the plate-glass windows on the front of the diner, trying to figure out what was going on. The Volvo was still parked at the far end of the lot, and he could see the kids inside, doors open, lights on. They'd wear down the battery if they weren't careful. Where was Kate? Why hadn't they gone home?

He finally realized that Kate was sitting in Dixon Bell's truck. The lights were on there, too, because the door was still open. L.T. could see the silhouette of her head and, beyond, the shadow of Bell's face. They appeared to be talking. About what?

Shaking his head, he picked up his iced tea and drained half the glass. Old times, probably, the ones he'd never been a part of. He'd come into this town as a stranger. Sure, he was Kate Bowdrey's husband, and that gave him some leverage. But most of her friends and their parents had looked at him as if he belonged on another planet instead of in a different town. He had never really fit in.

He'd made money, though, and that had bought him acceptance. He built their new houses, renovated their old ones, and they liked him for it. Unless something went wrong, of course. Nobody realized that you couldn't get perfect work at reasonable prices. The economics just didn't add up. L.T. gave them the prices they liked, and they just had to live with the flaws.

"Chicken salad plate and fried chicken." Charlie set down their plates and a basket of biscuits. "Abby'll be here to refill your tea in a minute. Anything else?"

L.T. shook his head and attacked his meal. But with a piece of chicken in his fingers, halfway between plate and mouth, he looked outside again to see the Volvo driving away. Dixon Bell came around the front of his truck and then he, too, was gone.

Good riddance. Crunching into Abby's crispy chicken crust, L.T. thought about Bell's attitude that afternoon at the house. Wouldn't sell. Well, they'd just see about that. It took a strong man to resist L. T. LaRue. A strong one, or a very, very rich one. He'd have to find out whether Dixon Bell fit in either category.

And then find a way to break him, anyway.

CHAPTER THREE

MISS DAISY WAS ALREADY bustling around the house when Dixon came downstairs at six-thirty on Friday morning. She stopped long enough to kiss him on the cheek.

"The housekeeper will be here at nine," she reminded him. "We have to have everything straightened up before then."

He followed her through the parlor as she took the cats' towels off the furniture and bundled them up in her arms. In several cases, she had to remove a cat, too. Dixon knew he was guilty of exaggerating when he'd told Kate there were too many cats to count. In fact, there were only four—Audrey, Clark, Cary and Marlon. But they moved silently and appeared out of nowhere when he least expected it, so he felt as if he was living with at least twice that number.

"Forgive my confusion, Miss Daisy, but isn't that what you have a housekeeper for? To straighten the house?"

"I don't need to hire somebody to pick up your dirty socks." She handed him the pair he'd left by the couch after falling asleep in front of the television waiting for her to come home. He'd woken up about three in the morning with the long-haired white cat—Audrey?—snoring on his chest. "I get the clutter out of her way so Consuela can do the real cleaning."

"That's clear as mud." Dixon followed his grandmother into the kitchen. "Can I pour you a cup of coffee?"

"I've had my daily quota, thank you. I'll be glad to fix you some breakfast, though. We still have time. Eggs and bacon? Pancakes?"

He toasted her with his coffee mug. "I'm fine. What can I do to help you?"

Miss Daisy was busy putting away the clean dishes still in the drainer from yesterday. Magnolia Cottage didn't own a dishwasher. "Just be sure your room is neat, dear. And the bathroom upstairs. That will be sufficient."

Coffee in hand, Dixon climbed the wide, uncarpeted staircase to the second floor, appreciating the fine woodwork. At the same time, he noted a couple of missing balusters and the desperate need for a refinishing job on the banister. In his bedroom, he picked up his shirt and slacks from last night and caught, along with a flurry of white cat hair, a whiff of Kate's rose-washed perfume clinging to the cloth. Or imagined he did, anyway. His first waking thought, as it was on many mornings, had been of Kate. He wondered if she'd spent time thinking about him last night, or if she'd gone home and straight to sleep. He couldn't help but notice that she looked exhausted. Beautiful, but exhausted.

In the bathroom, he hung his towel over the rack, as opposed to the shower-curtain rod, stowed his shaving gear in his bag and put it under his arm to take to his room. There was no linen closet, no storage cabinet of any kind in the tiny, white-tiled bath. The sink rested on a stainless-steel frame and the tub was the ancient, freestanding variety. Big but difficult, he was certain, to clean behind.

Dixon decided he'd better get out a notepad and start writing down all the things he wanted to fix in the house. There were too many to keep a mental list.

He spent a couple of pleasurable hours surveying the second floor, thinking about converting a small bedroom into a bath, creating a walk-in closet for Miss Daisy so she wouldn't have to store her wardrobe in every closet but his. Just as he reached the foot of the stairs again, the front doorbell rang. He opened the door to a short, plump lady with glossy black hair and a sweet smile.

"I am Consuela Torres. You must be Mr. Dixon."

He took her hand and drew her into the house.

"I'm glad to meet you, Mrs. Torres. Miss Daisy says you've done a wonderful job taking care of the house, and of her. I really appreciate that."

"She is easy to care for. And I am glad to have such steady work." Consuela set the big shopping bag she carried on the floor by the stairs and bent over to extract cleaning cloths and bottles of various kinds. Dixon saw that she winced as she straightened up again.

"Are you okay?"

She gave him another smile. "Of course. These old bones just take some warming up in the morning. I think I will start upstairs today, if that's all right with you."

"That's great." He watched her as she went up, noted that she was breathing hard by the time she reached the middle of the staircase. She wasn't an athletic woman, but she wasn't really "old," either, and it seemed to him that climbing the steps shouldn't be that hard.

"Are you sure Consuela's okay?" he asked Miss Daisy when he found her in the kitchen. "Is this job too much for her?"

His grandmother considered the questions with her delicate eyebrows drawn together. "She's worked hard since she was a teenager, that I do know, mostly cleaning houses and offices. She has a number of children, several of them very young. I imagine she is tired most of the time, and feels a little older than her years. But I wouldn't presume to pity her," Miss Daisy warned. "And I wouldn't think of firing her. Her husband can't hold a job, and some weeks her housekeeping money is all they have to eat on."

Dixon shook his head. "No, I wouldn't fire her. I just wonder how to make things easier for her... and for you. This place is a wreck, Miss Daisy. We've got to get it fixed up."

Now her bright blue eyes widened in surprise. "Fixed up? What's wrong with this house?"

For an answer, he walked to the wall beside the back door and chipped off a piece of crumbling plaster with his fingernail. "For starters. And you need new bathrooms, a new kitchen. More phone connections. What would happen if you fell upstairs and needed help? You couldn't even make a telephone call."

"I seem to have managed well enough all these years." Her tone was frosted with injured pride.

"Sure you have." Putting an arm around her shoulders, he brought her to the table, brushed a fat calico cat—Marlon?—off the chair, and sat her down. The cat immediately jumped onto Miss Daisy's lap. "And I don't have any right to criticize when I stayed away for so long, leaving you to take care of everything all by yourself."

She shrugged a thin shoulder. "You needed to go, and I gave you my blessing. Anyway, I was used to being in charge. Your grandfather died a long time ago. And then your mother and father…" Her sigh spoke of an unhealed sorrow.

"But I'm here now, Miss Daisy, and I want to make this a comfortable, easy place to live in. For you, and for me, for the family I hope to have someday."

Daisy sat up straight. "Dixon Crawford Bell! You're planning a family already? And just who might the lucky woman be? Or do I already know?"

He put a finger on her lips. "Don't say anything—I don't want to jinx it. But I do want to set things to rights around here, if you'll let me."

Her shoulders slumped a little. "I'm comfortable enough, Dixon, but I don't have the money to do the kinds of things you're talking about. How are we going to afford all this?"

Though he hadn't really doubted that she would go along with his plans, he felt better having her permission to begin. "I've got the money, Miss Daisy—they're paying me pretty well to write songs these days, remember? And I have a lot of time and energy to do at least some of the work on the house myself. Don't you worry about anything but picking out wallpaper and paint colors and countertops. Leave the rest to me."

By lunchtime, he'd made a survey of the downstairs and his list had grown to twelve closely written pages. More than a little daunted by the task he'd set himself, he went outside into the hot July sun, where mad dogs, Englishmen and crazy ex-cowboys belonged.

There, the grounds met him with their own demands—knee-high grass, overgrown gardens where weeds formed the primary crop, wisteria and poison ivy vines gone crazy as they climbed over pine trees that should have been pulled up as seedlings fifty years ago. The giant magnolias for which the house was named had fostered their own crop of sprouts, smaller trees which, though beautiful, detracted from the majesty of the originals. Dixon thought he would like to transplant those sprouts rather than just cut them down. But that would entail a monumental amount of extra work.

As he stood staring, feeling his shirt stick to the sweat on his back, caused by a combination of heat, humidity and sheer trepidation, a blue Taurus came down the gravel driveway and stopped at the front walk. The driver was young, and his olive skin and black hair easily identified him as Consuela's son.

"Good afternoon." Dixon extended his hand and got a firm shake in return. "I'm Dixon Bell."

"Sal Torres. My mother works here." The words held a certain defiance. An arrogant tilt to the boy's chin indicated resentment.

"I met her for the first time this morning. I really appreciate all she's done for my grandmother—it's not easy for an eighty-four-year-old woman to manage on her own."

Sal Torres didn't intend to be placated. "My mother always does a good job. She takes pride in her work."

"As well she should. I've done my share of dirty jobs, chores other people turned up their noses at. Work done well is work to be respected."

The youngster looked a little surprised, then nodded. "That's true." His gaze moved beyond Dixon, to the wilderness around the house. "And it looks like you need a lot of work done out here."

"Yeah. Inside, too. Your mother keeps things clean, but there's a mountain of repairs to be made."

"I know people who do landscaping, carpentry, painting." Before Dixon could reply, Sal gave a shrug, rueful and angry at the same time. "'Of course you do,' you're thinking. Hispanics are the new labor class. We've replaced the African slaves."

"You know, that wasn't what I was thinking at all." Dixon unclenched his jaw, got his irritation under control. "I can't help that my ancestors ran a plantation and owned slaves, and I won't apologize for that fact. But, as I believe I just said, I respect anybody who does a decent day's work and I expect to pay them a good wage when they work for me." He turned on his heel and headed for the house. "I'll tell your mother you're here."

Sal watched the other man go into the grand, sad old house, then went to sit in the Taurus with the air-conditioning blowing full blast. He hadn't really meant to start an argument about slavery and prejudice, especially not with his mother's employer. Something about the atmosphere surrounding the mansion, some remnants of past lives, maybe, had stirred resentment in him, and a need to take a stand. Dixon Bell had probably been more tolerant than Sal deserved. L. T. LaRue would have picked him up bodily and thrown him off the place. Or tried, anyway.

Of course, Mr. LaRue had already laid hands on Sal once, for kissing his daughter. Dixon Bell probably wouldn't be too tolerant, either, when his children wanted to date outside their own class. Kelsey's mother managed to be polite, but it was obvious she had serious doubts about Sal as somebody worthy of her little girl. All because he had dark skin and came from the south side of Boundary Street, the line dividing the haves in New Skye from the have-nots.

The heavy front door of the house shut with a thud, and Sal looked up to see his mother ease her way down the steps, the heavy shopping bag she always carried in one hand, her other hand holding tight to the rail. She looked tired, and it was only a little past noon. How would she feel at five, when she finished her second cleaning job of the day?

Sal jumped out of the car and ran around to open her door, taking the bag out of her hand. "Let me get that."

She sank into the front seat with a sigh of relief. "Ah, the air-conditioning feels good. That house is always too hot."

In the driver's seat again, Sal flipped the fan up a notch. "Don't they have AC?"

"Yes, but not enough. And when you're working…" She shrugged. "Did you go to class this morning?"

He cleared his throat and put the car into gear. "No."

"Salvadore, you must go to class. You need these credits to graduate next year."

"I know, Mama, I know. I'm going this afternoon. But I had a job this morning, unloading furniture at Joe's. I earned fifty dollars. So this afternoon I'll figure out how to do algebra."

With another sigh she closed her eyes, leaning her head back against the seat. "The fifty dollars is nice. But you need a diploma to get a good job. In the long run, a diploma is worth a lot more than fifty dollars."

He didn't argue with her, just let her doze a

little as he drove across town toward one of the brand-new subdivisions where her afternoon job was located. These big, new houses were easier to clean, she said, because they had all the modern conveniences. She didn't work nearly as hard there.

Sal only wished she didn't have to work at all.

They stopped for a fast-food lunch before he dropped her off at the big house on a street where all the trees were too young to make real shade. "I'll be here at five," he promised as she leaned in the window to give him a kiss.

"Go to class," his mother ordered.

And because he promised her, he went. He was late, of course, which meant checking in through the office and getting a lecture from the secretary. School schedules never took into account that teenagers might have real lives. If he didn't drive his mother to work, she couldn't get there. If she didn't get there, she didn't get paid, and his brothers and sisters didn't eat. That was a pretty simple equation, he thought. Maybe the algebra teacher could explain it to the front office.

After two hours of algebra, the teacher gave them a fifteen-minute break. Sal went in search of a cold drink and the one person who made him feel as if the future held promise for someone like him.

He found Kelsey lingering by the vending machines. The way her face lighted up when she saw him was worth all the hassle of going to summer school.

"Sal!"

"Hey, *querida*." He put an arm around her waist, felt her yield to him with a surge of pride. She was gorgeous, she was sweet as candy, and she was his. "How are you?"

"Better, now. Where were you all morning?"

Sal didn't like being questioned, but he did like it that she cared. "I had some work to do. Judging from the last two hours in class, I didn't miss anything."

He let go of her long enough to get a drink from the machine, then grabbed her hand and pulled her down the hall after him. "Let's get out of here for a few minutes."

The afternoon was scorching hot, even in the shade of the tree they had chosen as their special place. Sal leaned back against the trunk, then took a long swig of his drink. "That's better. You and a cold soda—that's about as good as a summer day gets."

"You're so sweet." She smiled at him, her brown eyes bright, her mouth full and soft. "You deserve a kiss."

"You're right. I do."

"Mr. Torres, Miss LaRue...must I remind you

again about the school rules prohibiting public displays of affection?"

Kelsey gasped and stepped away from him as Sal opened his eyes to see the principal glaring at them from barely ten feet away.

The big man crossed his arms and tapped his foot on the asphalt. "Well?"

"No, sir." Sal straightened up and sidled out from underneath the tree branches. "You don't have to remind us." They'd been caught last Friday afternoon, but that was inside the building. Sal had hoped being outside would keep them off the radar, so to speak.

"One more incident, and I will notify your parents and assign both of you detention. Do you understand?"

"Yes, sir."

"As it is, you are going to be late for class." The bell rang to emphasize his point. "Your teachers may be assigning detention, as well."

A glance at Kelsey as they trailed Principal Floyd into the building showed Sal her red face, her scared eyes. He understood her fear—if the principal talked to her dad about him, Kelsey would have hell to pay. Hard as it was, for her sake, he would have to stay away from her during school hours.

But school hours took up so much of the day. After class, he picked up his mother, took her to the grocery, helped her at home with the younger children. By the time he got free, Kelsey's curfew was in effect. He'd spent a lot of evenings this summer watching movies with her at her house. At most, they found enough privacy for a goodnight kiss.

Couldn't anything in life be simple?

He saw Kelsey again after class ended for the day. This time, the complications came in the form of her little brother walking down the hall beside her. Trace LaRue had inherited his dad's redneck attitude. He hated Sal on the principle that he was Hispanic, which made them about even, because Sal hated Trace on the principle that he was a bigoted jerk.

So he made sure to demonstrate how things stood between him and Kelsey every chance he got. "Hey, beautiful," he said as he reached her, putting an arm around her waist. "Missed you." He bent to kiss her cheek.

"Sal!" She drew away. "Remember what Mr. Floyd said."

"I remember." He pushed open the door and ushered her ahead of him out of the building, then let the heavy panel swing back on Trace. "But we're out of school now. The big man is watching the bus line in back. We're safe." Lifting her thick blond hair in one hand, he placed a kiss on the nape of her neck.

A hand grabbed Sal's shoulder and jerked him around. "Take your hands off her." Red-faced and sweating, Trace looked just like his old man when he got mad.

Sal shoved back. "Make me."

Before either of them could move, Kelsey pushed in between them. "No, you will not. Neither of you is gonna start a fight at school over me. Do you hear? I swear, Sal, if you take this any further, I won't see you or talk to you again for…for…for weeks. Is that what you want? Is fighting Trace worth it?"

He was tempted to take the boy on in spite of her warning. But…

Sal knew he couldn't live without seeing Kelsey. She kept him sane, gave him a reason to get up in the morning.

"Go," he said through clenched teeth, with a nod across the parking lot to the Volvo where their mother sat waiting. "Just go."

Trace grabbed Kelsey's arm. "You heard the jerk. Let's go." She went with her brother, looking back over her shoulder at Sal the whole time.

Sal watched them drive off, then went to his own car and sat in the heat, fuming. The situation was impossible—he and Kelsey should have the right to see each other without so many hassles. He was beginning to think they would have to change the whole world, just to be together.

But this afternoon, changing the whole world looked like way too big a job for one Hispanic kid to handle on his own.

KATE WAS BETTER PREPARED to face L.T. when he came to get the children for breakfast on Saturday morning.

She opened the door and managed a smile as she stepped back to let him in. "Good morning." Beyond him, she could see his girlfriend…fiancée?…waiting in the car at the end of the walk.

"Are they ready?" He went across the hall toward the living room, but stopped on the threshold. "What happened to the furniture?"

"I've done some rearranging, that's all."

"Why would you do that? You've got the dining-room table in the wrong place. Who wants to eat in here?"

"I thought we might enjoy our meals with a fire in the fireplace, come winter. Especially for Thanksgiving and Christmas dinner. And this way, we can sit on the love seat by the big window at the other end and look out at the garden. It's just an experiment."

"I think it's a disaster. Put the furniture back the way it's supposed to be."

She drew a deep breath. "L.T., you don't live here anymore, so it really doesn't matter what you think. Trace and Kelsey and I like this arrangement, so it's going to stay this way until we want to change it."

He faced her, his eyes narrowed, his fists clenched. "You're turning the kids against me, aren't you? I've suspected all along that was what you were doing. Brainwashing them, getting them to believe what you say is right, instead of me."

Her knees were shaking, but she held her ground against the urge to back away from him. "No. We don't talk about you at all, if we can help it. We're just getting on with our lives, L.T., the same way you have. And that includes moving the furniture around."

Footsteps on the floor above heralded the appearance of Trace and Kelsey at the top of the stairs. L.T.'s face smoothed into a welcoming smile. He was a handsome man when he wasn't angry. "Hey there. Good to see you both. Let's go get something to eat."

The kids descended slowly, not sure what kind of mood their dad was in, but when they reached the bottom, L.T. was surprisingly gentle with his greeting. He put a hand on Trace's shoulder and gave him an affectionate shake. "How's it going, son?" For Kelsey, he had a kiss on the cheek. "You're looking pretty this morning, sweetheart." As he ushered them out the door, he looked back. "I'm thinking we might drive up to Raleigh to do some shopping, if they don't have plans for the rest of the day. Any problem with that?"

Kelsey whirled to face Kate, her face alight with eagerness. "Oh, please, Kate, please? They've got such cool stores and a brand-new mall we've never been to. Please?" Even Trace conveyed an interest in spending some of his dad's money.

In the face of such desperation, a legitimate reason would have been hard to maintain and Kate didn't have one, anyway. "That's great. I'm sure y'all will have a good time." As they moved down the walk, with Kelsey practically dancing, Kate called out, "Can you give me an idea of what time to expect them home again?"

L.T. waved a careless hand in her direction. "It'll be late."

"Oh." She drew back inside the threshold. "Thanks so much for the specifics." Closing the door, she leaned against it and listened to the empty house. "Now what?"

The hours passed quickly enough, filled with her usual Saturday chores plus an impulsive trip to the garden center to buy a new planter for the terrace and a selection of herbs to plant there. About six o'clock, she finally sat down in a nearby chair with a glass of iced tea, set to enjoy the scents of earth and oregano and marjoram, the fading heat of the day radiating from the stones under her bare feet, the changing colors of the sky.

But after a few quiet moments, she found herself longing for company. She enjoyed Trace and Kelsey—except when they were fighting, of course. Their minds were lively and they always seemed to have something interesting to talk about. Tonight, L.T. would reap the benefit of their imaginations, their curiosity. Kate had to wonder if he really appreciated the treasure he had so recklessly thrown away.

And tonight *she* would be alone. She could take a long bath, make herself a salad for dinner, watch one of the movies she truly enjoyed, rather than going along with the kids' choice. Most women with children would, she thought, leap at the chance to indulge themselves that way.

Kate would rather have had somebody to talk to.

Where the idea came from, she wasn't sure. But suddenly, Dixon was in her mind. She could almost see his grin as he helped her grill the steaks she had in the refrigerator, hear the rumble of his voice as it would sound in her house, picture his long legs stretched out in front of him as they sat here in the growing darkness with candles on the table. The rightness of the idea took her breath. She was on her feet and standing by the phone in the kitchen before she realized she had moved.

That was when the terror hit. How could she do this? She had never in all her life called a man and asked for a date. Growing up, she'd learned that nice girls simply didn't call boys. That rule had fallen by the wayside, of course—nice girls did anything they pleased these days.

But she wasn't free to date. She was still a married woman. How would Dixon interpret an invitation to dinner? What did she really know about him? He might expect…more…if he came to her house and it was just the two of them alone. A dinner party, even supper with the kids, would be one thing. A tête-à-tête meal, with candles, surely implied something else altogether.

Her sister would tell her to stop thinking and call him. Kate had no doubt at all on that score. Mary Rose was high on the euphoria of first love regained and newlywed bliss. She stood at the beginning of her marriage, certain of the inevitability of happily-ever-after.

Her sister hadn't failed, as Kate had. Hadn't managed to somehow alienate a husband of ten years so that he sought other women's company. She didn't face the daily shame of running into people who knew what had happened—friends and acquaintances, L.T.'s business associates— and trying to ignore the embarrassment of being rejected. Mary Rose didn't understand the ultimate implications of separation and divorce in a small town like New Skye.

Kate let her hand slip off the phone. Calling

Dixon would be a mistake. Even if she intended only friendship, he might misinterpret the gesture. One of the neighbors might see him arrive, or leave, and draw the wrong conclusion about what they were doing together on a Saturday night.

Worst of all, Kate knew that she might, herself, mistake the nature of her relationship with Dixon. Something about him appealed to her as no man had since her high-school crushes. She found him gorgeous and strong and oh, so perfect.

And completely out of her reach. Even if she were free, what chance was there that she would make a man like Dixon happy? She hadn't kept L.T. more than marginally content during their whole marriage. Standing in her darkened kitchen, Kate could not ignore the fact that she was simply nowhere near enough woman for Dixon Bell.

She ate a turkey sandwich and a pear for dinner, then watched a series of news programs on television until L.T. brought the kids home at midnight. When they all went upstairs, she tuned the radio in her room to a country-music station and got into bed, hoping sleep would help her escape.

"And now," the announcer said, "we've reached the top of the countdown with a tune that's been at number one on the country charts for three weeks and shows no sign of giving up its slot. This song has even started showing up on pop lists, amazing, considering its classic country sound. Here you are, folks, our number one song for the week, performed by the man who does country ballads better than anybody in the business. Evan Carter, with 'My Dream.'"

Kate rolled to her side as soft guitar chords and the sweet wail of a fiddle flowed into the room. The singer's deep voice picked up the waltz.

Deep in the night, dark as your hair,
I open my eyes to find you're not there.
The dream feels so real,
I hold you so tight,
But you're a lifetime of lonesome away.
Me lovin' you—it's only a dream
And dreams are for fools, so they say.
Me lovin' you—that's all I would ask
You're the dream I won't let slip away.

What would it be like, Kate wondered, *to have a man feel that way about you, think of you with such tenderness?*

Before the song had ended, the gentle lyrics broke her control. Hot tears filled her eyes and rolled down her cheeks. Burying her head in her pillow, she cried herself to sleep.

CHAPTER FOUR

KELSEY SHOWED OFF at least five hundred dollars' worth of clothes to her mother and her aunt Sunday afternoon, a fashion show that took almost an hour to complete. Trace had new clothes, too, plus new computer games and a stack of video games to add to his collection.

"Bribery," Mary Rose Bowdrey Mitchell pronounced. "L.T. is using his money to get the kids on his side."

"So I'll change the furniture back?" Kate squeezed her tired eyes shut and took a sip of iced tea. "Pretty drastic measures, even for L.T."

"'Dog in the manger' is just L.T.'s style. He doesn't want to be here, but he doesn't want anything to change. I bet he'd go ballistic if you cut your hair."

"I won't push him that far." The idea had her combing her heavy curls up off her neck, though, to feel the cool air-conditioning blow across her nape.

Mary Rose, a financial advisor, was used to looking at life's little details. She cocked her head and considered her older sister critically. "I think you'd be thrilled with a shorter cut. Sometimes your hair looks too heavy for your neck to support."

"Well, thanks."

"Not that it isn't lovely. You never look less than your absolute best."

"Oh, yes, I do." Kate recounted last week's thunderstorm. "And who should I meet on the sidewalk, when I'm looking like a drowned rat, but Dixon Bell."

Mary Rose frowned. "Who?"

"Dixon Bell. He was in my graduating class. Daisy Crawford's grandson."

"I don't remember him."

"You will when you meet him again. He's…" She didn't have words. "Unforgettable."

"Oh, really?" Mary Rose sat up a little straighter. "That's interesting."

"Don't start." Kate went to the counter for the tea pitcher to refill their glasses. "Dixon is just an old friend. He's been gone ever since graduation—I don't even know if he's here visiting his grandmother or planning to stay in town for a while."

"I can tell you that." Pete Mitchell came into the kitchen, put his hands on his wife's shoulders and leaned down to kiss her cheek. "He ate breakfast with us yesterday morning after the game. He's planning to renovate the family mansion and take up permanent residence." Pete and some of his friends—Adam DeVries among them—had been playing basketball together on Saturday mornings since high school. The traditional game was almost always followed by a traditional breakfast at the Carolina Diner.

And now Dixon had returned to take part in the male-bonding ritual. Kate let her curiosity get the best of her. "That's a big project, restoring Magnolia Cottage. Did Dixon say…"

"Where the money would come from?" Pete grinned. "He worked in the oil business, and I gather he's made good money there with investments. Plus, he said he does some kind of freelance work he earns royalties on."

"He writes books? Articles?"

"We never got to specifics. Maybe some kind of consulting. But I definitely got the impression he's played it smart the last few years and doesn't have to worry about finding a job here in New Skye. Dixon was always a bright guy, so I wouldn't be surprised to learn he'd made himself a fortune."

Kate was, but didn't say so. Maybe she hadn't paid enough attention to Dixon Bell when she'd had the chance.

"There you are." Mary Rose put one hand over her husband's and gestured with the other. "An intelligent, unforgettable—not to mention rich—

man has moved into town just when you need him." She looked up at Pete. "He's not married or engaged, is he?"

"Don't think so."

"I am," Kate reminded them. "And Trace and Kelsey don't need more upheaval in their lives."

Mary Rose stuck out her lower lip in a pout. "You always say that."

"Because it's always true. They're my first responsibility, especially since L.T. can't be bothered most of the time."

"But you deserve a life, Katie!"

Pete squeezed his wife's shoulders and she subsided with a sigh. "Speaking of the guy upstairs, Dixon wants to play ball with us next Saturday and wondered if Trace would join us and even out the teams."

Had Dixon acted on that small moment so quickly? "Y'all are sure you want to play with a thirteen-year-old?"

He grinned again. "Yeah…we're dying to prove we can outrun a kid twenty years our junior." The grin faded. "But I'm doubtful that Trace will accept the invitation coming from me. I'm down near the bottom of his list of people to hang out with."

In a fit of rebellion last spring, Trace and two of his friends had engineered a bomb threat during a street fair in downtown New Skye. Pete, a

North Carolina State Trooper, had been the one to arrest Trace and turn him over to the police. Her son was still doing community service and going to counseling as the result of that incident.

"So Dixon said he'd call," Pete continued. "If you don't mind letting Trace play with us."

"Of course not. I'm sure Trace will be thrilled." Kate hoped she wasn't blushing at the idea that Dixon would call, that she would get to talk to him again. "L.T. doesn't give him that kind of time anymore."

She fidgeted through the hours after her sister and brother-in-law left, not wanting to venture out of the house in case the phone rang. Which was silly, Kate knew, because Dixon might call any time during the week. She couldn't hold her breath all week long.

But the July afternoon was muggy and unbearably hot, not suitable for working outside. After putting together a pasta salad for supper, she sat down at the kitchen table with her checkbook and bank statement, determined to get the balancing done this time. Trace and Kelsey were in their rooms and the house was completely quiet except for the low thud of Trace's music vibrating through the ceiling.

And Kate did manage to concentrate, so completely that she actually jumped and gasped in surprise when the phone rang. Only one ring, though, and she sank back into her chair when she realized that Kelsey had no doubt answered. After several months of restriction, her daughter had recently regained phone privileges, which were being liberally enjoyed. The call was probably from one of her friends. Or Sal…whose very name conjured up a whole different set of problems.

But the feet pounding down the staircase a few minutes later belonged to Trace, not his sister. He burst into the kitchen, holding the cordless phone from her bedroom in one hand.

"Hey, Kate, this is Dixon Bell, that friend of yours, you know? And he wants me to play basketball with him and his friends next Saturday morning. Mr. DeVries and Mr. Crawford and—" he took a breath "—Pete. That's okay, right? It'll be just grown-ups except for me. I told him I thought you'd say yes. You will, right? I can go?"

Kate stared at her son for a moment, speechless. She hadn't seen him this excited in months. Certainly not since his father had left. And maybe not for a long time before. One miracle, courtesy of Dixon Bell.

"Please, Kate?"

She shook her head to clear it. "I think it sounds great. Be sure to thank him for the invitation." The urge to ask to speak with Dixon was almost overwhelming, but she managed to keep control as Trace put the phone to his ear.

"It's okay," he said, still with that Christmas-morning eagerness in his voice. "What time should I be there? Oh, okay. That'll be good. I'll be ready. What? Oh, sure." He put the phone on the table beside Kate's hand. "Dixon wants to talk to you."

Breathless, she picked up the receiver with a shaking hand. "Hello?"

"Hey, Kate. How are you?" His warm voice seemed to release all the tension in her shoulders.

She sank back in her chair. "I'm fine, thanks. And I really appreciate that you've included Trace in your ball game. He's thrilled, of course."

"I think it'll be fun. He'll give us old guys a standard to strive for."

"What time should I have him at the school Saturday?"

"Don't worry about getting out so early. I'll pick him up about a quarter to seven, if that's okay."

The conversation was coming to an end and she couldn't think of a good reason to extend it. "If you're sure…"

"That's set, then. Now…" He paused for a long moment. "What about us?"

Kate wasn't sure she'd heard correctly. "Us?"

"Yes, ma'am. That dinner I wanted to share with you. Can we set something up?"

Be careful what you wish for, she thought, *because it hurts so much when you have to refuse.* "I—I don't—"

"If dinner doesn't work, what about lunch? I could bring Trace home after breakfast on Saturday, grab a shower and a change of clothes, then pick you up and we could have a sandwich together. Or," he added when she still hadn't found her voice, "you could meet me somewhere."

Unable to resist any longer, Kate sighed. "I think we could do that. I—I would like to have lunch with you."

"That's a d—...that's great." She thought she heard him blow out a long breath. "I'll look forward to seeing you...and Trace...on Saturday."

Kate hung up the phone, feeling a wide smile crease her cheeks, stretch her lips. Dixon had such wonderful manners. He would "look forward" to seeing her on Saturday.

But not half as much as she would look forward to seeing *him.*

DIXON DIDN'T PUSH to keep Kate on the phone, though he couldn't think of a nicer way to pass the Sunday afternoon than listening to her soft southern voice in his ear. An idea occurred to him—the possibility of writing a song about a woman's voice, her words, her tone, and how they affected the man who loved her. The concept had potential, he decided, and went upstairs to fetch his pad of paper and make some notes. Sitting on his childhood bed in the sleepy quiet of the old house, he found it easy to think about Kate, to imagine words she might use in love, in laughter. Next weekend, he'd have hours to listen to what she had to say and how she said it. He only had to get through five long weekdays first.

This afternoon, though, thinking too much about Kate unsettled him enough that he decided to get out of the house, despite the July heat. Miss Daisy had curled up on the sofa with the cats and the newest Tom Clancy novel, then slipped into a genteel nap, so Dixon tiptoed across the front hall and shut the door carefully behind him. On the right side of the house, where there had once been a rose bed and boxwood parterre in a knot pattern, he found shade and a weed-free spot under a tulip poplar. He checked for ant beds at the base of the trunk and settled in with his notepad on his knee to consider landscape plans.

But in only minutes his mind wandered back to Kate. Convincing her to have lunch with him had been a significant effort. She acted for all the world as if she was afraid that he would hurt her if she let him get too close. Which would make sense, Dixon thought, if he were L. T. LaRue.

Did Kate believe all men were cut from the same cloth?

He looked around at the sound of a car door being shut and nearly growled aloud when he saw LaRue's SUV parked in front of the house. Kate's ex had brought someone else with him this time, a man Dixon didn't recognize.

Already irritated, he got to his feet, dusted the grass and dirt off his pants and went to confront LaRue and guest before they could get more than halfway up the walk. "Can I help you gentlemen?"

L.T. grinned, as if he knew a really great secret. "Afternoon, Dixon. I thought I'd bring the mayor over and introduce the two of you. Mayor Curtis Tate, this is Dixon Bell, one of our newer residents. Miss Daisy Crawford's grandson, of course."

The mayor put out a thin, manicured hand. "Glad to meet you, Mr. Bell. Your grandmother is quite…uh…well known to those of us in New Skye government." Tate was probably six foot three, gaunt and bony, with dark hair and a shifting gray gaze that Dixon immediately distrusted.

But he shook the man's hand and even resisted the urge to wipe his palm on his slacks immediately afterward. "Good to meet you, Mr. Mayor. Miss Daisy does tend to speak her mind when she's got something to say."

"Yes, yes, she does." He looked past Dixon's

shoulder at the house, then surveyed the tangled chaos of the garden. "This was a lovely place once."

"And will be again. I'll be doing a lot of work inside and out, but I expect to bring Magnolia Cottage back to its former glory in pretty quick order."

L.T. put his hands in his pockets and rocked back on his heels. "Gotta have inspections for this kind of work, y'know. Rewiring, heating, AC, plumbing...all that takes approval from the right departments."

"Your point being...?"

The mayor shrugged. "You can't always count on these things going through in a timely fashion. Or at all."

Dixon straightened up to his full height. "I believe I hear a threat in there somewhere."

"Just a warning." L.T. gave him another one of those grins. "You might find that your little... um...renovation project doesn't go as smoothly as you expect. Whereas I could take this property off your hands in a matter of days." He snapped his fingers. "Easy as pie."

Behind Dixon, the front door squeaked open. "Do we have visitors, Dixon?" Miss Daisy called from the porch.

"They were just leaving." Dixon refused to

budge from his place, which left Tate and LaRue no choice about approaching the house.

And when he took a step forward, the other two men backed up. "Let me explain this very slowly." He kept his voice low. "You two are leaving this property right now and you're not ever setting foot here again. Because if you do," he continued as they retreated toward the SUV, "I will greet you from the porch with a shotgun. Any part of that you don't understand?"

Safe inside his vehicle, L.T. rolled down the electric windows. "You think you've got this settled, don't you, Mr. Bell? Well, I'm telling you that I've got connections in this town. You haven't heard the last of this issue, believe me. And I think you'll be surprised at how our little disagreement gets resolved." He revved the engine, then fishtailed his way down the driveway with a spray of gravel and dust.

Dixon joined Miss Daisy on the porch. "Scalawag about covers it as far as L. T. LaRue is concerned," he said.

"And was that the mayor?"

"Yes, ma'am. Appearances can be deceiving, of course, but I can't say he inspired much confidence."

"He's as crooked as they come," Miss Daisy said, leading the way into the house. "He owns a lot of the downtown real estate—or co-owns it with L.T., which is why we've been successful at the New Skye Historical Society in getting approval for renovations in the business district. We've increased the property values and made them more money. I take it they're badgering you to buy this place?" She perched on the sofa and was immediately joined by cats, one on either side and the third in her lap.

Dixon dropped into a threadbare armchair. "You've heard from them before?"

"Off and on for several years. I was fortunate to be able to say that the property was in your name and I didn't have the power to sell." Her smile was mischievous. "Passing the buck, they call it."

"I'm glad you had an easy way out, and that I was useful for something while I was gone. What do they want to do with the land?"

"Condos." Miss Daisy said the word as if it were not used in polite company. "L.T.'s got this grand plan to build luxury town houses up here. Even wants to keep the name—Magnolia Cottage Condominiums, or some such." She sniffed in disdain. "Given the quality of work he delivers, the place would be falling down around people's ears within a year or two. Why, Gladys Sykes had him build her a pool house—against my advice, of course—and it wasn't halfway through the summer that she had nails popping through the walls and boards warping, and she had to have the stucco completely replaced…"

She continued the litany of L.T.'s failings as she fixed bacon, lettuce and tomato sandwiches for supper, and even as they washed dishes and straightened up the kitchen afterward.

"L. T. LaRue is cheap and mean," she concluded. "He'll take advantage of his clients in any way he can find. How he manages to make so much money—not to mention acquiring the influence he appears to exert over what goes on—is a complete mystery to me and every well-intentioned, thinking person in this town."

How he'd managed to convince Kate to marry him was an even bigger mystery, Dixon thought. But at least that problem was on the way to getting solved. And with L.T. out of the way, he and Kate could finally get started on the rest of their lives.

L.T. FLIPPED the air-conditioning a notch higher as he drove through the brick pillars marking the driveway for Magnolia Cottage. "Dixon Bell is a jerk. The man's been gone for thirteen years—what does he want with a crumbling disaster like that house?"

Curtis Tate shook his head. "He'd be doing the city and himself a favor to get rid of it, have us build something decent on one of the best pieces of real estate in the entire county. It's a waste, pure and simple, letting that prime land sit there unused." Then the mayor flashed L.T. a sideways grin. "I imagine you've got some ideas on how we can 'persuade' Mr. Bell, though, don't you?"

"With a little cooperation from the powers that be, Mr. Mayor, I think I can guarantee that Magnolia Cottage will become a real showplace, a development that'll do this city proud."

His passenger laughed and clapped him on the shoulder. "Well, L.T., civic pride alone demands that we in the government cooperate in such a worthwhile endeavor."

After dropping the mayor off at his home, L.T. drove around town for a while, trying to figure out where he wanted to go. If he went to the apartment, Melanie would be there expecting attention, probably wanting to go out somewhere. New Skye wasn't a lively place on Sunday nights, but some of the restaurants had bars where folks gathered for a good time. Or she might have a movie she wanted to see. Melanie wasn't much for staying home and just kicking back with the remote in one hand and a soda in the other.

But L.T. didn't feel like a movie, or a rowdy time in a bar. So he ended up all alone in the cool quiet of the impressive brick building he'd erected to house LaRue Construction, Inc. Nobody could deny that this was a pretty fancy place of business for the son of a no-account dirt farmer and his wife. Although L.T. was really proud of the two-story reception area, with its man-size potted plants in the corners and framed photographs of his projects on every wall, he went in through the back door, resetting the alarm to accept motion inside the building. No sense calling out the police when he had every right to be here. In his own office, he sat down behind the big mahogany desk, propped his heels on the top and leaned back in his blue leather chair to think.

He didn't need to turn on the computer and call up the accounting files to know what his situation was. That bottom-line figure had been blinking red at him for almost a year now. Good thing he kept the books himself—the accounting degree he'd earned had sure proved its worth over the years. L.T. didn't have to depend on some outsider to keep his records, or even figure up his taxes. He couldn't imagine giving up that much control to anybody else.

But it also meant he didn't have anybody else to blame when the numbers were bad, like now. Real bad, and getting worse. If he didn't get some positive cash flow going soon, LaRue Construction would be in danger of bankruptcy. He had debts all over town for materials, and Ray Calhoun at the bank had extended him more credit than he was worth. Calhoun had even hinted, last time they went fishing together, that he shouldn't show up again with his hand out until he'd paid down the balance.

What he needed was for his new project to take off: "Magnolia Cottages, *The* Address in New Skye." Knock down that derelict mansion, clear out the grounds…or better yet, spruce up the downstairs of the place, which would cost less, and turn it into the sales center. Folks were tired of tending lawns and trimming trees. They would flock to a town-house development where they could leave the outside work to somebody else, have their ritzy parties in the restored mansion, with a new pool added on. And there were enough people making money in New Skye these days—doctors, lawyers, smart businessmen— who would come flocking to put down their six-figure deposit for one of his classy condos.

All that stood in his way was Dixon Bell.

Mr. Dixon Bell was about to discover just who really ran the store in New Skye, North Carolina.

KATE HAD BEGUN SETTING her alarm clock so that she woke up with the country-music station, a much gentler beginning to the day than the buzzer L.T. had preferred and she'd never before thought to change. On Saturday morning, the song she heard first was that lovely ballad she found herself listening for these days—"Me lovin' you, that's all I would ask…" She was smiling as she went down the hall to wake Trace for his basketball date.

But her son was already up and showered and downstairs draining a tall glass of orange juice. He turned an expectant face her way as she came into the kitchen. "I didn't miss him, did I? He hasn't come by yet?"

"I doubt it, sweetie. He's not due for another ten minutes." She poured a cup of coffee and sat at the table. "Would you like me to make you some breakfast?"

"Nah, I'm good. Dixon said we'd eat after the game. Don't want to be too full to play." He paced around the kitchen, drumming on any available horizontal surface. "This is so cool. I mean, these guys are really cool, you know?"

"Even Pete?"

The drumming stopped for a few seconds. Trace shrugged, then his shoulders slumped. "He caused me a lot of trouble."

Kate reflected on the advice she'd received from the therapist Trace was talking to. "Are you sure that's the way it happened?"

He rolled his eyes. "I know, I know. I caused the trouble. I screwed up and I have to take responsibility for my own actions."

"And Pete cares about you, Trace. He wants to see you make a success of school, of your life."

"Yeah, yeah." The doorbell rang, and he brightened up. "That's Dixon. See you later."

Kate followed him down the hallway, her heart fluttering in her chest as fast as she thought her son's might be. The week had been so long, waiting to see Dixon again and yet hoping to run into him around every corner. Finally, the moment had arrived.

Trace had the door open and was halfway down the walk when she reached the front of the house. Dixon grinned at her as she joined him on the porch. "I guess he's ready to play some ball."

"He's so excited, I think he can take on all of you single-handed." She turned and her fingertips on Dixon's arm. "Seriously, I can't thank you enough for this gesture. Trace has been so lost since L.T. left, and there are issues between him and Pete that make it hard right now. This means the world to him."

Dixon's hand covered hers. "My pleasure, I assure you." His brown eyes were still a little sleepy, but warm and lighted with an expression she couldn't interpret. "I'll be back for you about noon, if that's all right."

She stepped back on shaky knees. "That's j-just fine. See you then."

All morning, she carried the sight of him in her mind, his long, tanned legs in navy shorts, his strong arms, equally tanned, and wide shoulders under a loose yellow T-shirt, his chestnut hair slicked back and shiny, still wet from a shower. Dixon Bell took her breath away. She barely had enough left to get up the stairs without panting.

Choosing what to wear could have been tricky, with Kelsey around. In true teenager fashion, though, her daughter stayed asleep until after eleven. By then Kate had dithered herself to death trying to decide on clothes and spent a long hour in the bathroom with makeup and her curling iron. She decided Mary Rose was right—she should get her hair cut. But there was no time this morning. Did Dixon think she had too much hair?

Down in the kitchen again, she found Kelsey waking up over cereal and bananas and Trace downing a liter bottle of water. He still glowed with enthusiasm.

Kate leaned against the door frame. "I don't have to ask if you had a good time."

"It was so cool. I played with Dixon and Mr. DeVries against Pete and Mr. Crawford and Mr. Warren. They were awesome, let me tell you, and Mr. Crawford might be kinda short, but he can shoot and block like nobody's business." The accolades went on for quite some time. "We won, finally, but only by three points. I made one of them," he said proudly. "Pete fouled me and I took a free throw that was nothing but net. Whoosh!"

Kelsey glanced at Kate and her heavy eyes widened. "You look nice. What's going on?"

"I'm…going out to lunch. There's pizza in the freezer for you two when you're hungry."

"That would be now." Trace dived into the icebox.

But Kelsey wanted details. "With Mary Rose? Where are you going?"

"I'm not sure where I'll be." Kate took the easier question first. "But I have my cell phone if you need me. I'm having lunch with…with Dixon Bell."

As momentous as the fact seemed to her, the kids didn't appear to notice. Kelsey returned to her breakfast. "Have fun." Trace was intently reading the cooking instructions on the pizza box.

The doorbell rang and Kate's heart pounded. Dixon was early. "No visitors until I get back. Right?"

Kelsey rolled her eyes. "Right, Kate. Sal's working today, anyway. And everybody else is at the beach."

Kate gave her a kiss. "Thanks. I'll see you both later."

Then she was walking down the hall toward the front door, trying not to gallop in eagerness as Trace had this morning. Whatever she hoped to pretend, this was a significant step in her life—a private lunch with the man she was seriously attracted to. Who knew what would happen next?

Taking a deep breath, she put a shaky hand on the doorknob, turned, pulled.

And looked into L.T.'s impatient face. "I thought I'd see what the kids were doing this afternoon. There's that new sci-fi movie out they wanted to see."

Disappointment drowned her, and Kate couldn't speak for several moments. Fortunately, L.T. didn't require an answer. He stepped past her into the house just as Dixon's truck pulled up at the curb.

Kate closed her eyes. Wasn't this going to be fun?

Leaving the door open, she turned to follow L.T. into what they now called the great room. "The kids are in the kitchen. Kelsey just got up. And I'm…going out."

He was shaking his head. "I hate the way you have this room."

"I know. I'll get the kids." She went back into the hall and saw Dixon on the porch. "Hi."

"Hi, yourself." He gazed at her for a long moment. "You look wonderful."

Kate felt a blush rise up over her neck and face. "Thank you. Um…L.T. has come by unexpectedly." She emphasized the word. "He wants to take the kids to a movie and I need to get them motivated. It'll just take a minute."

Dixon smiled and shook his head. "No problem. We've got plenty of time. Whenever you're ready."

She felt pressured, anyway. Enough so that she rudely left him standing in the foyer while she scurried back into the kitchen. Though both kids were happy to be headed for a movie, Kelsey was not pleased at the idea of having to run upstairs in her robe with a strange man in the house.

As they came down the hallway, though, there was no one in sight. The kids rushed to their rooms with a quick hello call to their dad. Kate looked into the great room to find Dixon and L.T. confronting each other across the fireplace.

Dixon turned as she came in. "This is a beautiful room, Kate. I had dinner with Pete and Mary Rose the other night and she said you had done the decorating for your house as well as the landscape planning."

"Y-yes. I did." L.T. was seething like a pot of rice about to boil over. "The kids will be down in just a minute, L.T. They're excited about the movie."

"And you were just going off and leaving them here for the afternoon by themselves? After all the trouble there's been?" He shook his head. "I don't think the judge would be much impressed with your idea of close supervision."

Kate felt something inside her start to shut down. "I think we're past that episode. Trace and Kelsey both have had to suffer the consequences of their behavior. Things are better now." She cast an apologetic glance at Dixon, who really shouldn't have to listen to them air their family's troubles.

"As for what people will say when a woman who's still married just takes off for a date with another man…" He clicked his tongue.

She pulled up every ounce of gumption she possessed. "Probably not anything worse than what people say when a married man sleeps with women other than his wife, L.T."

His face turned dark and his mouth twisted. "Why, you—" Fists clenched, he took a step toward her. L.T. had never hit her, though at times she had thought he might. Like now.

Somehow, Dixon stood between them. "Back down, LaRue."

"You get out of my way."

Dixon laughed. "Not likely."

"She's my wife, and this is my house. I'll thank you to remember it."

"Not anymore." Kate heard her own voice with surprise. She stepped out from behind Dixon, though not very far. "There's a divorce pending, L.T. Remember?"

He snarled, clenched his fists and took another step toward her. She felt Dixon tense; for one instant, she thought there would be a brawl right there in her great room.

But the kids came clomping down the stairs, all eager and innocent and ready to take their dad up on his unusual generosity. The violence in the room disintegrated, and both men retreated. Kate could breathe again, and think.

For some reason, it seemed very important that she be the one to leave the house first. She couldn't explain it to herself, but she couldn't ignore the compulsion, either.

So while the kids were still talking and Kelsey was checking her makeup one more time, Kate looked at Dixon. "Are you ready to go?"

"If you are."

She nodded. On the way to the door, she put a hand on Kelsey's shoulder. "Be sure the door is locked when you leave, okay?"

The girl nodded absentmindedly, intent on her hair. Kate turned to Trace. "Check the door lock and be sure you have a key with you," she told him, interrupting his conversation with his father. L.T. glared, and Trace shrugged a shoulder in acknowledgment. It was the best she could do.

"Okay, then." She went to the chair in the hall

and picked up her purse. Turning to Dixon, she gave him the brightest, bravest smile she could muster. "Shall we do lunch?"

Holding the door, he grinned widely in return. "I thought you'd never ask."

CHAPTER FIVE

DIXON DIDN'T SAY MUCH as he drove out of town—
he thought maybe Kate needed some time to re-
cover from the encounter with her ex-husband. He
hadn't come that close to hitting a man in years,
and he hated having almost lost his temper. But if
one person on the planet could push him that far,
he had a feeling it would be L. T. LaRue.

As the traffic and strip malls fell behind them
and the country opened up into cotton and corn
fields edged by needle-straight pines, Kate drew
a deep breath and, finally, looked at him. "Where
are we going? Not somewhere nearby, obviously."

"Not too far away." He punched the button to
turn the music on, letting soft bluegrass flow into
the truck. "I remembered this place from a wedding Miss Daisy made me go to, back when I
was about fifteen. I didn't know much about atmosphere and good food, but I've always thought
I'd like to go back and see if it was as special as I
recall. And since they're still open, I decided I'd
find out with you."

"Are you talking about Moseby House Inn?"

"You got it."

"Well, I can tell you from here that it's every bit as special as you remember. It's a wonderful place to eat, to stay—" She broke off and cleared her throat. "And the shops are just lovely. I could spend hours in the garden store alone. There's the book and music shop, and a toy store, too. And I haven't been in ages." She smiled at him, a sweet, relaxed curve of those soft lips. "Thank you."

"Anytime." Dixon was grinning inside.

He shifted in his seat. "How's your week been?"

"Oh…" She seemed bewildered. "Fine. About the same as usual."

"What's the usual?" Dixon really wanted to know. For thirteen years he'd thought about what Kate Bowdrey was doing at any given moment, if she was happy, if she was in love, if the world was treating her right. He felt as though he had a lot of her life to catch up on. Might as well start with the present.

Turning a little in the seat to face him, Kate shrugged her slender shoulders. "Take Trace and Kelsey to school, pick them up in the afternoon. Grocery shopping, cooking, laundry, cleaning, yard work."

"Do the kids help?"

"Trace mows the grass. Kelsey is responsible for cleaning up the kitchen after dinner. And they're both pretty good about keeping their rooms neat."

"That's got to be a rare talent among teenagers."

She laughed, then sobered. "L.T. is fairly... strict...about having everything in order. When they were small, we always made sure all the toys were put away before he came home at night."

A simple enough comment, but all too revealing. Dixon sent a mental curse toward the man who couldn't enjoy his kids' playthings scattered around the house. "So what do you do in your spare time?"

There was a pause. "Well, during school I volunteer for the various events. I've been working with the historical society and the women's club on the renovations downtown. And I organized the Azalea Festival Street Fair this year. For better or worse." Her sigh was all the invitation Dixon needed to probe further.

"What happened?"

Kate's explanation of Kelsey's troubles and Trace's rebellion—poor grades, smoking, sneaking out at night, vandalism and a bomb threat that had disrupted the street fair—occupied the rest of the drive. As Dixon pulled the truck into the parking lot at the Moseby House Inn, she leaned her head back against the seat with another sigh. "Not exactly the ideal family, are we?"

He took her left hand in both of his, noticing with relief that she didn't wear any rings. "I'm not sure there is an ideal family. Everybody has their problems. Sounds to me like you handled yours pretty well, without much help from the person who's most responsible for the mess to begin with." Without thinking, following instinct, he lifted his hands and pressed a kiss on her smooth, cool fingers.

She made a small sound. With his mouth still against her skin, Dixon looked up to meet Kate's startled eyes. Her cheeks were flushed, her lips parted, and every part of him demanded *more,* urged that he pull her into his arms and claim that sweet mouth for his own.

Every part except his brain, which knew that he could lose her if he went too fast. The outcome would be worth the wait, he was sure of that.

So he pressed one last kiss on her knuckles and set her hand gently back on the seat beside her. "What do you say we get some lunch?"

Her smile was relieved and—maybe?—a little disappointed. "I'd love to."

Kate didn't know what to think about that moment of intimacy when Dixon had pressed his mouth against her skin. As the afternoon went on, he kept her laughing during their meal with stories about his exploits working as a cowboy, as a roughneck in the oil fields, as a short-order cook in a Kansas truck stop. But he didn't touch her again, didn't mesmerize her with the intensity of his gaze the way he had for those few seconds. He was more than patient as she browsed through the garden shop, carefully considering the statuary, the pots, the tools in a way that made her wonder if he had some garden plans of his own in mind. In the bookstore he gravitated to the hardcovers while she looked at the paperback novels. She was more of a romance reader than anything else, and the month's new selections had just arrived, but she didn't see herself walking out with a bundle of romances under her arm for Dixon to comment on. So she stared at the mysteries without seeing anything she really wanted to read and they both left empty-handed.

"Toy store?" he asked, slowing down as they passed the window.

"Do you have someone who likes toys?"

"Yes, ma'am. Me!"

Inside the shop, Kate followed Dixon around as he examined all the different boy toys—trains and cars and trucks, building blocks and chemistry sets and puzzles of all kinds. He even investigated the dolls. "This one," he said of an elegant beauty in old-fashioned pink flounces, "looks like you." He tilted the box and the doll's eyes closed. "Sleeping Beauty, awaiting her prince."

Kate laughed the idea away. "I've met the prince, thank you very much."

Dixon put the doll back on the shelf without looking her way. "No, you met the dragon. You haven't got a clue about what a real prince could do for you." He left her staring at him with her jaw hanging loose as he moved farther down the aisle.

The sun was still blazing hot when they stepped out into the courtyard around which the shops were clustered. Dixon bought fresh-squeezed lemonade at the tiny ice-cream parlor for each of them to enjoy as they walked the brick-paved path, where the sharp scent of boxwood shrubs mingled with sweeter flower fragrances from the gardens. Kate thought she could easily have spent the rest of the day taking notes on the different planting designs set in between and in front of the quaint buildings.

When they'd finished, though, she decided she'd better mention the inevitable. "It's probably time for me to get back home. I think I can trust Trace and Kelsey now, but I don't like to leave them alone too long."

Dixon nodded. "I understand. Dating a woman with responsibilities has its price."

Kate worried over that one for a while. A date? She had tried not to think of this as a real date. The implications were just too staggering to take in.

The ride home was silent, but not uncomfortably so. Dixon's choice of music was soothing, a ripple of guitar and banjo, the wheedle of a fiddle, and a sweet, plaintive voice singing of love lost and found. At one point they went over a bump in the road and Kate opened her eyes with the realization that she'd been dozing.

She sat up straighter. "I'm so sorry—I didn't intend to fall asleep on you."

"No problem. I've been thinking you could use more rest than you're getting."

He'd been thinking about her. Kate took a deep breath. "I had a lovely time this afternoon. Thank you very much."

"I enjoyed every single minute." He hesitated for a second. "And now I'm going to ask a favor."

"Of course. What is it?"

"Well, here's the thing. I want to get Magnolia Cottage back in order. I know what needs to be repaired, what needs to be updated, and I can tell that the grounds have to be cleared before anything meaningful can happen. But when it comes to actually choosing colors and furniture and curtains…I just don't have the practice, let alone the talent."

"Miss Daisy…"

"Is willing to go along, but I'm thinking it's a lot to ask of her, at her age, to make all those decisions. What I thought was that you could work with her, as a consultant, I guess—find out what she likes and what she wants, then use that as a starting point for the details that have to be considered."

"The entire house?"

"That's my plan."

"It's a really big project."

"I know. And I'm not expecting you to work for free. You're welcome to set a rate on your services, and charge me for labor and materials, of course."

"I couldn't do that, Dixon. We're friends."

"For now." Another second's pause. "But I also want advice on planning the gardens. This is really a full-time job, Kate. I can't use your expertise and not pay for it."

"Then we're at an impasse."

"Well, I think I'm usually fairly easy to get along with. Occasionally, though, I get real stubborn." His white grin flashed in her direction as he turned the wheel to take the corner of the street where she lived. "So you'll just have to give in."

Kate tried to consider the situation as Dixon pulled his truck into the driveway and walked her to the front door. Her thoughts were jumbled—her desire for the opportunity to bring Magnolia Cottage back to its gracious self conflicted with a very real concern that she wasn't up to the challenge. She didn't have any formal training, had never worked on any house other than her own.

Scarier still was the possibility of seeing Dixon on a regular basis, because she now knew just how vulnerable she was to his charm. She'd been dreading the end of this afternoon almost from the moment she saw him at the front door. Could she keep "business" and personal feelings separate? If this was business, she should probably charge him something. But how could she take money from Dixon, or his grandmother, whom she considered a friend?

She reached the porch, still in a state of indecision. Only as she started up the steps did she see the paper wedged between the door and the frame. When she pulled it out, she recognized L.T.'s small, neat printing.

The movie was sold out all afternoon, so we have tickets for the 7:00 p.m. show. We ate lunch and thought we'd play around until then—batting cage, bowling, miniature golf, who knows? I'll get them home after the movie ends.

"Well." At a loss, she turned to gaze at Dixon, standing on the walk at the base of the porch steps. That meant she had to look down slightly, which gave her a new perspective on the smooth planes of his cheeks, the waves in his hair, and a greater appreciation for the deep brown of his eyes. "Um…the kids are still with their dad. I always hoped he'd recognize what he was missing when he didn't see them." She said it as much to herself as the man in front of her. "I wonder why he changed so quickly."

Shaking off the question, Kate pulled up a smile. "Anyway, thank you again—"

Dixon held up his hand, silencing her. "Does that mean you've got some more time on your hands? Nothing urgent calling for your attention?"

"Um…I suppose so." Her heart started to thud against her ribs. "Yes."

He closed his fingers gently around her wrist. "Then you could spend that time with me?"

Now she couldn't breathe, couldn't make a sound. But she didn't resist as he tugged her arm to lead her down the steps.

"You can come with me now, get a look at the cottage and let me give you an idea of my plans. You'll probably see things I haven't thought of doing. And you could get started on your own ideas, however it is you figure out what a room should look like."

The thought occurred to her, as he walked her back to the truck, that the whole day had been about his plans for the house. Maybe Dixon had taken her out to lunch just to put her under an obligation to him so she would feel compelled to help him renovate Magnolia Cottage. He had used that lady-killer smile and all the charm in his arsenal to soften her up so that she had no choice but to agree. And she'd taken the bait—hook, line and sinker.

What a fool she was when it came to men!

Kate suffered in silence as she followed Dixon across the grass to the driveway, let him open the truck door for her, even hold her elbow as she stepped up into the high seat. But that was as far as she could go. Then she turned back to face him. "Dixon…"

He hadn't yet closed the door, and still stood with a hand on the back of the seat, barely brushing her shoulder. "This is just an excuse, you know," he said quietly.

She could only stare at him as he confirmed her worst fears.

"I had to think of a way to get to see more of you. And when Mary Rose mentioned that you were so good at—what did she call it? 'dressing a room'?—I started thinking along those lines. I mean, your house really is beautiful, inside and out." He stroked his fingers down her cheek. "Just like you. So it seems like the perfect solution to me. If you don't mind too much."

There were reasons to be cautious. Kate was

sure of that. She just couldn't remember what they were. "I don't mind at all."

Dixon gave her a slow, sexy smile. "I was hoping you'd say that."

UNDER THE GRAY neon glare of the electronics store, Trace pulled his sister into the aisle behind the video cameras as their dad waited at the sales desk to pay for the latest gadget he'd decided they needed. "Why are you going along with him?"

Kelsey opened her eyes wide. "What are you talking about? What's wrong with getting the new tablet? You've been bugging Kate for months."

"Raleigh last weekend, a movie and all this family togetherness garbage today. What's he want?"

She shrugged. "To be a dad?"

"Why now?"

"How should I know? Maybe he's tired of the Bimbo," she offered, referring to the secretary their dad had decided he couldn't live without. "Maybe he just needed some time off and now he wants to be with us again. Why are you complaining?"

"Doesn't feel right. It's too good to be true."

His sister rolled her eyes, then softened up enough to put a hand on his shoulder. "Look, I don't blame you for not trusting him. He's blown it big time, over and over again. So be careful, protect yourself. But you might as well take advantage of what he's giving out these days. Sure beats a measly breakfast at the diner every two weeks."

Trace wasn't convinced. His breakfast at the diner that morning, with five men who treated him like a friend, had to be one of the best things that had ever happened to him. Dixon Bell was too cool, telling stories that always seemed to end up with him looking foolish, even ridiculous. As if he didn't mind being laughed at. Hard to imagine not minding what people thought of you. Dixon obviously liked himself well enough that other opinions didn't matter.

"All right, there we go." Their dad joined them on the aisle. "We pick up the box at the counter on the way out, and you guys are finally entering the twenty-first century. About time, isn't it?"

Trace shoved his hands into his pockets. "I guess so," he said in response to his dad's expectant stare. "Thanks."

"It'll be great." Kelsey was wearing her megawatt smile. "But we don't have the accessories."

"That's the next stop." With an arm around each of them, their dad headed toward another section. "Each of you pick out the extra things you want to buy. Think that'll do for a start?"

He's up to something, Trace thought. *What*

can we do for him? Who's he trying to beat out this time?

Only one logical answer occurred to him. *Kate.*

"So MY RAPSCALLION grandson has talked you into helping him with his grandiose plans, has he?" Miss Daisy had agreed to let Kate help her wash the dinner dishes, but only after Dixon threatened to carry her bodily from the kitchen otherwise.

"Well, it is a lovely building. Such gorgeous woodwork and these high ceilings…" Kate sighed as she dried the porcelain platter on which Miss Daisy had served ham and cheese sandwiches with the crusts removed. "Restoring some of its glory would be a real privilege." Dixon's tour had been long and detailed, and he'd successfully ignited Kate's enthusiasm for his plans.

"But new bathrooms and a new kitchen? I've cooked in this one just fine for sixty years now."

There appeared to be some ruffled feathers Dixon hadn't mentioned. "I'm sure of that, Miss Daisy. Your contributions to the historical society picnics and potluck dinners are legendary. I think Dixon is just trying to make things easier for you. I'm sure if you felt really strongly about something, he'd leave it just the way it is, for your sake."

The older woman let the water out of the sink, wrung out her sponge and set it aside to dry.

"You're right, of course. And I don't have the heart to do that to him. He wants to build his home here, raise a family, from what he says." Her smile was gentle, her usually fierce blue gaze soft. "Who am I to argue? I'd love to hold my great-grandbaby in my arms before I pass on."

Kate swallowed hard. A family? Babies? That would require a wife. Was Dixon thinking...? Her mind scampered away from the idea. "I'm sure there's plenty of time for that. You've got more energy in your little finger than I can claim in a whole week." She dried the last glasses and put them away. "So let's think about humoring the man in your life. What's your favorite color?"

They sat in the main parlor for a while talking about which shades of blue would take advantage of the light in the room. Dixon had been sent on an errand to fetch vanilla ice cream to eat with homemade pound cake and strawberries picked and frozen only three months earlier.

After finishing every bite on her plate, Kate sat back with a sigh. "You're right, Miss Daisy. You create miracles in that kitchen of yours. Dixon, I don't think you should change a thing."

"Not even a dishwasher?"

"I don't know. There's something soothing about washing dishes by hand. Time to think, to reflect, to talk. We've got all sorts of modern conveniences to make life easier, but I'm not sure they've made life better. We're in such a hurry these days, we don't take time to connect with the other people in our lives." Kate gave a self-conscious laugh. "That's easy for me to say, I suppose, when I can choose whether or not to use the dishwasher. For someone who doesn't have the option, I'm sure it would look like a gift from heaven."

Miss Daisy reached across the table and covered Kate's hand with her own. "My dear, don't apologize. I've lived long enough to have seen the miracle of one day become the bane of the next. People don't think ahead much anymore. If they ever did." She shook her neatly coiffed head. "Maybe that's mankind's besetting sin. A lack of forethought."

"This is getting really intense." Dixon stood up and gathered the dishes. "I'll let the two of you philosophize while I wash up." He lifted an eyebrow as both Daisy and Kate started to protest, which silenced them quite effectively. "Then I probably ought to get Kate home. The movie will be over in half an hour or so."

After promising to visit early in the week to talk more about the house, Kate left Miss Daisy on the porch and followed Dixon to his truck. She felt calm and relaxed as they wound their way through the tree-lined streets of New Skye. Dixon was so easy to be with, Kate kept forgetting to be on her guard, forgetting to watch what she said and how she said it. How many years had it been since she felt free to be simply herself?

In the driveway, she turned toward the man in the driver's seat. He already had his door open. "You don't have to walk me in. The yard's not that big."

He shut the door and came around the rear of the truck to open hers. "My grandmother taught me to be a gentleman. Can't disappoint Miss Daisy." Taking her hand, he helped her down and kept his fingers clasped through hers as they started across the lawn. Suddenly, Kate couldn't seem to draw a deep enough breath.

At the door, though, she had to disengage to find her key in her purse. She'd forgotten to turn on the lights before leaving and the house was dark, inside and out. Aware of Dixon just behind her, she pushed the door open, then stepped inside and went to the table in the great room to turn on a lamp.

"Don't." Dixon's voice was quiet in the silent, empty house. "You are so beautiful in the moonlight."

She looked around, realized that the summer moon was shining through the window on the front of the house, spotlighting her in its beams. "There's a song like that, isn't there?"

Dixon nodded as he came closer. "'Moonlight

Becomes You.'" He hummed a few bars. "We could dance."

Somehow, without her volition, that's what they were doing, dancing to the tune Dixon produced in a soft baritone, swaying, gliding, moving out of the moon's light and into the shadows of the hall. He put his arms around her, and his hands were big and warm on her shoulders, as they'd been that first afternoon in the rainstorm...

Then his fingers were tangled in her hair, his palms tilting her face up, his mouth taking hers. Warm...no, burning. Branding.

Kate knew she didn't possess that kind of passion. Didn't have the courage even to try.

She pressed her hands against Dixon's chest, turned her head away. He dropped his arms instantly and stepped back. After a minute, he ran his hand over his hair.

"I apologize. I...didn't mean for anything to get out of hand."

"No, don't. It's not you. I mean—" Outside, a car door slammed, and then another. Lights flashed through the open front door as the vehicle pulled away from the curb. Kate sighed. "The kids are home." She turned back to switch on the lamp.

"Yeah." Dixon stepped out onto the porch as Trace and Kelsey reached the steps. "Hey there. Looks like you've made a haul. I just brought your mom home—hadn't even had time to turn on the lights." It was clumsy, for Dixon. But the children wouldn't notice. He leaned back inside after they'd bustled in. "Thanks again, Kate. I'll call you next week about a meeting."

"Of...course." He was gone before she got the words out. And then she was caught up in the excitement of figuring out the tablet—Trace's department, since he was their electronics expert—and she joined the kids to watch one of the movies L.T. had downloaded onto it. More money spent on his children. Why?

The film didn't hold her attention and she woke up after a couple of hours to find the kids had gone upstairs, leaving her asleep in the recliner. Too comfortable to move, Kate sat alone in the dark, reliving the magic of Dixon Bell's kiss, wishing she could be the woman he seemed to think she was.

Wishing she could be the woman he deserved.

AFTER DROPPING OFF Trace and Kelsey, L.T. drove down the street and parked within the shadows of an old oak tree, waiting for the truck in his driveway to leave. He didn't wonder whose truck it was—he'd seen Dixon Bell's vehicle parked in front of the old stables that had been converted into a garage at Magnolia Cottage. The man hadn't gotten around to changing his Colorado license plate yet. That was another issue to be investigated—there were laws about how long he could wait before reregistering as a resident.

And L.T. sure didn't wonder what Kate and Dixon Bell had been doing in his house with all the lights off. The whole lunch excuse could have been a lie. They might have waited until the coast was clear to come back and spend the afternoon and evening together in *his* bed.

Except the truck hadn't been there when they'd stopped by to leave the note, at Kelsey's insistence. But it could have been hidden somewhere so the neighbors wouldn't notice...

The big diesel Ford backed down the driveway and headed toward the other end of the street. At least Bell had the decency to leave once the kids came home.

As the Ford turned the corner, L.T. eased his Yukon out of the shadows in pursuit. He wasn't exactly sure why he was following Bell, except that he figured he could use any little piece of information he came across to his advantage. Every man had his weak points. Might as well discover Dixon Bell's as soon as possible.

Instead of going directly home, Bell drove to one of New Skye's commercial strips. He stopped at a gas station, filled the truck's fuel tank and went inside to pay while L.T. watched from a drive-through burger place with a clear view.

When the tall man came out again, he was carrying a plastic bag, pretty clearly a bag of chips. L.T. was able to pick up his burger and cola just as Dixon Bell drove by, this time headed in the direction of Magnolia Cottage.

The Ford turned in at the brick pillars and L.T. was tempted to give up. The house was too far from the street for him to see, screened by overgrown trees and bushes, to boot. The man was probably going inside anyway. There wouldn't be anything to watch except the flicker of a TV through the windows, if that.

But something urged him to park the Yukon and walk down the driveway in the shadows of those trees, keeping his footsteps quiet on the gravel. He'd been a Boy Scout once. He knew how to stalk without being heard.

And his reward was a view of Dixon Bell sitting on the front porch of his dilapidated mansion with the potato chips beside him on the step. Elbows propped on his knees, the man ate the whole bag within what L.T. had to admit was an impressively short period of time.

Then Bell sat motionless for what seemed like an hour, with his face hidden in his hands. L.T. didn't dare move, hardly dared to breathe. Was the idiot going to sit out here all night long? He looked like a derelict with no place to go.

Eventually, the man on the porch dropped his

hands to his knees and pushed himself to his feet. Bell went inside and closed the panel behind him.

L.T. let out a deep breath, stretched his back and headed for his vehicle. He still kept to the shadows, just in case someone should look out the windows into the moon-bright night. But he didn't expect to be noticed.

And L.T. could see the beginnings of a perfect plan. Megabuck condos were all well and good, profitable in the short term. But who had the deepest pockets of all? Who never ran out of money, because the only certainties in life were death and, more to the point, taxes?

Why, Uncle Sam, of course.

CHAPTER SIX

DIXON WOKE UP on Sunday morning with a headache.

He'd kissed Kate Bowdrey.

Even after dreaming about that moment for half his life, he had been totally unprepared for the impact. He'd had his share of relationships since leaving home and he thought he understood the nature of give-and-take between a woman and a man. But Kate…

In high school she'd been bright, sharp, like a star he gazed at from a distance and could only wish for. Now the star had fallen, and from the earth where she'd landed had sprung a flower, soft and fragile, yet somehow containing that same brilliant energy of the star. One touch of her mouth against his, the sweet sigh she gave as she yielded to his hold, and he'd lost every shred of his control.

He might have lost Kate, as well. No question but she was surprised by—even afraid of—what he'd let loose last night. She'd had reservations before they went to lunch. How could she trust him now? Dixon wasn't sure he trusted himself anymore. After a lifetime of practicing self-discipline, he'd learned just how weak his willpower really was.

Groaning, he rolled to his back, eyes tightly closed against the light sneaking through the dusty windows. So much to do with this house. He needed to get started. Would it all be for nothing? Would Kate ever let him get close again?

The click of high heels sounded on the floor of the hallway. "Dixon?" Miss Daisy rapped on the closed door. "We need to leave for church in about thirty minutes."

"Yes, ma'am." Talking above a whisper was an exercise in masochism. "I'll be ready."

A shower, shave and clean clothes made him look conscious, even though the jackhammer inside his head still thundered on. Miss Daisy didn't believe in medicine, which was probably why she was so rarely sick, and there wasn't an aspirin in the house. Black coffee was the strongest drug he could find.

"I really enjoyed talking with Kate last night," Miss Daisy commented as they rolled down the driveway in her New Yorker. "She's a lovely young woman."

"That she is."

"And I think she'll be a pleasure to work with, if you're really set on taking on this project."

"I am."

He felt his grandmother's sideways glance. "You're not too talkative this morning. Did you sleep well?"

More a coma than sleep. "Not very."

She nodded. "Kate seemed to like the house."

"It's a beautiful place."

"Do you think she'll be willing to live there when you're married?"

"I hope so. I—" He braked too hard at the red light and looked at her in exasperation. "Miss Daisy."

"It's not very hard to see how you feel, dear. You practically glow when she's in the room."

"That's embarrassing. Grown men don't glow."

"Of course they do. Your father was the same about your mother. His eyes brightened every time he looked at her."

"I don't remember that." Against his will, the memories invaded. "I just remember the shouting."

"Shouting? What are you talking about?"

But they'd reached the parking lot of First Presbyterian Church, where his family had been among the founding members some two hundred years ago. Dixon was out of the car and opening Miss Daisy's door before he had to answer. Though she kept casting him puzzled looks, there were friends of hers to greet as they walked to-

ward the sanctuary, and their seats to occupy—
always the fourth pew from the front, sitting on
the right side if there was room. He'd never been
so glad to hear an organ start up. And Dixon did
not like organ music.

But with the preacher talking, at least he
wouldn't have to.

JOHN AND FRANCES BOWDREY joined Kate and her
children for Sunday lunch. As Kate removed the
salad plates and brought out the roast chicken,
Kelsey looked up. "Sal's coming over this afternoon, remember?"

"I do." Although she would have preferred not
to mention it in front of her mother.

Frances Bowdrey included both of them in her
frown. "You're still seeing that boy? After all the
trouble he got you into last spring?"

Kelsey stuck out her lower lip in a pout. Kate
stepped into the breach. "They're not sneaking
around anymore, Mama, because I agreed to let
Sal come here. I think that's an improvement."

"But he's completely...unsuitable."

"He's a nice boy. I don't mind that Kelsey has
him for a friend."

Her daughter brightened up. "I thought we'd
go swimming at the club."

Kate straightened up slowly from refilling her

dad's iced tea. Both grandparents stiffened in their chairs.

Trace gave a snort. "Yeah, right. Like they'll even allow you inside the gate."

"What are you talking about?"

His smile was mostly sneer. "The country club doesn't let just anybody in, you know. Even as a guest. I'm betting that Sal is on their 'No Way Do You Get Into Our Space' list."

Kelsey's cry of "Shut up!" clashed with Kate's stern warning, "Trace…" The boy shrugged and took a long draw from his glass.

"I doubt the club manager will be pleased if you appear with this…this Sal person." Frances dabbed her lips with her napkin. "If you must see him, you might be more comfortable at one of the public pools."

"That's stupid. He's as good as anybody else in that place."

Frances made her point with a delicate sniff. "Tradition is important, Kelsey. And the club's tradition has been to—"

"Be bigoted against anybody who isn't rich?" Kelsey surged to her feet. "Well, forget that. I'm taking Sal to the club pool and we will get in." With her hair bouncing on her shoulders, she stalked from the room.

"Such manners. Such behavior." Kate's mother

shook her head. "And I'm afraid she's setting herself up for a severe disappointment."

"She is right, Mama." Kate sank into her own chair, without the least desire to eat. "The club will have to change those 'traditions.' The world is a different place these days."

Her father cleared his throat. "Unfortunately."

At that point Kate knew her words were wasted. She continued to argue, for Trace's sake, because he seemed to have absorbed the same "traditional" beliefs as his grandparents. But by the end of the meal, she doubted she'd made headway with any of them.

Trace went out about two-thirty to show off his new gadgets to friends who lived nearby. When Sal arrived at three, Kelsey was bright, welcoming and defiantly committed to her course of action. Thirty minutes after the couple left, they returned through the front door.

Kate was just coming down the stairs with a basket of laundry. "You didn't swim?" Neither had wet hair or that telltale chlorinated look to their eyes and skin.

Kelsey threw her carryall bag down the hallway, where it slammed against the kitchen door, raining towels and assorted cosmetics all over the floor. "They told me they were closing for an hour to clean the pool."

"Was that true?"

"We waited, and they did pull everybody out. But Sal has to be home by five, so we wouldn't have had but twenty minutes to swim anyway." She brushed a hand over her eyes. "I think they just did it so they wouldn't have to let us in. Why clean the pool in the middle of a Sunday afternoon?"

Kate silently agreed with her. "Well, you have an hour to hang around here, anyway. Help yourselves to some ice-cream pie and iced tea." She looked at Sal. "I'm sorry your plans didn't work out."

He really was a very attractive young man, well built, with an angel's face. "It's okay." His shrug was eloquent with disdain. "I enjoy being with Kelsey whatever we do." Graceful with words, as well as with his body. Like Dixon Bell...which made him just about perfect.

Kelsey sighed and linked her arm through his. "You're so sweet. Let's get something to eat."

"First pick up your mess," Kate instructed with a nod down the hallway. "I can't get to the washing machine until you do."

Laughing, Sal and Kelsey did as she asked, and then Sal opened the kitchen door and the door to the basement for Kate as she made her way down to the laundry room. When she climbed up with a load of clean clothes, she found him opening the doors again. "Thank you very much. Would you like to come every day, just to open doors?"

His warm gaze cooled and his chin came up, as if she'd insulted him. But then he seemed to rethink her comment. "Anytime," he said easily. "Just give me a call."

But on the way to the bedrooms, Kate realized the young man probably expected her to classify him as a servant, only good for menial labor like opening doors. The idea made her want to weep.

She was still putting away clothes when she heard Sal and Kelsey arrive at the front door, heard the profound silence that indicated a good-bye embrace. Immediately, she was in the same place last night, locked in Dixon's arms with his mouth moving over hers, evoking what felt like a volcano of emotion inside her. If Sal did that for Kelsey...

Suddenly, the front door swung open with its distinctive squeak. Kelsey gasped, and there was a scuffle of feet.

"Get your hands off her," Trace growled. "And get out of my house."

"When I'm ready," Sal said in a menacing voice.

Kate stood at the top of the stairs. "Stop it, both of you. Sal, you should be going if you have to be home by five. Trace, I'll talk to you in your room."

The two boys held their battle stances for another instant. Kelsey gave Sal a push on the shoulder, and the tension broke. Trace jogged up the steps and rushed past Kate, slamming his door at the other end of the hall.

Kelsey looked up from the bottom of the staircase. "What am I going to do? Why are people so blind?"

"I don't know, honey." Kate shook her head, as baffled as her daughter and wondering what in the world she could say to change Trace's mind. "I just don't know."

WHEN SAL TORRES ARRIVED to pick up his mother Tuesday at noon, Dixon was waiting for him on the front porch. The boy surveyed him from the car for a few seconds without moving, then got out and propped his arms on the roof of the Taurus. "You want something?"

Dixon stood up. "I have a proposition to make if you've got time. Want to come inside and get a drink?"

He thought Sal was honestly surprised. "Uh… okay."

Dixon took him back to the kitchen and waved him into a chair at the table. "Water, tea or soda?"

"Water's good."

With two tall glasses of ice water in his hands,

he came to the table and sat down. They both took a minute to enjoy the cold drink.

Then Sal set down his glass. "So what's this all about?"

Dixon leaned back in his chair. "I want to do some work on this place. I'm acting as the contractor, so I need to line up labor for the projects. I've asked around and folks in the business tell me your dad has a lot of experience in construction and carpentry."

"They also tell you he's got a drinking problem?"

"Yeah, they did."

"So what's your point?"

"I'm willing to take a chance. I thought he might know a couple of other guys who would take on the work, too."

Sal stared at him. "Where's the catch?"

"Hard work."

"What do you pay?"

"DeVries pays twelve-fifty an hour. I'll match that."

"You made of money, man?"

Dixon decided not to explain the advantages of a decade spent writing songs for some of country music's biggest stars. Or the money to be made on oil rigs, if you didn't mind risking your life on an hourly basis. "I do okay. Will you talk to your dad?"

"My mom'll do that—she can convince him. When do you want him to start?"

"I'll look for him at 7:00 a.m. Thursday. We'll spend a couple of days surveying the job and start work Monday morning."

"Salvadore?" Consuela came into the kitchen, and both Dixon and Sal got to their feet. "What are you doing here?"

"Just getting a glass of water, Mama. Are you ready to go?"

"Of course." She bobbed a curtsy at Dixon. "Have a good day, Mr. Dixon."

"You, as well, Mrs. Torres."

Consuela cast him a questioning look and hurried Sal out of the room. Dixon sat down again and sipped his water until Miss Daisy joined him a few minutes later.

"So you've started?" She took a loaf of bread out of the cabinet. "Tomato sandwiches for lunch?"

"Sounds great. Yes, ma'am, I've started."

"Now you need to call Kate."

He pulled in a deep breath. "I need to call Kate."

What he really needed was to see Kate, but he would take it slow. While Miss Daisy was at the hairdresser that afternoon, he picked up the telephone. "Hey, Kate."

"Dixon!" He would swear there was pleasure in her tone. "How are you?"

Hearing her voice, much better. "Great. Miss Daisy and I were wondering if you're ready to get to work."

"Well…" Her voice held an undertone of laughter. "As a matter of fact, I've got some fabric samples and paint chips here."

"Excellent." Did that mean she wanted to see him again? Or at least wasn't afraid? "When can you come over?" She could drive her car, and feel free to leave anytime. Or to stay as long as she wanted.

"I have two hours before I pick Trace and Kelsey up at school. Should I come now?"

"Sounds like a great idea. But…" He had to be honest. "Miss Daisy isn't here. She's getting her hair done."

"Oh." Now he could hear the doubt. "I suppose it wouldn't be much use then, talking paint and curtains." She hesitated, came back timidly. "We didn't get a chance on Saturday to discuss what you want to do outside, though. And it's not too hot today. We could walk through the gardens and talk about your plans for the grounds."

Dixon heaved a huge sigh of relief. "I'll look for you when you get here."

To his delight, Kate arrived within fifteen minutes. He made himself wait until she rang the bell before opening the door. "Come on in. Would you like something to drink? Miss Daisy made tea this morning."

"I'm fine, thanks." She looked up at him, her smile fresh and wide, no caution obvious. "Let's walk through this jungle of yours."

"At your service, ma'am."

Outside, she put on the wide-brimmed straw hat she carried. "I think you might want to kill all this grass in front and start over with sod. It'll take years to get the kind of lawn you can enjoy, otherwise."

Dixon made a note on the pad he carried. "Nuke the front yard."

Kate laughed. "You have such a way with words." She followed the walk to the driveway. "And repair the bricks." Then she turned to the overgrown band of trees and bushes bordering the lane to the street. "What are we going to do with this?"

The time for her to leave arrived long before they'd surveyed even half the grounds. Kate stood in the shade of a tulip poplar and fanned her face with her hat. "I can come back earlier tomorrow so we can keep going."

"If you have the time." Dixon leaned back against the tree's trunk and held up his notepad. "I've got four pages filled so far. Even I am a little daunted by what needs to be done out here."

"You don't have to do it all at once. You can't plant until you clear. So the first job is clearing out what you don't want."

"I'm thinking I need to borrow an army from somewhere to get that done. Not exactly a spare-time project."

Kate gazed at the disaster surrounding them. "You know, Trace helps me in the yard and seems to like it. He may have a couple of friends who would join in. Kelsey will come out occasionally, if it's not too unbearably hot. You'd probably have to pay them something," she said apologetically. "But they've got huge amounts of energy. With some supervision, you could get quite a bit done."

"I think it's a terrific idea." They started the walk to her car. "Can you check with Trace?"

"Oh, I'm sure he'd be even more enthusiastic if the invitation came from you. Since the basketball game, you're pretty much at the top of his list."

"We're hoping he'll play again this weekend."

"Well, then, you've got two reasons to call him." At the Volvo, she turned to face him. "And I'll talk to Kelsey. That's a start on your army, at least."

"Sounds great. We can commence this Saturday, if that works for Trace and Kelsey."

"I think it will."

He waited while she opened the car door and then faced her across the panel, with his hands resting on either side of hers along the top edge. "Kate, before you leave, I want to apologize for Saturday night. I didn't intend to let things get out of hand. I'm really sorry."

"No, don't apologize. It was wonderful, it's just…" She lowered her chin, so all he could see was her shiny dark curls. "I don't think I can give you what you want."

"What do you mean?"

"If you're looking for something—someone—special, I-I'm afraid you're going to be disappointed." Her shoulders lifted on a sigh. "I'm simply Kate LaRue, housewife, mother. That's all."

Dixon gripped the car door even tighter. "That's all. Kate Bowdrey LaRue, beautiful, intelligent, charming, intoxicating." She looked up at him, shocked and disturbed. "Ah, Kate. Let me show you all you are." He bent his head, keeping his hands still beside hers, so that the only point of contact was their mouths.

And then he gave. All the years of his devotion—his adolescent longings, his loneliness, his homesickness, the nights he'd ached for her, the days he'd worked himself to exhaustion so he could sleep without dreams—given to her in his kiss, along with a very real love he couldn't conceal if he tried.

When Dixon lifted his head, Kate stood with

her eyes closed for a long time, unwilling to let go of such lovely feelings. She'd never been kissed like that in her whole life, and she wanted it to last forever. The sweet scent of honeysuckle threaded through the breeze, sealing the moment in her mind.

Finally, though, she lifted her eyelids and looked into Dixon's face, seeing his brown eyes so close, so intense, she felt as if he were still touching her.

He smiled, gently, regretfully. "You'd better go, or you'll be late to get Trace and Kelsey."

Kate drew a breath, nodded, and sank into the seat of the Volvo. Words were still beyond her. Dixon picked up her hat off the ground and handed it to her. "I'll see you tomorrow?"

She nodded again and he shut the door. After a minute, she lifted a hand to the ignition and turned the key. The sound of the engine grounded her in reality enough so that she remembered how to drive, remembered where she was supposed to go, and why.

But she had to force herself to focus on the traffic signals, the other cars, as she headed toward New Skye High School. Her mind showed an alarming tendency to drift back to Dixon, to that incredible kiss. She sat in the parking lot and waited without any sense of time passing, only to jump in alarm when her daughter dropped into the passenger seat.

"Let's get some music." Kelsey reached for the radio knob. "Oh, yuck, country." She fingered the tuning button, preparing to change stations.

But Kate had recognized the notes coming out of the speakers. She clasped a hand around Kelsey's wrist. "No, don't."

"Kate..."

But Kate ignored the protest and turned up the volume, so lost in the pleasure of "My Dream" that even when Trace got into the car, she didn't pull out right away.

Was it possible she could have a love like this? Was Dixon the man who would fulfill *her* dreams?

Was she brave enough to seize the chance to be truly happy?

MANO TORRES CAME HOME sober Thursday night. Sal was drawn out of his bedroom by the sounds coming through the open window—children laughing and giggling, with a deeper voice joining in. When he reached the front porch, he saw his father playing tag with the young ones. Mano had made himself "It" and was grinning as he chased them around the front yard, pretending to stumble, running slowly after them before suddenly catching one for a big hug. He moved that way at other times, too. Sal was always amazed at how quickly Mano could throw a punch.

His mother joined him on the porch. "It's good to see him enjoy them. He doesn't relax enough."

"He doesn't work enough to need to relax."

Consuela slapped him lightly on the arm. "Why are you so cynical?" Then she sighed. "No, I know why. You have suffered so much these last years, at the hands of someone you should be able to trust. I understand. But your father is a good man, Salvadore. He has suffered, too. You should try to understand."

Mano gathered the children for one last hug, then sent them to play on their own. He came up the porch steps, smiling and sweating. "Not too bad for an old man, was it? But they're all getting to be so big now. No more babies." He put his arm around his wife and gave her a squeeze. "Very sad."

Together they turned and went through the screen door, with Sal following. "Tell me about your job," Consuela said as she fetched a glass of water and handed it to Mano. "Did you like Mr. Dixon?"

"He's okay. Even gave me an advance on my pay. But he has so much work to do in that house—many months' worth of work for me. And he must be loaded with money, to do all he says he wants to." Mano took a long swallow of water.

"Still, it's good work. The carving in the house is beautiful. He wants me to find a couple of guys to work with us. I was glad to hear that—otherwise I'd be working until midnight every night."

Mano continued to boast of his job, but Sal went back to the front porch with uneasiness tugging at him. Something about the situation bothered him, though he couldn't see any real reason to worry. There was no connection he knew of between Kelsey's family and Magnolia Cottage. Consuela didn't clean house for any of Kelsey's friends. As long as everyone stayed in their own compartment, things would work out okay.

As he stepped outside, Ricky Feliz came up the sidewalk. Not exactly the person Sal wanted to see at that moment, but he didn't get to choose. "Hey, man. What's the word?"

"We haven't seen you in forever, that's all." Ricky looked up at him from the bottom of the steps. "We're getting together for a big party tonight, thought you might honor us with your presence."

Sal ran his hand through his hair. "I don't know. I'm pretty tired."

"You're always tired, man, or working. Or spending time with your girlfriend." Taking the steps two at a time, Ricky came close and lowered his voice. "You forget you're the head of Los Lobos, Sal? These days seems like you just give out orders and expect things to get done, without doing any of the real work yourself. The brothers are getting fed up with this garbage."

"Tough. They don't like it, they're welcome to face me down, choose another leader." Since the next in line was Ricky himself, and they both knew Sal could take him with one hand tied behind his back, that wasn't too likely. Still... "Okay, yeah. I'll come over tonight. It has been too long since I hung out. Where?"

"My house. We're planning on some serious fun for a change."

Sounded like trouble. And he was really tired of trouble. "That's cool. See you later."

Ricky roared off in his truck just as Mano stepped outside again. "You disappeared, but I got news for you, too."

Sal turned to face the latest disaster. "What's that?"

"Dixon Bell needs some work done in his yard."

"I noticed."

"So I told him you could work for him."

"I've already got a job. Plus summer school and homework." Not to mention seeing Kelsey. And Los Lobos.

"Yeah, but you can work for Bell on the weekends." Mano went to the doorway, smiling as if he'd done something really smart. "So you got yourself another paying job. I told him you'd start on Saturday morning."

CHAPTER SEVEN

SATURDAY DAWNED hot and humid, with the predicted high to be ninety-seven degrees, typical of southeastern North Carolina in July. Not hot enough to call off the basketball game, of course. Only a hurricane or a blizzard could justify canceling the weekly contest.

Bell, Crawford and LaRue lost that morning to DeVries, Mitchell and Warren.

Tommy Crawford shook his head as they crossed the street, headed toward the diner. "Us old guys blew it for you this morning, Trace. Couldn't get the lead out for love or money."

Trace didn't mind losing in company like this. "We'll get 'em next time." Then he realized how much he was taking for granted. "I mean…" He heard himself stammer, felt his face get hot.

Dixon Bell draped an arm across his shoulders for a second. "You're right, we will. Might even have to get in a little practice between now and then."

"N-no way," Mr. DeVries said. "This is strictly

a p-pickup game. You start p-practicing, next thing you know we've g-got referees…"

"And we'll have to start betting on the game," Mr. Warren finished for him.

"Mary Rose doesn't give me that much allowance," Pete said with an innocent look.

The men all hooted at that, and they went into the diner laughing. Trace didn't really get the joke, but he laughed, too.

Until he caught sight of his dad sitting alone in one of the booths and staring straight at him. Even as Trace sank into a chair between Dixon and Adam DeVries, his dad was on his feet and weaving through the crowd toward their table. He didn't so much as nod at the other men, but set a hard hand on Trace's shoulder.

"What are you doing here?"

Trace waited for help, but no one came to the rescue. "We…we were playing ball. Across at the school."

"And now we're having breakfast," Dixon said smoothly. "If you'll excuse us."

The grip on Trace's shoulder tightened until he nearly winced. "I'm taking you home, boy."

He didn't have much choice except to stand up when he was pulled. The men around the table stood, too. Trace wondered how the air had suddenly gotten so cold.

"Let him be, LaRue." Pete had his state trooper face on. "He'll get home when he's eaten."

As if he hadn't heard, Trace's dad turned him toward the door. "You leave with me. Now."

Behind him, Trace heard somebody move sharply. He realized that all the noise in the diner had died and everybody in the place was staring at him.

With a quick glance at Dixon Bell, he silently asked them all to back off. There was no sense in making things worse by interfering. Since he got out without an argument, they must have understood what he wanted.

His dad gave Trace a shove as they reached the Yukon. "Get in." Once inside, he grabbed his cell phone and started dialing. "What you think you're doing with those people is more than I can figure. They'd take the food out of your mouth if they thought they could ruin my business somehow. Hey, Mickey." The person he was calling had answered. "Yeah, something's come up. I'll catch you later, we'll get together for lunch. Okay? Yeah." He punched the button and tossed the phone into the box between the seats. "I would think Kate had more sense than to let you hang around with my worst enemies. What does she think they're using you for, 'cept to get at me? I swear, the woman has sawdust for brains."

The tirade continued during the ride home.

Trace slouched in his seat without buckling his seat belt, hoping maybe they'd have an accident and he wouldn't have to listen to this crap from his dad anymore. He wanted to defend Kate. She'd been good to him, better than he deserved. At least she'd stuck around when the old man walked out, which was better than he could say for his real mother.

But he kept his mouth shut. The best he could do was bolt from the car as soon as it stopped and continue running until he was upstairs with his bedroom door locked behind him. He lay face-down on his bed, breathing fast, and listened to his dad ranting at Kate in the room below.

What had started out to be a great morning now felt like just one more day in hell.

ONCE L.T. HAD SAID his piece and slammed out of the house, Kate went upstairs. Kelsey was waiting at her bedroom door. "Are you okay?"

She smiled and gave her daughter a kiss on the cheek. "Believe it or not, I am. His…disapproval…doesn't bother me as much as it has in the past."

Although that was true, she still felt a little shaky as she approached Trace's door. She never knew what to expect from him these days. The spring had been marked by rebellion and estrangement. Kate thought things were improving, but with L.T. behaving so erratically, there was no telling how Trace felt now.

She knocked and opened the door on his invitation, to find him sitting at the computer.

He didn't look at her. "Hey."

"Hey, yourself." She thought he wanted to appear unconcerned. But she'd made his bed just a couple of hours ago. Now the spread was wrinkled and the pillow dented, as if a face had been buried there. "You ran into your dad at breakfast?"

"Yeah. He was angry that I was there with Dixon and Pete and everybody, and he made me come home." Trace shrugged one shoulder, still without glancing away from the computer painting he was working on. "No big deal. I'll grab something to eat in a while."

"That's fine." She walked to the window, pretending to be equally casual. "As long as you realize that what your father says when he's angry isn't necessarily true."

There was a long pause. "Like what?"

"Well, I thought he might have suggested to you that Dixon and Pete and their friends were playing ball with you because they wanted to use you somehow to hurt your father. And, of course, that's not the case." She waited, but Trace didn't answer. "They like you, that's all. Dixon noticed you were interested in their game, and he thought it would be fun to play with you in the same way that he enjoys playing with the others. That's all there is to it. No sneaky plans to ruin LaRue Construction through you."

"Does sound kind of dumb."

"I think you give them a challenge, because they're older and a little slower. You're the mark they're trying to reach. You have to humor people as they age, you know."

She looked over with a smile, and got a grin in return from Trace. "Yeah, I know." Finally, his shoulders relaxed. "Dad does kinda let loose when he gets mad. Says whatever comes into his head."

"He does." Kate put a hand on his shoulder for a second as she crossed to the door. "I thought I'd take you over to Dixon's to work at about two this afternoon. Okay?"

"Sure. I'll be ready."

Outside his closed door, she leaned back against the wall and blew out a deep breath. Trace had gotten the message, she thought. Hoped. What L.T. said and did was not his son's fault. She didn't much care what he said about her now. But she had to find a way to keep him from damaging his own children.

He'd done quite enough damage already.

As Kate had planned, Kelsey stopped the Volvo on the empty circular driveway in front of Magnolia Cottage just a few minutes after two. The old white house drowsed in the sun, its window shades closed like eyelids against the glare. In the stifling heat, the air was a damp blanket draped over their heads.

Dixon had said he would be outside all afternoon, and voices could be heard somewhere in the overgrowth off to the left, along with the crackling of cut wood, the brush of leaves. "Go tell him you're here," Kate said to Trace and Kelsey. "I'll get the tools out of the trunk and bring them over." Although Dixon would have bought some equipment, she knew there could never be too many clippers, loppers and saws for a work party like this.

As she walked around the house, lugging a canvas tote in which the tools were wrapped, she saw a pile of brush indicating where the work was taking place. The voices, however, had ceased. Birds, frogs, insects, traffic…all continued with their afternoon business. None of the nearby humans made a sound.

Kate dropped the tools with a clang and stepped into a sizable clearing where the undergrowth had been cut away. Trace stood close to the opening, hands on his hips and a scowl on his face. Kelsey had crossed to the other side where Dixon had obviously been working only moments ago. With Sal Torres.

The two of them had stripped down to T-shirts, jeans and work boots in the humid afternoon. Sal's skin glowed bronze, slicked with sweat, streaked with dirt and a few scratches from the thorny vines he'd been taking down. His wet black hair clung to his skull, showing off beautiful bone structure. The Spanish conquistadors might have looked like this—elegant, arrogant, in command.

But Dixon…ah. The lankiness of youth had given way to solid muscle, subtly defined under the golden tan of his skin. This was not a man who sat at a desk all day and got his workout at the gym. He'd built his body the old-fashioned way, with hard physical labor. His arms were lean, smooth, tense with sinew. Kate found herself staring.

"What are *you* doing here?" Trace's voice could be as harsh as his father's when he chose.

"Working my tail off," Sal told him. "So what's your problem?"

Trace turned on Kate. "You didn't say he was gonna be here."

"I didn't know." She put a hand on his arm. "It doesn't matter. You're here to help Dixon. Remember?"

"I'm not working with that idiot."

Kelsey strode across the circle and punched her

brother in the arm. "I told you to be nice. Take it back."

He folded his arms over his chest and stared at her with contempt.

Sal came up behind her. "I don't need you to protect me from your brother." He moved Kelsey out of the way, turned and pushed at Trace's shoulder with the heel of his hand. "Back off."

All at once, they were both in battle stance. Trace drew back an arm, fist clenched. "Make me."

Dixon stepped between them, put a hand on each boy's chest and shoved them apart. Sal and Trace landed on their rear ends in the dirt. "Enough. You want to beat each other to a pulp, do it off my property."

"Fine." Sal's gaze was fixed on Trace.

"Oh, yeah." Trace scrambled to his feet, followed by Sal. It looked like they were prepared to stalk off and, Kate presumed, do just that.

"Hold it." Dixon blocked their exit. "I have a contract with each of you. I'm holding you to that contract, but since you're both minors, that means your parents are legally responsible. Which of you is going to explain to your father that you didn't want to work for me after all?"

As the daughter of a lawyer—as one who had once planned to attend law school herself—Kate wasn't sure his argument would hold up in court.

But that didn't matter. What mattered was Sal thinking about explaining to his father why he wasn't earning the extra money. And Trace trying to tell L.T. why he'd even considered working for Dixon Bell in the first place. She didn't know which boy faced the more intimidating prospect.

The stiffness went out of both sets of youthful shoulders, and Dixon nodded. "Right. Now, it's a big yard, and the two of you can work far enough apart that you don't even have to see each other. Since Sal's got a handle on things here, I'll take you to the other side of the house, Trace, get you started."

With a final challenging glance at Sal, Trace followed Dixon as he picked up tools and crossed the overgrown lawn. Sal and Kelsey looked at each other. "I'll work with you," the girl said, pulling her long blond hair through the hole in the back of her pink baseball cap. "What do I do?"

Sal began explaining which plants to leave and which to pull or cut out, and Kate returned to her car. She should leave, because the invitation to work didn't actually include her. She'd dressed in gardening clothes, just in case—jeans and sneakers and a sleeveless T-shirt—and she wouldn't mind staying to help. In fact, she wanted to stay, badly, just for the chance to catch a glimpse of Dixon now and then, maybe take the opportunity to talk for a while over a cool glass of water.

His footsteps on the gravel driveway startled her out of her thoughts. She turned to face him. "I'm sorry. Trace isn't very…broad-minded… these days."

"My fault entirely. I didn't think about the possibility of friction."

"There's no reason you should. I don't think I'd ever mentioned that Sal and Kelsey are dating. And even if I had, it's completely out of line for Trace to act like this." Shaking her head, she sighed. "But the example he gets from his father is not the best."

"Judging by what I've seen of the man, I'd say not." His tone was stiff, as close to anger as she'd seen him come.

The sun was beating down without mercy. Kate wiped her damp forehead, then shaded her eyes with her hand. "That's another thing I should apologize for. This morning, L.T. obviously—"

"No. No way." To her surprise, Dixon grabbed her wrist and pulled her across the driveway, beneath the high limbs of the same poplar they'd stood under on Tuesday. "No way am I letting you take the least responsibility for the jerk you used to be married to." He cupped her face in his hands. "Don't even try."

His intensity left her breathless. His hands were surprisingly cool on her cheeks, overheated from the sun. Her gaze fell on his bare throat, the vulnerable hollow gleaming with sweat. Kate felt an overwhelming urge to kiss him.

And she was terrified. Fists clenched, she stepped back, out of his reach. Putting him out of hers. "O-okay. I won't. Take the responsibility. L.T. is a grown man."

Dixon saw the fear, though he wasn't sure of the cause. Except he had let his temper loose some. After living with that jerk, Kate probably saw anger as a serious threat.

He reined himself in, wiped his palm across his face. "Glad to hear it." His voice was as smooth as he could make it, given the way she always stirred him up, just by being so beautiful, just by being Kate Bowdrey. "I guess I'd better be getting back to work. The boys—and Kelsey—shouldn't have to do this by themselves."

"Right." She turned toward the driveway, then turned back again. "I don't suppose…would you mind if I helped?"

Fireworks shot through him, but Dixon managed to hold his reaction to a grin. "Where would you like to start?"

TRACE SAW THEM together. He stopped for a minute in surprise, then realized if it got too quiet they would realize he was watching. So he went back to digging, lopping, in general working his…

He wasn't going to repeat what the moron had said.

Dixon had detailed him to clear brush from around the old stable they'd converted to a garage. This was where Sal had parked his stupid Taurus, so they hadn't noticed it when they got here. If he'd seen the car first, Trace wouldn't have stayed for a minute, let alone the whole afternoon. Too late now.

From where he worked, he had a view of Kate and Dixon, standing close together, with his hands on her face. What was happening there?

Why were all the adults in his life so totally messed up? First, his dad, falling for the Bimbo and walking out on all of them. Aunt Mary Rose had come to live with them for a while and that was okay, until she got involved with Pete Mitchell. Then everything went to hell, and he'd ended up in court and in counseling and just generally screwed.

Was Kate going to make the same mistake? He'd counted on her ever since he could remember. His own mother had left while he was a baby and never come back. Kate was all he had.

Would Dixon Bell take her away?

L.T. MET WITH THE MAYOR at the diner on Saturday afternoon. "He's got people lined up to work on that house already. I've got to stop him as soon as possible. He gets too far, we won't be able to get the place condemned."

"Relax, L.T." Tate settled more comfortably against the booth. "Already taken care of. There'll be a cop out there early next week with an injunction notice. Not a problem."

"Good to hear." He kept quiet while Abby Brannon set glasses of tea and pieces of key lime pie in front of them. "Thank you, sweetheart."

She gave him a half smile and walked away.

L.T. took time to savor a bite of tangy pie. "If he does get around the injunction, I've arranged to make the work substandard. He'll never pass inspections."

"Sabotage?" Tate swallowed some tea. "Don't mention my name anywhere near it."

"Of course not." L.T. waved away the very suggestion. "So what'd you shoot this morning?"

"Eighty-three. Can't seem to break eighty, even with those high-priced, new clubs. I'm thinking about taking one of those golf clinics over in Pinehurst. Or maybe out West. You can play some great golf in Palm Springs."

L.T. let the mayor ramble, pretended he was listening. Not that he cared about golf one way or the other. He hadn't had much time for sports while he was building his business and he didn't have time while he was trying to save it.

But he did know what side his bread was buttered on. If the mayor wanted to talk about golf, if the banker wanted to sit in a boat all day and drone on while the fish didn't bite, well, then, L.T. was all ears.

THE FIVE OF THEM worked until the sun sank behind the tall magnolias on the edge of the property. A small breeze sprang up about six o'clock, and the air became breathable again. Kate had started clearing out what used to be flower beds at the base of the house, while Dixon alternated his time between the two opposing sides in the current adolescent war. At seven, he declared an end to the day.

"That's enough," he told Kate as she knelt in the dirt by the front porch. "Time to sit back and enjoy the rest of the evening in peace." He put a hand under her elbow to steady her as she got to her feet.

"You're probably right. The boys will need dinner."

"I could use some, myself." Miss Daisy had spent the afternoon bringing out snacks and beverages, from lemonade and chocolate cake to crackers and cheese and soda, with lots of cold water, candy bars and nuts thrown in for good measure. Now the time had come for real food. "I'm going to light the grill, we'll cook some burgers and then sit and watch lightning bugs come out. Sound good?"

Her eyes widened. "You don't have to make dinner for us."

Dixon grinned. "I am making dinner and I expect y'all to stay. We'll keep Trace and Sal on opposite sides of the terrace. It's about sixty feet long—that should be safe enough, don't you think?"

When he came downstairs again, in clean jeans and shirt, Kate and Miss Daisy had spread a cloth on the wrought-iron table at one end of the brick terrace and set out plates, glasses and all the fixings for great hamburgers. The charcoal was just about ready. "I'll round up the kids."

He went to Trace first, found him with his teeth gritted and his forehead wrinkled as he fought to get a huge chokeberry bush out of the ground. "Whoa, there. Call it a night."

But without even acknowledging his comment, Trace continued to struggle. Finally, Dixon stepped in and grabbed the boy's shoulder. "That's enough, son. It's gonna take two of us. Leave this for another day and come have some dinner."

With a violent shrug, Trace freed himself. "Let me alone, you—" He broke off before completing the insult. "Don't call me son."

What was this all about? Dixon held up his hands in surrender. "No problem. Work's over for now. Miss Daisy'll tell you where to clean up. We've got burgers for supper."

"I'm not hungry."

"I believe that one." Dixon slipped his thumbs into the pockets of his jeans and walked off, whistling. The boy would have to figure the rest out for himself.

On the other side of the house, everything was quiet. Real quiet. Dixon decided he'd better make some noise of his own, so he started singing the first tune that came to mind. "Deep in the night, dark as your—" He broke it off quickly, remembering.

Kate was here. And he wasn't ready to get into a discussion of that particular song. Not with her. Not yet. So he changed channels, so to speak, and sang snippets from "Streets of Laredo."

By the time he reached the clearing, Kelsey and Sal had stopped working. "Supper's on the fire," he told them. "Kelsey, Miss Daisy'll tell you where to clean up. Come on, Sal, I'll take you in through the front." And avoid another confrontation as long as possible.

Not surprisingly, though, the thick, juicy burgers and cold, sweet iced tea displaced any impulse the boys felt to continue the fight. The night settled comfortably around them all, blessedly cool after the miserable day. Miss Daisy had put a couple of candles on the table so they could see to eat. When darkness fell, the real light show was up underneath the trees, as fireflies left their perches to float toward earth, seeking the company of their kind.

Kate helped Miss Daisy clean up, of course—the woman couldn't just sit and enjoy herself. Finally with bowls empty of ice cream, they were all quiet around the table, free to enjoy the display.

Miss Daisy put a hand on his arm. "I haven't heard you play since you got home. Will you get your guitar?"

Too risky. "I don't want to bore everybody..."

Kate looked over. Her eyes glistened in the soft candlelight and her face was a pale circle surrounded by curls that blended with the dark. *Deep in the night, dark as your hair...* "You still play?"

"A little."

"Oh, Dixon. Such modesty." Miss Daisy sat back in her chair. "Why, he—"

Before she could finish, he flashed her a look. She raised her eyebrows, but changed the train of thought. "Why, he's quite good."

"I'd love to hear," Kate said. "That's what I remember about you, always sitting in the corner, playing your guitar."

There wasn't much she could ask that he wouldn't give her. And as long as he was in control of the music, his secret, such as it was, would stay safe.

"Sure." He fetched his guitar from the bedroom. Not the new model, handmade and signed by a craftsman in Nashville, but the sweet lady he'd been playing since junior high, when Miss Daisy had given in and bought him the best she could afford for Christmas.

Back out on the terrace, he tuned carefully and strummed lightly, thinking about what to play. With a smile, he started in on James Taylor's "Goin' to Carolina" and the more recent "Copperline." Then he surprised himself with "Mockingbird." A little close to the bone, but Kate's voice joined his, and that was worth the risk.

"Wonderful," she said, applauding. "I had no idea you were so good. Did you try out the music business when you were in Nashville? You know, you never did finish that story for me."

Beside him, Miss Daisy cleared her throat and got up to collect ice-cream bowls. This time she was firm when Kate rose to help. "No, dear. You worked all afternoon. I think I can manage a few dessert bowls." She walked into the house with her back straight, the picture of injured pride.

But Kate understood. "She's good at getting her way, isn't she?"

Dixon nodded. "The best." He searched his brain for some safe songs, went with a couple of Jim Croce's funnier numbers, and Gordon Lightfoot's "Wreck of the Edmund Fitzgerald." Nothing romantic there.

The kids had drawn closer. "Do you know any new music?" Kelsey asked.

He grinned. "You call it music?" But he lashed out with a couple of songs from the hotter pop stars, one of which he'd written, as it happened. Just because he could do it didn't mean he liked it that much.

Kelsey sat back. "Very cool."

Kate leaned forward. "One more real song. Please?"

Tempted. So tempted to do *her* song. Dixon couldn't think for a moment, the urge was that powerful.

Then he mastered himself, more or less, and settled for "You've Got a Friend."

There was a long silence when he finished. Dixon didn't look up from the strings until someone else spoke. "Kelsey, you have ten minutes to say good-night to Sal." Kate stood up. "Trace, do you want to start the car?"

"Sure." He sounded nearly as enthusiastic as he had during the ball game this morning. Kate threw him the keys and he vanished into the darkness on the side of the house. In a minute, the Volvo engine purred gently in the distance.

Dixon blew out a breath, got to his feet and set

the guitar gently on his chair. "Thanks for coming this afternoon. I really do appreciate the help."

Kate had blown out the candles. "Thank you," she said as she straightened up, just a ghost in the night. "You handled several really tricky situations today, much better than I could have."

He shrugged it off. "Sal's coming back tomorrow afternoon, and I'll pay him then. I can give Trace his money now."

She put a hand on his arm. "Why don't I bring him back? I can't stay—I have a meeting at the historical society. But I can leave him here. And if Miss Daisy's going to the meeting, I'll be glad to drive her there and back."

"Sounds good." Felt good, her palm on his skin. The scent of honeysuckle filled the air, and he wasn't sure whether it was her perfume or the yellow-blossomed vines growing in the jungle around the house. All he knew for sure was that it made him crazy with wanting. He hadn't realized how hard it would be, needing Kate Bowdrey, seeing her, and not having her.

And he thought he'd suffered in high school.

In high school, though, she had never touched him. Had never stepped closer, like now. Had never reached up to let her fingers drift along his jawline, the curve of his ear, through his hair to the nape of his neck. Had never drawn his face down to hers so that she could initiate a kiss, featherlight.

And then over, as the radio in the Volvo blared and Kelsey called good-night to Sal across the length of the yard. Kate stepped back, and her hand fell away from his arm.

"'Night, Dixon. Sleep well."

Oh, sure.

SATURDAY NIGHT, Kate had been too tired even to dream, though she went to sleep with the sound of Dixon's rich baritone in her head.

Sunday, though, would surely be a less strenuous day, physically and emotionally. Her parents had lunch plans, so she and Kelsey and Trace went to a restaurant, which meant no dishes to wash. She dropped them both at Dixon's around two-thirty and took Miss Daisy to the New Skye Historical Society meeting for a lecture on the Scottish settlers of New Skye. During refreshments afterward, she caught more than a couple of surreptitious glances cast in her direction by some of the other women, and there seemed to be whispers in the air she wasn't privy to. Kate sighed silently. This had been going on ever since L.T. walked out. She really should be used to it by now.

As she waited for Miss Daisy in the foyer of

the house that served as the club headquarters, Jessica Hyde, the D.A.'s wife, joined her.

"That's a lovely dress, Kate. Linen always looks so cool in the summer, doesn't it?"

"Thank you." She never knew whether to take Jessica at face value or look for hidden meanings. "I wish it didn't wrinkle, but the blends just don't have the same feel."

"I'm afraid not." Jessica glanced at the slight creases in Kate's green sheath and shook her head. "I understand you're going to be working with Miss Daisy on the renovation of that derelict house of hers."

Now she saw the attack. "Hardly derelict. Just in need of attention."

"And as a side benefit, you'll get to see that grandson of hers on a regular basis. That's quite a fringe benefit."

"Dixon's been a friend for more years than I really want to remember."

"Well, seeing as you're a single woman now..."

Behind Jessica, Miss Daisy was approaching. "I'm not, actually, and won't be for quite some time. So Dixon and I will stay...just friends. Are you ready to leave, Miss Daisy?"

"I am, thank you." She nodded to Jessica. "Good to see you again, dear." As they closed the door behind them and walked slowly down the steps toward the parking lot, Miss Daisy leaned close to Kate. "She always was the snippiest girl. Never liked her, not even as a child."

Jessica did have a way of bringing home the truth, though, which was that Dixon Bell was out of reach, as far as Kate was concerned. There was little doubt that the gossip today concerned the time she'd spent with him. You couldn't do much in a town the size of New Skye that somebody didn't find out about, even if you went to lunch in a restaurant an hour away.

If she gave in to her longing for Dixon, the whole town would know. Including her parents.

She wouldn't be free for most of a year. The law stipulated a year's separation before a divorce could take place, and L.T. hadn't filed those papers until two months ago. Dixon couldn't possibly be expected to wait so long for her.

But they had agreed to work together on the house. Every time she saw him, the need inside her grew stronger. The fire in his eyes burned higher. Something in this situation was bound to break.

And Kate was very much afraid it would be her.

CHAPTER EIGHT

SOMETHING—or somebody—had gotten to Kate.

When she brought Miss Daisy back from the historical society meeting, it seemed to Dixon that every inch of progress he'd made in the last couple of weeks had been erased. He couldn't get her to look him in the eye, couldn't get a single private smile or a personal word. She spent some time in the house showing his grandmother the wallpaper and fabric samples she'd selected, but when Dixon came to join them, Kate almost immediately decided she had been there long enough. She apologized profusely for taking Trace and Kelsey away from their jobs and couldn't be persuaded to have a drink on the terrace with him while they continued, or even for the ten minutes it would take to put the tools away.

He brooded over dinner and through most of the kitchen cleanup afterward. When Miss Daisy settled in the parlor with the cats all around her and the last fifty pages of Clancy to read, Dixon followed.

She glanced up as he sat in the armchair. "Was there something you wanted, dear?"

Dixon took a deep breath. "Did you notice anything strange at the meeting today? Anything that might have upset Kate?"

His grandmother put her book aside and drew Audrey into her lap. The cat immediately rolled to her back, exposing a white belly to be stroked. "There was some gossip, yes. Not too ill natured, but I'm sure a sensitive woman like Kate would be disturbed."

"Gossip about what?"

"You, of course."

He dropped his head back against the chair and groaned. "What could there possibly be to gossip about? I've barely seen her, and never in private. Well…" He reconsidered, remembered those minutes in her house. "Almost never."

"There are lots of busy tongues and curious minds in New Skye. It doesn't take much to set them to work."

"So now Kate's convinced the town has painted her as a scarlet woman. Great." He closed his eyes, rolled his head from side to side. "I'm doomed."

"No, you simply have to wait until she's free." The tone of Miss Daisy's voice implied what he would have to wait for.

"I will." Sitting forward, he propped his elbows on his knees and put his head in his hands. "I can. But I have to be able to see her, at least. Talk to her. I can't be here and not see Kate." Dixon looked up at his grandmother. "And I don't want to leave home again. I just want to make a real life. With Kate Bowdrey at its center. Is that too much to ask?"

MANO TORRES SHOWED UP for work Monday morning with the two guys he'd said he would get to help him—Danny Stark and Miguel Cruz, whom they called Mickey. Dixon hadn't slept much the night before, but he was revved up with coffee and the excitement of starting his project. The four of them put in a solid twelve-hour day of work.

And late that night, when he thought the kids might be asleep, or at least in their rooms, he let himself call Kate to report on the progress.

"Most of the plaster along the staircase was falling off anyway, so we chipped it all away from the lath underneath, which is still surprisingly intact. Adam DeVries knows a plasterer who can restore the wall. He'll be over next week to give me an estimate. Meantime, we can strip the banister and steps for refinishing. What do you think—stain or paint?"

Kate couldn't help smiling at the enthusiasm in Dixon's voice. The house meant so much to him. "Are you going to refinish all the floors?"

"Definitely."

"The wainscoting is stained now—are you going with paint or staining there?" She set aside the romance she'd been reading in bed and snuggled down into her pillows.

"That's the next question. What do you think?"

His deference to her ideas was both frightening and stimulating. She'd never made decisions like this without someone else's opinion to consider. "What does Miss Daisy want?"

"I quote, 'I'm sure Kate will know just what we should do. She's exceptionally talented and thoughtful and I trust her completely.'"

"She did not say that."

"Oh, yes, she did. Word for word."

"Dixon." Kate shook her head, hardly believing him, thrilled at the opportunity. "Do you want to take the house back to its original state, or do you want to simply make it as beautiful as it can be?"

"It's not the same thing?"

"Some people like the decorating ideas of the mid-Victorian era and some don't."

"Victorian…like horsehair sofas and heavy drapes and those lace things everywhere?"

"That's one version."

"Let's go with simply beautiful. Like your house."

She had to catch her breath. "Okay. Then I would plan to paint the wainscoting and the ballusters, stain the handrail and the steps."

"Sounds great. How was your day?"

The sudden swing to personal caught her off guard. "Not as much fun as Saturday." Too late, she realized where this would take her.

"You had fun pulling four-foot-high weeds out of the flower beds?"

Surely she owed him honesty, at least. "Well, yes. And having dinner and listening to you play." She hoped he would let it go at that.

Dixon, she was learning, didn't let things go. "Me, too. It was the kind of night I thought about a lot over the years."

"You mean you were homesick?"

There was a pause. "You could call it that. West Texas doesn't offer quite the same quality of magic as your typical southern summer night."

"You said you worked in the oil fields there? That's a hard and dangerous job, isn't it?"

"Has its moments. The pay is good, though."

"But you weren't there all this time."

"Nope. The company got bought and they laid off a bunch of people, so I moved on. Worked on a ranch near Amarillo for a while, then decided I wanted to get out of the heat, so I moved up to Colorado."

"How old were you then?"

"Let's see…twenty-five, I guess. Why?"

"Just wondering." At twenty-five she'd been here with Kelsey, who was nine then, and Trace, seven. L.T. had worked until ten or later almost every night, building the construction company, handling the paperwork by himself after hours. "So where did you end up in Colorado?"

"You're not bored yet?"

"Not in the least." She found it easier to be curious over the phone. "Did you go to another ranch?"

"I worked construction in Denver for about three years, but I really did miss ranch life. So I went looking for a job and wound up in a little town in the middle of the mountains. They ran cattle and horses. I'd still be there if—"

Another pause. "If?"

"If Miss Daisy hadn't written and reminded me that this is where I belong. I had to leave my horses in Boswell, though. I'm hoping to find a place nearby to board them so I can get them shipped over."

"You have your own horses?"

"Yes, ma'am. A nice cow pony, Brady, and a quarter horse mare, Cristal. I was still working on breaking her to saddle when I left. I'll be glad to see them again."

It sounded as if he'd left in a hurry, which seemed strange. "Was there a special reason you came back?" Was Miss Daisy sick, or in trouble? "I mean, after so long…"

"I can hear the worry in your voice, Ms. Bowdrey. No specific reason. It was just time for me to come home."

"I'm glad." An understatement, if ever there was one. "Do you remember Jacquie Lennon? She graduated in our class."

"Horse-crazy, right? She rode English, as I recall. Wanted to go to the Olympics."

"That's her. She was gone for several years, but she's come home, too, and she's a farrier now. I'll bet she could give you some help finding a stable for your horses."

"That would be great. You know everybody and everything in this town, don't you?"

"I have lived here most of my life." Which seemed even more uninteresting, compared to Dixon's adventuring. What could she possibly offer a man who had seen so much of the country? "Have you been outside the U.S.?"

"A few times, mostly before I got to Texas. It's easier to pick up and leave when you're not working a steady job."

"Where did you go?"

As he told the tale of his travels in Spain and Portugal, Greece and Russia and Italy, Kate curled onto her side and turned off her bedside lamp. With just a few promptings from her, Dixon offered such marvelous stories—people he'd met, horses he'd ridden, museums and castles and bazaars and food...

"Kate?" She hadn't said anything for quite a while. Dixon listened carefully to the silence on the other end of the line. "Kate?" Her breathing was deep, even. He'd talked the woman to sleep.

He rested the phone against his chest and chuckled. Was this a good omen, or bad? Good, he decided. She was so relaxed, she'd fallen asleep while they were still on the phone. The only thing better would have been if she'd been lying here beside him, and fallen asleep in his arms.

The thought brought an ache to his throat, his chest, deep in his belly. Kate would be free one day. Free of L. T. LaRue's shadow, free to step out into the sunlight and see the world without any clouds blocking the view.

And, as he had for thirteen years, Dixon swore that when the time came, he would be the man by her side.

KATE WAS STILL BLUSHING in embarrassment when she parked in the driveway of Magnolia Cottage just a few minutes after she'd dropped the kids off at school. She'd fallen asleep on the phone with Dixon last night. Hadn't heard the phone buzz when he hung up, hadn't awakened until this morning when Kelsey looked in to ask if they were staying home today.

She had no doubt that Dixon would forgive

her—he wasn't a man to take offense. But she did need to apologize.

Or maybe she just needed to see him.

Two vans and a motorcycle occupied the driveway in front of the house. The front door stood open and a faint cloud of dust danced in the sunlight slanting over the roof of the porch. When she stepped inside, the cloud thickened, tickling her nose with dry, dusty powder and making her sneeze. All the doors into the hallway were shut and taped off with sheets of plastic, meaning the only light came from outside. On the staircase, the wall had been replaced by a latticework of thin wood strips, the lathing on which plaster walls were built. Upstairs, she followed the pounding of hammers, plus intermittent grunting and tearing sounds, to the source of today's labor.

Yet another door had been sealed with plastic up here. Inside a small, empty room at the back of the house, they were pulling down a wall. Plaster dust filled the air and coated the figures within. Dixon was sweating as much as the three men struggling beside him as they pried plaster and lath away from the timbers of the wall. Kate waited and watched without comment. As hard as they were working, they'd have to take a break for breath soon.

They stopped when they had the plaster completely torn off the wall. Then Dixon stepped back and pulled off his dust mask. "Let's take a break. I could use some air that doesn't coat my throat with white." He turned to the door. "Kate!" At the plastic, he stopped. "Good to see you. But I'm a wreck and I hate to contaminate you with this dust. Did you need something?"

She glanced beyond him to the workmen. She knew their faces from seeing them on L.T.'s construction sites. And Mano Torres looked like a heavier, older version of his son—a very attractive man. "Um...I just wanted to talk for a minute. I don't mind the plaster."

Dixon ran his hands over his face and through his hair, gave his shirt a shake and stepped out into the hallway. "Mano, if I'm not back inside when you're ready, take down the door and the frame, then start on the timbers." He motioned Kate to precede him toward the stairs. "We're expanding Miss Daisy's closet into that room, and using the rest to make a bathroom. Messy work, though." They stepped outside onto the front porch. "Come on around the back and I can get you some coffee from the kitchen. Miss Daisy's gone to her book club meeting, but she left a pot on the stove."

Kate let him lead her to the terrace and seat her at the table. When he came back with a delicate porcelain cup for her and a tumbler of water for himself, he was miraculously cleaned up—plaster dust rinsed out of his hair and off his face and arms, and a new shirt replacing the coated T-shirt he'd worn just minutes ago.

"You didn't have to change," she told him as she accepted the cup. "I understand you're working and I don't intend to keep you long."

"Stay as long as you like. I'd much rather talk to you than rip out boards." He sat down across from her, then took a long drink of water. "That's better—the plaster is making a cast of my stomach. Now, what did you come to say?"

Kate sought courage in a sip of coffee. "I just wanted to apologize for falling asleep while we talked last night. I usually try to behave better than that."

"So I've noticed." He grinned at her. "You tie yourself in knots trying to be sure you aren't making a wrong move."

That didn't sound good. She sat up straighter. "I don't deliberately set out to offend people, if that's what you mean."

"No, that's not what I mean." Dixon put his glass on the table and leaned forward, propping his elbows on his knees. If he'd wanted, he could have held her hands in his. "I mean that you are so concerned about taking care of everyone else, meeting their needs, not getting in their way or interfering with their plans, that you completely forget to take care of yourself, meet your own needs and make your own plans. Live your own life."

"I—" Protest was futile. What a weak-spirited, spineless mess he must think her. And he was right. "I'm sorry."

He grabbed her hands, held them tight. Drawing his hands together, he brought her knuckles to his lips and set a kiss on each hand as he gazed up at her. "Stop apologizing. Better yet, stop even being sorry. Kate, I fell in love with you when I was fourteen years old. Okay, maybe that was an adolescent crush. But I left here thirteen years ago knowing you were the only woman I would ever want to spend my life with. Nothing's changed in that regard. We're older, with separate histories to handle. You've been crushed by marriage to a cruel, inconsiderate man, and it's made you afraid to be yourself."

He drew a deep breath. "But I still love you. I still want to marry you. What do you think this is all about?" He freed his fingers and gestured toward the house behind him.

Kate couldn't think, period. "I—"

Dixon recaptured her hand. "Most of all, what I want is for you to be yourself with me. Not the person you think I want. Just you. Say what's on your mind. Do what seems right to you, or what's wrong, I don't care. I can disagree or disapprove as it suits me. Go back to being that bright, ambitious girl who led the graduating class, if that's who you are. Tell me what you want for the rest of your life, and we'll try to make it happen, whether it's law school or a string of babies or safaris on the Amazon. Just don't hide from me. I've waited so long, Kate, to be the person you shared with. Whatever you have, I'll take, and treat you with all the care and courtesy you deserve."

Dixon ran out of words then. Lowering his chin, he set his forehead against their clasped hands and sat completely still for a long time. He felt Kate's fingers tremble in his grasp, knew that the tremor shook her entire body. Oh, boy, he hadn't meant to blurt all of that out this morning, or any time before she was ready. Chalk it up to yet another bad night's sleep.

He was steeling himself to look up, to get things back on some kind of lighter level, when he heard the sound of footsteps crunching on the gravel driveway running along the side of the house. With a gasp, Kate jerked from his hold, got out of her chair and stepped back. Way back.

He put out a hand. "Wait. Don't leave. We need to talk."

Mano came around the corner. "Mr. Bell, we got a problem you have to see."

"Sure. I'll be there in a few minutes."

Kate shook her head. "No, it's okay. I have to go."

At the same time, Mano said, "You really need to see this now."

Frustration surged in his chest, but Dixon choked it down. "Fine. I'll be right there." He looked at Kate. "Please stay."

"I can't." On the words, she turned and practically ran back the way Mano had come. Dixon followed, but by the time he reached the front, the green Volvo was heading toward the street.

"Mr. Bell?" Mano stood in the open front door. Blowing out a deep breath, Dixon raked his hair back from his face and vaulted the steps to the porch. "What's the—"

The problem was impossible to miss. Shattered crystal and splintered boards covered the floor of the entry hall. Looking up, Dixon located the source—the Waterford teardrop chandelier that had been hanging in the stairwell since 1886, when a Crawford brought it back from Ireland. Not every piece was broken—just most of those hanging on the side nearest the staircase. Following that line of sight, he saw Mickey standing on the steps, the epitome of guilt. In the wall beside him, the lathing had been shattered, leaving a big, empty hole.

"What happened?"

Mickey shrugged. "I was carrying out some of the boards we took down. Missed a step, stumbled, and the boards banged into the wall. When I tried to swing them away from the wall, they went flying…" He lifted his hand toward the chandelier. "Over there."

Dixon choked down the rage. "We'll have to get it cleaned up—can't leave a hazard like that lying here. Maybe there are some pieces that didn't break when they fell." Unlikely—the floor looked as if it had been sprinkled with magic dust. A rainbow of light shimmered through the plaster dust in the air.

"Mr. Dixon Bell?"

Not a voice he knew. Turning to the front door, he found himself confronted by a uniformed policeman. "Can I help you?"

The officer held out a folded sheaf of papers. "I'm assigned to deliver these into your hands."

Unfolding the papers, Dixon read the first word. "Injunction?" The legalese was obscure and obstructive, but he got the point. "This is an order to stop working on my house?"

"I didn't read it, sir. I was assigned delivery."

"Right." He wasn't going to waste breath arguing with somebody who didn't know what was going on. He was saving all his breath for the jerks who thought this one up. "Have a good day."

"Yes, sir."

Dixon looked back at his three workmen. "Get this mess cleaned up. Get the room upstairs swept. I'll let you know when we can start working again.

Meantime, here's your pay." He handed the cash out as he went by them. "Thanks for your time."

And then he went to his room and checked out his closet. He wasn't taking on this fight in anything less than full body armor.

KATE DIDN'T HAVE ANYONE to talk to—Mary Rose would be at work. Her friends, even the closest ones, couldn't know about her feelings for Dixon. As for what he'd just confessed…she thought perhaps she'd been dreaming. He wanted to *marry* her?

But she was still married to L.T., for another ten months, at least.

She drove around aimlessly, thinking she had errands to run but unable to remember what they were. At about ten-thirty she realized she had driven by the school twice. Trace and Kelsey wouldn't be finished for another six hours.

Charlie's Carolina Diner was open, however, the parking lot empty after the breakfast rush. She could get some tea and sit in the quiet and think. Or maybe not think, but simply try to bring reality back into perspective.

There was noise coming from the kitchen, but the front room of the diner was empty. Kate sat in a booth with windows facing the highway and let herself drift. The crepe myrtle trees in the median were at the height of their glorious, watermelon-colored bloom. She would add some pink crepe myrtle to her yard this fall, she decided. It made such a nice contrast to the white.

"Well, good morning, Kate LaRue. It's good to see you again."

She jumped a little, startled to find Abby Brannon standing beside her. "Hi, Abby. How are you?"

"Just fine. I didn't mean to scare you, though. Are you here for breakfast? Or we can do early lunch. It's almost eleven."

Kate shook her head. "Just iced tea, thanks. Un-sweetened."

Abby nodded. "I remember." She returned with two glasses of ice and a full pitcher. "Do you mind if I sit down a minute? I like to get a break between breakfast and lunch, and I'd feel kind of silly sitting all by myself in one booth while you sat here alone in yours."

Company might be even better than mere thought. "Be my guest."

They sipped in companionable silence for a few minutes. Then Abby refilled their glasses and glanced at Kate. "I hear you're going to be working with Dixon and Miss Daisy on renovating that gorgeous old house."

Why should simply agreeing seem like such a commitment? "I am."

"Should be a lot of fun. I remember Dixon had

a party once, oh, in tenth or 'leventh grade. Only time I've been inside, but I remember how impressed I was with the wood paneling and chandeliers and everything."

Kate thought back. "I don't remember a party at Dixon's. Did everybody in the class go?"

"Sure. You were dating Trent Bishop. Y'all showed up for about five minutes and then took off again. Too bad." She smiled. "We had a good time."

"That was rude of us." She felt her heart sink at the idea of treating Dixon so badly, especially after what he'd said this morning.

Abby shrugged. "You weren't like everybody else, though. We knew that and it didn't bother us."

"What does that mean?"

"Well…" She seemed to realize that she might have said the wrong thing. "We just thought you were meant for bigger places, a different kind of life than the rest of us. You were smart and pretty and witty. And you had great clothes. Everybody liked you. We were just a little in awe, I guess."

Kate put her head in her hands. "And look how wrong you were."

"Oh, honey." Abby set a hand on her hair. "I'm sorry. The last thing I meant to do was make you feel bad."

"It's okay." She didn't look up. "This has just been a strange morning."

"I think you need something to eat." Abby slid out of the booth. "I'm going to bring you a chicken salad sandwich with some fries. If you're smart, you'll eat every last bite."

To her own astonishment, Kate did finish the entire plate. She even allowed Abby to persuade her into having a piece of key lime pie for dessert.

"I haven't been so stuffed in years," she told her friend as she cleared the table. "I'll have to skip dinner tonight."

Abby lifted an eyebrow. "You're too thin, if you ask me. I think you should eat dinner tonight and breakfast tomorrow. Then think about going light on lunch." She winked and bore the dishes away.

Kate realized that she'd been sitting in the diner for almost two hours and hadn't done any real thinking at all. The respite felt…wonderful. She might even be able to face the rest of her day now. Picking up her purse, she slid out of the booth just as a slim blond woman in a T-shirt and jeans moved by. Kate placed her fingers on a surprisingly muscular shoulder. "Jacquie? How are you?"

The farrier turned, saw who had spoken, and smiled widely. "Hey, Kate. I'm great, how about you? Haven't seen you in forever."

"I guess I should spend more time around horses."

"Or I should spend more time around people."

They both laughed at the suggestions. Jacquie had been horse-crazy from their earliest school years. All her drawings in kindergarten had been of horses, her creative writing had been about horses, and as soon as she'd graduated, she'd left to make her name as an equestrienne.

Kate might have fallen asleep on him, but she hadn't forgotten the longing in Dixon's voice when he'd talked about his horses. "I have a question to ask you, if you've got a minute."

"Sure."

"Dixon Bell is looking for a place to board his two horses. He had to leave them in Colorado when he came home, but he'd like to move the horses here, too. I told him you might be able to recommend somewhere nearby."

"Of course. I'd heard he was back, but I haven't run into him yet." Jacquie flipped her long blond braid over her shoulder as she thought for a minute. "There are plenty of boarding facilities all around the county. But I've just started working with a lady who bought a farm fairly close to town, with a big barn and great pastures that are much more than she needs for her two horses. She mentioned that she wouldn't mind taking on some boarders, just for company. Dixon should give her a call. Her name's Phoebe Moss. Let me get you her number."

Moving quickly, Jacquie went back outside to her truck. Kate paid her bill while she waited and said goodbye to Abby, then met the farrier at the door.

"Her work and home numbers," Jacquie said, offering a business card and pointing to the writing on the back. "Really nice woman, takes care of dogs and cats and horses like they were her kids. I know Dixon's animals would be in good hands."

"I'll tell him. Thanks so much."

"And make sure he sees my number on the front. I expect to hear from him when he needs horseshoes."

"Count on it."

Of course, that meant she had to figure out how to face Dixon at all, after this morning. He had loved her, he said, since high school. Then why had he left so suddenly? Why had he never said a word about his feelings? She couldn't recall that he'd ever asked her for a date.

Had she been so unapproachable? So wrapped up in her own consequence she couldn't notice the shy boy who wanted to be with her? This morning, she'd bragged about not offending people. But it looked very much as if she'd brushed off Dixon Bell without a second thought.

Kate decided she desperately wanted to know

what had driven Dixon away. And, even more important...

Exactly what had brought him back.

CHAPTER NINE

DIXON PROPPED the heels of his hands on the edge of the desk and leaned over until his face was very close to the administrative assistant's. "I've been waiting to see Mr. Hyde for an hour now. I'm going to wait until he either comes through that door or jumps out the window. Since we're on the fifth floor, I think the door would be a better choice. Why don't you tell him again that I'm here? That's Dixon Bell, in case you've forgotten."

The young man blindly felt for the intercom button, his round eyes fixed on Dixon's face. "M-Mr. Hyde? M-M-Mr. Bell is…is s-still waiting to s-see you."

"I told you to… Oh, never mind. Send him in."

As the red-faced admin started out of his chair, Dixon held up a hand. "Thanks. I can find my way." He crossed to the polished wood door marked District Attorney James Hyde and opened it wide. "Hey, Jimmy."

"Dixon Bell." The grin, the enthusiastic handshake, indicated that this was a meeting the D.A. had waited for all day long. "How are you? It's been years since we saw you. I think Jessica mentioned she'd run into you recently downtown. Is she still beautiful, or what? Come in, come in. Have a seat. Can I get you a drink?"

"No, thanks." But Dixon took the offered chair. "You've done yourself proud in your hometown. District Attorney Hyde. Very impressive."

"I feel like I serve the community. That's what counts. We're gonna have to get you over for dinner some night soon. I'd love you to meet my boys." He turned a frame standing on the desk so Dixon could see the family picture. "Gonna be great ballplayers, every one of them. That's Jim Jr., there, he's thirteen…Jeff, ten…and Alex, seven. We have a great time together, though Jessica feels outnumbered sometimes."

"She's a strong lady. I imagine she holds her own."

"You got that right. Orders us all around with a lift of her finger." He set the frame in its place, then looked up with every appearance of innocence. "So what can I do for you today? Not expecting to be arrested, are you?" He grinned.

Dixon didn't grin back. Reaching into his suit coat, he pulled out the injunction and tossed it onto the desk in front of Jimmy Hyde. "Explain this to me, if you would."

The D.A. picked up the paper, but he was looking at Dixon's jacket. "Nice suit. I like good tailoring."

"Thanks. There's no place like Italy for clothes."

Jimmy's eyes widened. "Uh, yeah." He opened the paper and read the contents. "Well, this is a court order barring you from pursuing further renovations on the house located at 111 Magnolia Lane. That would be Miss Daisy's house, right?"

"Technically, the property belongs to me."

"Oh. Well, then, you're not supposed to work on the house until a hearing can be held."

"Yes, I can read. What I don't understand is where this came from and how it can possibly be legal to prevent a man from improving a house he owns."

"That's a legitimate question." He pulled a notepad across the desk and scribbled a few lines. "Let me make some phone calls on this, see what I can find out. I should have answers for you in a day or so."

"No. I want some answers now."

"It's after two o'clock. People'll be at lunch, in court, you know. I'm not likely to reach the folks who have the answers on the first try."

Dixon settled more comfortably into his chair. "I'll wait."

Jimmy's harassed frown said what he thought of that suggestion. He did start dialing, talking, following a trail of sources Dixon could only guess at. After thirty minutes, he put the phone down.

"Okay." He reviewed two pages of notes. "As I've been told, this injunction was granted based on the fact that there's a dispute over the disposition of the property."

"Not as far as I'm concerned."

The D.A. didn't look up. "It appears the Public Housing Authority is interested in securing this land for the purpose of building public housing."

"That's a bunch of bull."

Jimmy shrugged. "That's what I'm told. I know the city council has been looking at sites for a while now, considering possible options on where to put up this new project. I guess somebody decided Magnolia Cottage would be a good choice. And that somebody convinced Judge Harnett to sign the injunction."

"Somebody being who?"

Jimmy shifted in his seat. "That's where I get stonewalled. There's a trail of paperwork through the system, but there aren't any names attached."

"Well, I can give you the most important name. LaRue."

"L.T." He didn't look surprised and he didn't look Dixon in the eye. "He does want to build there, doesn't he?"

"I'm not selling, so he's trying the bureaucratic route."

"When L.T. sets his mind on something, he usually gets what he wants."

"There's a first time for everything." Dixon got to his feet. "And you can tell him, when you report what went on here this afternoon, that he's not getting Magnolia Cottage to build on. He might have the mayor and the D.A. and a couple of senile judges in his pocket." Picking up the injunction, he tore it in half, and in half again, dropping the pieces on Jimmy's desk. "But that house and that land belong to me. I've got a deed dated 1832 and all the paperwork from the last one hundred seventy years. He'll have to start— and win—another Civil War before I'll let go of what's mine." He walked across the room, opened the door, then turned back to give the D.A. a grin. "Have a great afternoon. Be sure to tell Jessica I said hello."

Dixon left the office with a nod to the admin and waited patiently for the elevator. He thought he had his face under control, keeping all the rage tamped down deep inside him. When the doors slid open, however, the two women in the elevator looked startled, and then a little uneasy as they slid past him. Maybe he wasn't doing as good a job as he thought.

As he sat in the truck, reminding himself not to rip the gearshift off the steering column, he had to admit that his temper was breaking loose as it hadn't in years. He didn't get mad. Didn't want to get mad. Anger only made a situation worse. He'd learned that lesson when he was three years old.

He glanced at the clock on the dash. Not quite three. Where could he go with this…this fury beating at him inside? Not home to Miss Daisy. She didn't deserve the hassle of dealing with his malfunction. Especially not after returning from her book club to find her chandelier shattered. He'd thought for a minute she would faint. But not Miss Daisy. She'd fetched a broom and set to work with Mano and Mickey and Danny. She would have faced the War of Northern Aggression, as she called it, with equal aplomb.

But she wasn't going to have to face the loss of her home. Not as long as he had breath in his body. Surely even L. T. LaRue wouldn't commit murder for a piece of land. He could have the whole rest of the planet to build on. He just couldn't have Magnolia Cottage.

The traffic light turned red. Dixon stopped the truck and realized that, without being aware of it, he'd driven up The Hill toward Kate's neighborhood. *Like a homing pigeon,* he thought with an almost-smile. *Heading back to the roost.*

Kate wouldn't want to see him, not after his confession this morning. He shouldn't have poured all that out to her, but at the time he couldn't stop. So now he ought to leave her alone…

Except that she was the one person he needed at this particular moment. Not to carry his burden to, but if she would allow him to share just a few minutes of peace in her company, he thought he might be able to get himself under control.

The Volvo sat in the driveway under the shade of a row of maple trees. Crossing the lawn, Dixon stopped thinking should or shouldn't, right versus wrong. If this was a bad idea, he'd pay for it later. All he could manage was now.

IN THE MIDDLE of Tuesday afternoon, Trace walked into the boys' bathroom and stopped in his tracks. Sal Torres stood at the sink, washing his hands. Trace thought about turning around and walking out again, then decided he wasn't going to let Sal chase him out of the john.

Torres was still there when he stepped up to the sink. He sent a sneering grin through the mirror. "Couldn't hold it till you got home?"

Trace rolled his eyes. "I notice you're in here, too."

"Yeah, well, some of us have things to do when school gets out. You wouldn't know anything about actually having to work in order to eat."

"You wouldn't know anything about keeping a job for more than a couple of weeks. That's why my dad had to get rid of your old man—couldn't afford to keep him on the payroll when he didn't show up every day."

Torres turned to look at him directly. "What do you mean?"

"You heard me. My dad fired your dad because he came to work drunk, or didn't show up at all." Trace shrugged. "Like father, like son."

"You're telling me." Torres tore off a paper towel and dried his hands. "I can't figure out how you and Kelsey could possibly be part of the same family. She's a human being. And you—" He dropped his towel into the trash can and walked to the exit, then looked back over his shoulder. "You're the black ooze at the bottom of a dead river."

Trace stood speechless as Torres left. *Black ooze?* What kind of stupid insult was that?

Unfortunately for him, he couldn't think of a single decent comeback.

KATE HEARD THE DOORBELL with a start of surprise. She wasn't expecting anyone this afternoon—that she remembered, anyway. True, since this morning's encounter with Dixon, she'd been wandering around in a daze. When she came upstairs from the laundry she took a glance at the calendar on the refrigerator, just in case. Blank for today. The caller would be a salesperson, or maybe a child selling candy. She didn't even check through the sidelight before she opened the door.

"Dixon?" The sight of him always stole her breath. But she hardly recognized the sophisticated gentleman on the doorstep, in his dark, elegantly cut suit, white shirt and silver tie, with his hair combed back smoothly and soft, tasseled loafers on his feet.

"Hey, Kate. How are you this afternoon?"

Ah, but his voice was the same rich, soft, Southern baritone. His deep-brown eyes sparked with laughter, as always…and, today, a sharpness she wasn't used to. His mouth was downright hard.

"What's wrong?"

He sighed. "May I come in?"

"Oh, of course." She stepped back and let him move past her. "Come sit down. Let me get you something to drink. Iced tea?"

"That would be wonderful." He sounded weary and yet on edge at the same time.

She poured a tall glass for each of them and brought the drinks to the great room with a plate of lemon cookies. "Sit down here by the window. I'll close the shutters some, because the sun comes in pretty brightly in the afternoon. It'll be wonderful in winter, but in the summer it's too much." Once she'd run out of things to do, she turned to look at him where he'd settled on the love seat. He wasn't drinking or eating. Just sitting. Watching her.

The last vestige of self-consciousness left her. Kate sat down beside him and took his hand in hers. "What's wrong?" she asked again.

"I'm sorry." He shook his head. "I shouldn't have bothered you, but—"

She put a finger on his mouth. "Some advice I've gotten recently—stop apologizing. Just tell me."

Dixon smiled against her fingertip…and then kissed it. "Right. Well, after the chandelier got broken this morning—"

"The one in the hall? Oh, my stars, how?"

"One of the guys swung a board the wrong way."

"That's…" Kate shook her head. "I'm so sorry. Has Miss Daisy seen it?"

"She was helping them clean up when I left."

"And where did you go, dressed so fine?"

"To find out who initiated an injunction to keep me from working on my house."

"A court order?" She was, after all, a lawyer's daughter. And the deduction didn't take much effort. "L.T."

"'Fraid so."

"Probably in cahoots with the mayor, his buddy."

"Probably."

"I hate that man." She pounded her clenched fists against her knees, realizing just how true it was. At least at this moment. "I hate him. He ruins lives without a second thought, as long as he gets what he wants when he wants it."

"L.T.?"

She looked at Dixon, caught his grin. "Well, the mayor, too. But, yes. My ex-husband." Even if the paperwork would take a year, she knew for a fact that she would never again let L.T. into her life. Not even for the children.

"Well, you've got cause." He sighed and slouched a little deeper into the sofa. "Me, too."

Kate handed him his tea. "You're awfully calm about it."

"Not at all. I came here because I was so worked up I could've chewed nails." He took a long drink, eyes closed. "You calmed me down."

"What are you going to do?"

"Ignore the injunction. Work on my house. Figure out how to destroy L. T. LaRue."

"Dixon…"

"I don't mean that." He hadn't opened his eyes again, but he smiled. "I just have to demonstrate to him that he's not winning this one. He's gonna keep trying until there's no option left. And I don't want to spend the next thirty years wondering what his new plan will be. So I've got to take over the strategy." With a sigh, he opened his eyes and straightened up. "But that'll wait until tomorrow. You've got to pick up your kids in a few minutes, right? I should get out of your way."

"Actually…" This would be terribly dangerous. If she told him the truth, who knew what would happen? "Trace and Kelsey attend the RE-WARDS program Pete runs at the high school."

"The juvenile offender rehab?"

"Yes."

"Things really did get serious this past spring, didn't they?"

"Oh, yes. So, anyway, on Tuesdays, Mary Rose picks them up at school and takes them home for dinner, then they all go to REWARDS. Mary Rose teaches a course on finances, and Pete does auto engines, with Sal's help. Anyway…" She took a deep breath. "Tonight I'm here by myself. Until about ten," she added, just to be safe.

Most men would have pounced. Dixon just settled back a bit. "So it'll be okay if I hang around for a little while?"

Kate relaxed completely. "Drink your tea, have some cookies. I need to put laundry in the dryer." She let her hand rest on his knee as she got to her feet. "Be back shortly."

"Great."

When she returned in a few minutes, he was asleep. He'd loosened his tie, but otherwise was still formally dressed in that exquisite suit.

She left him there in the shuttered afternoon light and went about her work with an amazing lightness of heart. Something about having him in the house—not a sulky teenager liable to pout over the least implied criticism, not an angry, stressed, impatient husband looking for the smallest mistake—soothed and comforted her in a way she'd never known before. Climbing two flights of stairs to put away the clean clothes cost her no effort this afternoon. She took steaks out to thaw, made a salad and put potatoes in the oven to bake for dinner, a routine that was somehow special because she was doing it for Dixon.

Upstairs again to neaten her hair and put on a clean, unwrinkled shirt, she took a moment to call Miss Daisy. "I wanted you to know that Dixon's at my house. I'm hoping he'll stay for dinner, unless you have plans."

"Oh, no, dear. That's wonderful." She sounded tired and sad. "I'll be really happy just to make myself a sandwich and go to bed early."

"He told me about the chandelier. I'm simply horrified."

"Yes. That piece was one of our treasures." After a long pause, she cleared her throat delicately. "But it was, after all, just glass. Having Dixon back is much more important. Seeing you two together, enjoying your precious children while they're here...those are the real treasures of life."

"Miss Daisy, you are a treasure all by yourself. I'll send your grandson home before ten. He needs a good night's rest."

"Thank you, dear."

Kate was in the kitchen making biscuits when Dixon woke up. He came to the door and leaned against the frame. "Don't I feel like a lazybones?"

She looked around and smiled. His sleek hair was mussed, his eyes still heavy with sleep. "You're allowed to take time off now and then. I'm hoping you'll stay for dinner—I'd love to have somebody else cook the steaks for a change. As a former cowboy, you're expected to know all about steaks."

"I know the most about them when they're still walking around on four legs. But I manage." He came a little farther into the room. "Anything else I can help with? And are those really homemade biscuits? I thought only Miss Daisy refused to eat biscuits from a can these days."

"I tolerate canned biscuits. But I had a little time, and it's a special occasion, so..." She shrugged, feeling her cheeks heat up.

"Is it? A special occasion?" Dixon came close, put a palm on her shoulder and turned her to face him. "Because I'm here?"

Her hands were covered in flour—she couldn't

move and risk marring that suit. She stared into his face, defenseless. "Why else?"

"Ah, Kate." He bent his head, grazed his lips across her forehead, her closed eyelids, her cheek. When he reached her mouth, he gave her gentle, tender kisses. No passionate assault. No erotic intimacies.

When he stepped back she was nearly dizzy.

So much for the peaceful afternoon.

"Uh…" He dragged his fingers through his hair. "Where can I get washed up for dinner?"

"In the hall." Her voice was as unsteady as his. "Under the staircase."

"Right."

When he returned, he'd taken off his jacket and tie and rolled up the sleeves of his crisp white shirt. "Ready for duty, ma'am. Where's the beef?"

They laughed together, recalling the television commercial with that punch line from so long ago. But the laughter had a self-consciousness to it, Kate thought. They were alone in the house.

And both of them were now very aware of that fact.

WHEN SAL BROUGHT his mother home after a trip to the grocery store, all the younger children were huddled together under the pine tree in front of the house. Not playing. Just sitting. Mano's truck was parked by the curb.

Sal turned off the engine and sat gazing at the scene. "He must be drunk. Four days on the job and he's drinking again."

His mother opened her door. "That is not necessarily true. Perhaps he wanted a nap after starting so early, and told the children to be quiet." She straightened up off the car seat with a soft groan. "I'll go in and see him, if you will get the food."

"Sure."

He carried the groceries in through the back door and set the bags on the counter. Mano's voice rang through the house.

"No, I didn't get fired." The words were lightly slurred. Six beers, Sal figured. Maybe eight. "Might as well have. Some kind of legal paper got delivered. Just like that, work is over. Maybe he'll call. Maybe he won't. Give a man a job with one hand, take it away with the other."

Consuela asked a question Sal couldn't hear.

"He paid me. What difference does it make? A few days' pay ain't gonna keep the house going. Might as well toss it away as anything else."

Sal heard the sound of a stumble as Mano got to his feet and tried to get around the coffee table in front of the couch. In another second, he lurched into the kitchen.

"Standing there listening, boy?" Mano headed for the refrigerator, where he pulled out two more beers. "I'm betting you're out of a job, too. Goes to show—working for rich folk is worthless. Can't trust 'em. They'd just as soon screw you as look at you, and they always take care of themselves first. Got that?"

Argument would be useless. "Got it."

"Goes for that girl you're so crazy over, too."

Sal clenched his fists at his sides. He held his temper with every ounce of his will. For his mother's sake, he would not get into a fight with his old man.

"Well, you just be ready. Something better comes along, you're history." He toasted his claim. "Guarantee it."

"And you know so much." Sal stepped past his father, heading for the living room.

"You don't talk to me in that tone of voice." Mano grabbed for him, stumbled and missed. "Come back here."

Without bothering to answer, Sal let the front door slam shut behind him. His mother was sitting on the ground with the children, coaxing them back into giggles and smiles.

She looked up as he came down the porch steps. "Salvadore?"

He stopped dead, gazing across the dusty grass at a woman who somehow managed to bear her life, despite its pain, without complaining. Without running away...as he had intended to do.

Mano sought the coward's way out in a bottle. Sal decided he could be at least as brave, as strong, as his mother.

"I'll stay with them," he told her, extending both hands to help her to her feet. "You make dinner and we'll be out here playing."

Her sweet smile blessed him. "Thank you. Just a few minutes," she told the little ones. "*Arroz con pollo* for everybody."

The children cheered and Consuela made her way back to the porch, leaning heavily on the rail as she climbed the steps. Sal blanked his mind, refused to consider anything beyond the moment. Even thinking about Kelsey was too much for him to handle right now.

"So what shall we play?" he asked the little ones. "Simon Says? Red Light, Green Light? Duck, Duck, Goose?"

Or how about *Ring around the rosies, pocketful of posies. Ashes, ashes, we all fall down?*

"I WANTED TO TELL YOU," Kate said as Dixon helped her load the dishwasher, "that I might have found a place for your horses. I ran into Jacquie this morning and she knows a woman who would like to have some boarders in her barn." She went to her purse on the kitchen chair, pulled out a business card and brought it back to him. "Phoebe Moss is her name, and her numbers are here. Jacquie said to be sure you call her when you need horseshoes. Her number's on the other side."

Dixon grinned as he slipped the card into his shirt pocket. "She always was an upfront kinda gal. I'll be glad to. And I'll talk to Phoebe Moss soon. I'd really like to get Brady and Cristal over here before the end of the summer."

"Well, here that would be October, but I suppose Colorado gets cold weather a lot sooner."

"Oh, yeah. Some years there's snow before Halloween."

"Will you miss the cold? We don't get much of it here, remember."

"I do remember that." He leaned his hips back against the edge of the counter as Kate rinsed the sink and wrung out her sponge. "I expect I'll enjoy not having to shovel a couple of feet of snow to get out of the driveway in the mornings. That routine gets pretty old by the end of January."

"I can't imagine living with that much snow for months and months. We go skiing for a week, and it's fun. Or it was. I'm wondering if we'll go this year at all, since L.T...." She shook her head. "Never mind. I didn't intend to bring up his name again."

"Good thinking." Dixon put his arm around her slender waist and led her back into the great room. "Let's sit and watch the sunset through the window."

She opened the shutters, and they settled on each end of the love seat, staring out into the backyard. Dixon felt the tension in Kate as if it were in his own.

"Those yellow flowers are daylilies?" He shifted sideways a little to see Kate and the yard. She nodded. "And the white-blossomed trees are crepe myrtle?"

"That's right." Her back was straight, her neck stiff.

He stretched his arm along the top of the sofa, letting his curled fingers touch her shoulder lightly. "What about the purple spikes?"

"Russian sage."

"And the pink?"

"Geraniums." Finally, she looked at him. "And I'm betting you know most of this, given Miss Daisy's fondness for garden flowers."

"I didn't know Russian whatever-it-was. But you don't seem so nervous when you're talking about the garden."

"I'm not…" She sighed. "A very good liar."

"I don't mean to make you nervous, Kate."

"You don't." Now she turned to face him. "I mean…it's not you. It's the—the situation."

"Us being alone?"

She looked out the window again, and nodded. "Nothing's going to happen."

Her hands, balled up in her lap, fell open.

"Except what you want," he said.

The sun dropped suddenly behind the tops of the trees. Kate drew in a deep breath. "That's the problem." Her wide eyes came back to his face. "I'm afraid I want…a lot. Maybe too much."

Her confession nearly knocked the breath out of him. He covered it with a small laugh. "You couldn't possibly want too much from me, Kate Bowdrey. There's nothing I wouldn't give." Dixon edged a little closer and set his palm on the sweet nape of her neck.

The trust in Kate's green-gold eyes was worth the price. "Why didn't I ever realize how wonderful you are?"

Before he could answer, though, she leaned into him and set her lips against his.

Kate couldn't believe she'd been so bold. And then she couldn't believe she'd waited so long. Kissing Dixon had to be the richest experience she'd ever known…coffee and chocolate from the cake she'd served for dessert, plus a flavor uniquely his own, something dark and warm and intoxicating.

"Ah, Kate." His fingers twined in her hair. "You don't know how many times I've dreamed about this."

This, *this,* was why she'd been born. To love Dixon Bell.

But then a thought came at her like lightning out of a clear sky. *I'm married.*

In an instant, her body cooled, stiffened, all the lovely fire in her blood dowsed by that one inescapable fact. Dixon lifted his head to meet her eyes. "Kate?"

"I can't do this." She closed her eyes, but the tears formed anyway. "I'm so sorry... I just can't."

CHAPTER TEN

DIXON HELD KATE against him, with her damp curls under his cheek. "It's okay, Kate. Sweetheart, please…it's okay."

She wouldn't—couldn't—stop crying. There were words amidst the sobs, but he didn't understand most of them. "Coward," he thought he heard once, and "wrong." "Sorry," he heard at least a hundred times. There didn't seem to be anything he could do but let her weep.

The room was completely dark when she finally calmed down and rested in his arms, hiccuping now and then, sniffing, wiping her cheeks. Eventually, she sighed. "I'm so sorry."

He pressed a kiss onto the top of her head. "One hundred one."

"What?"

"That's the one hundred and first time you've said you're sorry."

"Oh." As he'd hoped, she chuckled a little. Then drew another deep breath and let it out. "I don't think that's enough."

"What are you sorry for?"

She lifted a hand. "For…leading you on."

"For taking me closer to heaven than I've ever been in my life?"

"Dixon, you are such a kind man." She sat up and he reluctantly let her go. "But I know it's not fair."

"Fair isn't an issue between us. Honesty is."

"I didn't want to stop kissing you." Her voice was just above a whisper. "I had to." She got to her feet, letting her fingers slip slowly out of his grasp. "I'm…still married."

With a murmured apology, she hurried off to the bathroom. When she returned, Dixon had turned on a couple of lamps. Kate smiled at him gratefully, perching on the edge of one of the armchairs. "Can I get you something to drink?"

"I'm fine, thanks. Would you sit here beside me?"

The fear was back in her eyes. "I don't think…"

"I won't start anything. I just want you close."

"Dixon…" She shook her head, pressing her lips tightly together. But after a few seconds, she joined him on the love seat.

"That's right." With an arm around her shoulders, he eased her into his side. "Not so bad, is it?"

"It's wonderful. That's the problem."

He didn't reply, didn't say anything for a while. Outside the window, lightning bugs did their nightly dance in Kate's backyard ballroom. Gradually, the tension left the air, her shoulders, her body. She let her head nestle into his shoulder.

"I've told you before," Dixon said finally, "and I expect I'll say it many more times. There's nothing you can do to change the way I feel about you. Any reasonable guy would have given up the day you blew me off in high school. I'm obviously not a reasonable guy."

"What day? What are you talking about?"

Dixon chuckled. "See, you don't even remember, and it changed the direction of my whole life."

"You're killing me." She turned to face him and pounded a fist lightly on his arm. "Tell me what you're talking about."

"Spring of our senior year, you broke up with your then boyfriend...Ryan Kingman, I think it was...about three weeks before the prom."

"He had a one-track mind and I was tired of having to derail it."

"I'm not surprised. Anyway, as far as I knew, you didn't have a date for the prom. So I figured I might as well take my shot." He shook his head. "I found you alone in the library that day. You were looking for books on worms for a biology report. Round worms, to be specific."

Kate shuddered. "What a fun assignment."

"So I pulled a couple off the highest shelf for

you, handed them over and said, 'Can I take you to the prom?' Maybe I said it too fast, or too soft, I don't know. You checked the books off the list in your notebook, smiled and said, 'Thanks for the help,' and left me standing there with what I took to be no for an answer."

"I didn't even acknowledge the invitation?" She covered her face with her hands. "I'm completely mortified. I can only imagine how hurt you must have been."

"Enough to take my wounded pride and broken heart and hit the road for a decade or so. But the point is, Kate, that I never forgot you. Never stopped loving you, and don't expect to anytime short of eternity."

She sat with her head bowed, her face hidden. Dixon waited for her to say something, but whatever was going on in her mind, Kate wasn't ready to share.

Easing his arm from behind her shoulders, he got to his feet. She looked up then, and he managed a smile. "It's almost ten. I think I'll take my leave before the kids come home. No, don't get up." He put a hand on her shoulder. "You just stay there, and my intentions will stay good." A kiss would have been nice, but risky. So he drew his finger along her cheek as he stepped back. "Sleep tight. I'll talk to you tomorrow."

Dixon shut the front door carefully behind him

and crossed the grass to his truck, focusing on the scent of honeysuckle in the air, the night sounds of crickets and frogs, the crescent moon rising over the housetops. He didn't want to think about the ache of tension in his body, or the bruise on his soul from listening to Kate's sobs. What should make them both happy seemed to be causing nothing but heartache.

And he was beginning to wonder if sheer determination and a heart full of love would be enough to set things right.

TRACE KNEW someone had been there the minute he came in the front door. The air in the house felt different, had a different scent. Not perfume, not even aftershave. Just the trace of a person who didn't belong.

And then he saw the coat and tie on the chair in the hall.

Kelsey stomped up to her room to pout because Torres hadn't shown up for the REWARDS classes tonight. She was no help. Kate said hello, then she and Mary Rose went in the kitchen to talk. Nothing unusual there. Except for the coat and tie.

When he picked them up, the silver tie slithered back to the seat of the chair. The dark coat weighed next to nothing, which was weird, considering its size. Trace couldn't read the label—

Italian, he thought. He'd only taken his first year of Spanish at school. And planned to switch to French.

The jacket, he decided as he held it up by the shoulders, was too big for his dad. His grandfather—stepgrandfather—would never have left it here to begin with. What other man would be visiting Kate?

Dixon Bell, of course.

Since the tall man would probably come back for the jacket and tie, Trace folded them as he'd found them on the chair. He wanted something to eat, but he wasn't about to go into the kitchen and find food while Kate and Mary Rose tried to pretend they hadn't been talking about Dixon Bell before he came in and couldn't wait for him to leave so they could start again. He'd rather starve.

In his room, he checked his e-mail and found nothing but senseless jokes. Might as well go to bed. But as he lay in the dark staring up at the luminescent posters on his ceiling, he had to wonder what came next.

Sure, he liked Dixon Bell. Was Kate going to marry him? The divorce would have to come through first, he supposed. She had explained that they were required to wait a year by North Carolina law. Which would be maybe ten months from now.

And after ten months, what then? Though

he'd invited Trace to play ball with him and his friends, why would Dixon take on two kids who weren't his? Who weren't even Kate's? Would Kate move out of the house, and their dad and the Bimbo move in?

Trace thought about that possibility with his eyes squeezed tightly shut. He loved his dad—no other option there. But he'd gotten used to living without him. No cold silences over a B in math. No eruptions at dinner, or breakfast, over toys left out in the yard and sneakers by the kitchen door. The house was still neat, but not so perfect as his dad liked it. More livable.

The Bimbo wouldn't stand up to their dad. Kate hadn't either, she'd just worked double and then triple-hard to make up for his and Kelsey's mistakes and avoid the fallout. If Kate left, they wouldn't have any protection.

Most guys went to military high school as a punishment. Trace rubbed his eyes and wondered if he could get there as an escape.

KATE WALKED her sister to the front door. "Thanks for taking the kids all evening. Give Pete my love."

"I will." Mary Rose sent her yet another searching look by the front-porch lamp. "Are you sure you're okay?"

"I'm fine." She hadn't explained about Dixon's visit and didn't intend to. "Go home to your husband." Kate pushed lightly at her shoulder to start her down the steps, but stayed watching until Mary Rose was in her flashy red Porsche with the engine on and the doors locked. Only then did she shut the door and flip the switch for the outside lights.

Automatically, she made her nightly rounds, turning off lamps, checking the back-door lock, straightening a book here, a magazine there… until she reached the sitting area in the great room. Her knees gave way and she dropped into the armchair by the window, unable to stop staring at the love seat.

It didn't seem possible that this had been only one day…starting with Dixon telling her he wanted to marry her and ending with the two of them kissing. All that had stopped her from giving him more was the bitter, belated recognition that she still legally belonged to another man.

In the silent darkness, something about those words struck her as wrong. She listened to her thoughts again…*legally belonged*…

As if she were a piece of property. A possession to be bought, sold, bartered. What had happened to Kate Bowdrey, the person? Had there ever really been one?

"Mama's baby." "Daddy's little girl." She remembered those titles from childhood. "Me sista,"

Mary Rose's infant name for her, still brought a smile. John Bowdrey's daughter, the future lawyer. New Skye High School valedictorian. L. T. LaRue's wife, Trace and Kelsey's mother.

When had she played, worked, lived for herself alone?

The word *never* came to mind.

Kate closed her eyes and dropped her head back against the chair. She wouldn't claim to be a victim. She'd liked belonging to people, knowing her place, understanding the rules of who and what she should be. The terror of college, she thought, had come from not knowing where she fit in and having no one to tell her.

This spring, Mary Rose had helped her stand up to her father and to L.T. But she couldn't use her sister as a prop for the rest of her life.

She couldn't use Dixon, either. He would allow that, she thought. He was so strong in himself that he would gladly let her lean on him, whenever and however she wanted.

That wasn't, however, the kind of woman he deserved. Maybe more important, that wasn't the kind of woman she wanted to be. Loving Dixon meant giving him the best of herself.

Decent cooking and a flair for choosing fabrics didn't seem enough, somehow. Organizing school events and charity parties…useful, even helpful. But was that her best?

Dixon's words came to mind—"Tell me what you want for the rest of your life, and we'll try to make it happen, whether it's law school or a string of babies or safaris on the Amazon."

What in the world did she want to do with her life?

The real problem, Kate admitted to the night, was that she didn't have a clue.

L.T. WAITED UNTIL the woman in bed beside him had fallen asleep, then got up carefully, dressed in the dark and left the condo. Melanie was a sweet girl—not really bright but with none of Kate's reproachful silences and rigid behavior. He'd never known where he was with Kate, which had been kind of exciting at first. After being married for a while, though, a man liked to think he was hitting the mark most of the time. Kate always made him feel as if he'd forgotten to do or say something. Usually something important.

The streets of New Skye were deserted at 2:00 a.m. Once inside his office, he sat at the computer and ran through his accounts. The numbers hadn't changed since this morning. Between the stock-market fall and his overextended credit, LaRue Construction was running on fumes, so to speak. And, like a car with no gas in the tank, this particular engine was about to sputter and die. Everything he'd worked for would be sold in bankruptcy court to cover his debts, with all his enemies—and L.T. didn't kid himself, he knew he had plenty—looking on and laughing.

Foremost among them, no doubt, would be Dixon Bell. Jimmy Hyde had reported their talk today concerning the injunction. Neither the judge nor the mayor nor L.T. had really expected Bell to halt work—the injunction was a warning shot more than anything else. The hearing would be legitimate, of course. One way or another, he planned to get his hands on that land. Magnolia Cottage Public Housing Project would be the salvation of LaRue Construction. Mr. Almighty First Family Bell would not be allowed to mess up this deal.

Even if he was dating L.T.'s wife. Driving by the house this evening before going home, L.T. had seen the silver truck parked in the driveway. The kids went to that stupid rehab program on Tuesdays, so Kate had to be alone with the man. Who was she to criticize *him?*

And what about the kids? L.T. knew he'd made mistakes where they were concerned. He couldn't explain to Kelsey and Trace that he'd had to get free before his life crushed him like an empty aluminum can. He was forty years old, and he'd been working since he was their age, saving money for school—he knew his misbegotten parents weren't going to pay for college—and for his own business. He'd married too fast, and his first wife was a better con artist than he would ever be. Took all those savings and disappeared, leaving him with two babies. At least in Kate he'd found a good mother for the children. Too easy on them, too apt to excuse instead of discipline, but she'd stuck with them. And her family connections had helped him build a decent business without his missing savings.

L.T. turned off the computer and rubbed his hands over his face. John Bowdrey would not be pleased to lose his investment. He'd be even less pleased to appear as part of a news story if some of LaRue Construction's shadier operations came to light.

L.T. stood at his office window and watched as night faded into day. He would turn up the fire under Bell and his grandmother. Too many people had too much to lose, otherwise.

Dixon Bell could just consider it his civic duty to rescue them all.

Dixon worked by himself all day Wednesday, taking down the rest of the wall in the back room. Once Miss Daisy had gone to bed and all the cats had taken their favorite places on the available chairs, he sat on the steps under the ruined chandelier and called Kate. "How are you?"

"I'm...okay." Not, he was glad to note, her

usual polite "fine," given out to everyone regardless of how she truly felt. "You left your jacket and tie."

He hadn't even missed them. "Sorry about that. Shows you how often I wear a suit."

She didn't laugh. "Trace noticed and mentioned it to me this morning. He was a little stiff about it."

Warning bells. "He probably wonders what'll happen if you have a relationship with somebody besides his dad." Kate didn't respond. "You know there's no problem, right? As far as I'm concerned, Trace and Kelsey are part of being with you. I wouldn't for a second have it any other way."

"I knew you would say that." She sighed. "The problem is convincing them."

This wasn't going to be a cozy talk, or a long one. Dixon decided not to pester her any further. "Well, I just wanted to check on you, let you know I was thinking about you. But it's late, so maybe we should both get some rest."

"Maybe."

They said a pretty formal good-night and he hung up the phone feeling less sure of himself and less optimistic than he had since reading Miss Daisy's letter back in March.

Maybe I shouldn't have come home after all.

S AL HADN'T INTENDED to avoid Kelsey at school. It just seemed as if they were always missing each other.

That's what he told himself, anyway. And what he told her when she finally caught up with him Friday afternoon during their last break.

"I haven't seen you or even talked to you since Sunday," she said. "Did I do something wrong?"

"No, *querida*. Honest." He ran his knuckles along her bare arm, glanced around them and then bent to give her a quick kiss. "It's just… complicated."

Her eyebrows drew together over her big brown eyes. "Complicated how?"

"At home…things are a little rough right now."

"But I thought your dad was working again. For Mr. Bell."

"Something happened Tuesday and he got laid off. They all did."

"And so he…"

"Right." No need to explain that his dad was drinking again. Kelsey knew the story, understood why she could never come to his house and meet his brothers and sisters.

She put a hand on his arm. "I'm sorry. At least today's the last day of summer school. We can see each other more, right?"

He couldn't promise, but he couldn't deny the

hope in her face, either. "I think that can be arranged." The bell rang, calling them back to class.

"Are you working for Mr. Bell tomorrow?"

"Far as I know." His family needed the money.

Kelsey gave him her sweet smile. "I'll see you then."

Feeling better than he had all week, Sal turned toward his class, only to find Trace LaRue leaning against the corner of the hallway. "You're asking for trouble," he said as Sal walked by.

"I'm real scared."

"My dad's gonna kick your butt when he finds out you're still following Kelsey around."

"He's welcome to try."

"Why don't you do us all a favor and stick with your own kind?"

"Why don't you do us all a favor and drop dead?"

Trace grabbed Sal's shirt and jerked him around to face a clenched fist. Sal didn't wait to be hit; he brought his own fist up into his attacker's belly. Trace doubled over with a gasp, then reached out, clenched his hands around Sal's knee and pulled his leg out from under him. Both of them crashed to the floor.

They were rolling across the empty hallway, struggling for a grip, for leverage, for the chance to hit again, when the principal and the basketball coach pulled them apart.

"That's enough." The coach shoved Sal up against the wall. "I said, back off."

Across the hall, the principal had Trace in his grip. "My office, both of you. If this weren't the last day of school, there'd be hell to pay for this one, I can tell you that much." He shook Trace's shoulders. "You've had enough trouble already this year. Where're your brains, son?"

Of course, Mrs. LaRue was at school within fifteen minutes. And, of course, neither of Sal's parents were at home when the principal called. He was due to pick his mother up at work. Who knew where Mano was? Who cared?

Sal sat through the standard lecture on fighting in school without paying much attention. He'd heard it all before. He made the right sounds, apologized without meaning a word, put on a repentant face.

And when he finally escaped, he called Ricky Feliz. Their brothers—Los Lobos—had a job to do.

WHEN THE PHONE RANG Friday night, Kate hoped to hear Dixon's deep tone on the other end.

"What is going on over there?" L.T. demanded. "I got a call from Harry Floyd telling me Trace was fighting in school today."

Kate sat at the kitchen table and braced her

head on one hand. "He picked a fight with Sal Torres."

"About what?"

She wasn't prepared to tell him how much Trace resented his sister dating the Hispanic boy, because L.T. felt the same. "Trace wouldn't say."

"He should know better than to carry on like that during school. I've told him before to save that kind of thing for elsewhere."

"He shouldn't be fighting at all, L.T."

"Sometimes a man's gotta stand up for what he believes. Anyway, just wanted to let you know I'd be picking the kids up for breakfast tomorrow and then we'll do something for the rest of the day. Maybe go to the beach."

"Trace and Kelsey have something already scheduled for tomorrow afternoon."

"Well, they can just unschedule."

"They're doing some work for…a friend, L.T. He pays them and he expects them to be there to do the job. Could you see them Sunday, instead?"

"I'm supposed to rearrange my life so the kids can earn a few lousy bucks I'd be just as happy to give them? I don't think so."

"They're learning responsibility and commitment. You can't object to that."

Being L.T., he could and did. But in the end, he conceded. "I guess Sunday'll work. Unless you're going to tell me they have to go to church, too."

She would have preferred that option, but decided to make her own concession. "I'll have them ready about nine on Sunday. Will that be convenient?"

"It'll have to be, won't it?" Before she could answer, he hung up.

And Kate sat staring at the buzzing phone, wondering whether L.T. had always been such a…a jerk, or if living with her had changed him so drastically.

SATURDAY DAWNED humid and still, headed toward scorching. But when Sal and Trace faced each other on the driveway at Magnolia Cottage that afternoon, everybody felt the chill in the air. Dixon looked from one to the other with raised eyebrows, but neither boy said a word. Then he looked at Kate.

"They got into a fight at school yesterday," she said, with weariness evident in her voice. "Trace has been warned not to give you any trouble. But I would put them on opposite sides of the yard again."

She clearly wasn't staying. She wore a slim green dress and high-heeled shoes and looked as cool as a dish of lime sherbet on a hot day. Definitely good enough to eat.

"I think we'll be okay," he assured her. "Sal's been working over near the road. Trace, you can pick up where you left off last week. Just stay out of each other's way." Trace shrugged, grabbed some tools and shuffled toward the garage. Sal gave him a contemptuous glance, shook his head, then turned to smile at Kelsey. "Ready to work?"

But Kelsey had her arms crossed and her chin in the air. "I think the two of you are behaving like little boys and I don't want anything to do with it." She looked up at Dixon. "Do you have somewhere I can work by myself?"

He managed to keep a straight face. "It's a big yard. In the back we have a weed farm that needs serious attention. How's that sound?"

"Perfect. See you later, Kate." Sal stared after her as she carried gloves and clippers and marched away from him. At last, without a sound, he turned and headed for his own precinct.

"If Trace causes problems..." Kate closed her eyes and drew a deep breath. "I don't know. Hang him by his feet from the tallest tree and I'll cut him down when I get back."

Dixon managed to step in front of her before she could open the car door and escape. "Looks to me like you have somewhere special to go."

She stared at the keys in her hand rather than at him. "A birthday tea party for a friend."

"Should be fun."

"Of course."

He couldn't stand it any longer. Putting his fingers under her chin, he gently forced her to meet his eyes. "Kate, I didn't mean to make you unhappy. If that's what my being here does, just tell me. I can be gone in an hour."

"No." Her fingers closed around his wrist and gripped hard. "No, I don't want you to leave. Please...don't."

"Shh. Okay. Don't worry." He shifted his hand to cup her cheek.

She relaxed her grip. "I'm not unhappy. But I am confused. There's a lot to think about, and then Trace... I just need some time."

"All you want." Bending down, he kissed her nose. "I won't mess up your lipstick...till later."

Finally, she smiled. "Good idea."

On that smile, he stepped back and let her go, watching the dust from her wheels drift in the humid air long after the Volvo had disappeared.

CHAPTER ELEVEN

THE BIRTHDAY TEA PARTY was for Kellie Tate, the mayor's wife, at Jessica Hyde's big, elegant house on The Hill. Kate would have preferred to be almost anywhere else, but she had accepted the invitation weeks ago. She had no excuse for not going. Except cowardice.

Her "friends" didn't disappoint her. There was a moment's lull in the conversation when she came into the living room where most of the women had gathered. She kept her chin up and the smile on her face. But she was quaking inside.

"Kate, how are you?" Jessica gave her a hug and a cool kiss, along with a whiff of Chanel. "I was beginning to wonder where you were. Let me take this..." She eased the gift out of Kate's hands. "You go say hello to Kellie. She's in the dining room by the fireplace. Do get yourself something to eat and drink while you're there."

There was a line of well-wishers, and Kate found herself at the very end next to Candy Scot, the mother of one of Trace's friends.

"Hey, honey." Candy gave her the requisite embrace. More Chanel—it must be the scent of the season. "Isn't this just wonderful? Jessica always does such beautiful decorations." They gazed for a moment at the ice sculpture of a rearing horse in the center of the table. Kellie Tate was quite active among the horsey set. "I hear Trace got into some trouble at school Friday. I'm so thankful Bo's settled down. I just about died when the police came to get him last spring for that bomb threat. Where do boys get these kinds of ideas?"

Kate thought about current events in other parts of the world, and in the U.S., but didn't waste breath trying to explain. Besides, Candy usually carried the conversation without much help from anybody else.

"And you're going to be redecorating Magnolia Cottage for Miss Daisy and that grandson of hers. Aren't you the enterprising one? Though they do say he's run into some roadblocks. The bureaucracy is so picky about permits and things like that." Her husband, Reese Scot, was on the city council. "Maybe Dixon didn't get everything filled out just right." They had reached the top of the line. "Oh, Kellie, honey, happy birthday. I swear, you don't look a day over twenty. Does she, Kate?"

"Not at all." Kate leaned over for yet another perfumed hug. "Happy birthday, Kellie."

"Thank you so much." The words were warm,

but Kellie's expression was cool. "I'm glad you could be here. I know how busy you must be these days, taking on the renovation at Magnolia Cottage and all."

"I'm just advising at this point. Dixon's doing the real work. Although I do understand that he's supposed to wait until some kind of hearing takes place on whether or not he can continue. Thank you, Jess," she said as Jessica brought her a plate filled with tea sandwiches and strawberries dipped in white chocolate.

Returning to the table, Jessica ladled a cup of punch for each of them. "Jimmy was saying that Dixon paid him a visit the other day and didn't seem too cooperative."

"Surely he doesn't think he can disobey the law?" Kellie sipped her drink and stared with raised eyebrows at Kate.

"I think Dixon believes he has a right to improve the house and the grounds around it that have belonged to his family for generations."

"He's not giving much thought to the welfare of the community, is he?" Candy waved a cucumber sandwich in the air. "I mean, one family can live in that one house. But if the land was developed properly, a hundred or more families could live in the same space."

"Exactly," Kellie said. "The city needs more multifamily housing."

Kate took a deep breath. "Probably not five-hundred-thousand-dollar condos, though."

"Well, of course not. I understand L.T. is planning to bid on the public housing project the council has been considering. I'm really surprised at you," Candy said when she'd swallowed her sandwich. "It's your husband who's spearheading the plan. I would think you'd be supportive."

Jessica had, no doubt, been waiting to pounce. "Ah, but you have to remember that L.T. and Kate are getting a divorce. Kate's got her eyes turned in a different direction these days, don't you, sweetie?"

"I—"

"Do tell." Kellie leaned forward. "Someone we know?"

"Kate doesn't want a housing project built at Magnolia Cottage because…" Jessica played out the suspense. "Because she wants to live there herself. With Dixon Bell."

The last words were loud enough to be heard by everybody in the room. There was a collective gasp at the announcement.

After a few seconds, Kate decided the earth wasn't going to open and swallow her up, because Jessica wouldn't allow that kind of escape in her own house. She had to face this down.

So she turned to the table and carefully filled her plate with all the delicacies, aware that every eye was upon her. She sampled a mini-quiche before saying a word.

"Actually, I would like to see Magnolia Cottage restored with some degree of accuracy because I think it's an important building in New Skye. We've lost so many of the original homes to fires over the years." She glanced around Jessica's lovingly preserved dining room from the early twentieth century. "I mean, most of the houses on The Hill are less than a century old. Hardly significant, really, in an historic sense." She heard Jessica's outraged sniff and quelled a smile. "Magnolia Cottage dates from the 1830s. That's almost two hundred years in the same family—a heritage to be proud of. The Crawfords and the Bells have done a lot for this town, fought in all the wars, and for the right side." A shot at the Scots, who joined the Northern army and came back with Sherman to loot the town. "Why wouldn't we preserve a landmark of such importance?"

The protests broke out, then—hardly tea party conversation, but rather an argument over civic issues. Jessica stood paralyzed, watching her elegant event disintegrate. Kate saw her pull herself together, finally, and secure the crowd's attention with a frantic waving of her hands.

"Let's go into the living room and help Kellie open her gifts." The D.A.'s wife managed a shaky smile. "Won't that be fun?"

BACK AT MAGNOLIA COTTAGE around five o'clock, Kate found the yard crew sprawled in lounge chairs on the terrace, obviously partaking of a serious cooling-down session. Dixon got up from a low chair and straightened to his full height without so much as a wobble or a creak. "Have a seat. How was your party?"

"Um…fine." Of course, he interpreted the comment correctly and gave her a questioning look as he held out a glass. But there was no point in going over what had happened. "How's your interior work coming?"

"Slow but steady. I have an electrician coming in Monday to talk about rewiring. I think having just one phone is a bit of a problem."

"You only have one phone?" Kelsey shook her head. "How do you manage?"

"It's tough." He winked at Kate. "Of course, everybody has their own cell phone now. But even teenagers might want to use the house phone now and then. Having more than one is a safety measure, at least."

Kelsey's eyes widened. "Are you planning to have teenagers here?"

"It's a distinct possibility."

She looked from Dixon to Kate and back again. "Really," she said slowly.

Trace stirred in his chair. "I'm going back to

work." He set his glass down hard on the tray and stalked toward the trees.

Kelsey sighed. "I'm sorry. I think I've had all the weeds and bugs and frogs I can take for one day."

Dixon nodded. "Perfectly understandable."

"I can take you home," Kate suggested. "And come back to get Trace later."

Kelsey couldn't hide her relief. "I'd really like to go home." She looked at Sal. "Okay?"

"Sure." He kissed her cheek. "Maybe I can come over tomorrow."

Kate stood up. "I'm afraid Kelsey and Trace will be with their dad all day tomorrow." Dixon followed as she left the terrace.

"What?" Kelsey sat up straight.

"You two can see each other on Monday. Meet me at the car in five minutes, Kelsey." Out of sight around the corner of the house, Kate let her resolve slip away. Dixon's arm behind her shoulders was a welcome support. "Nobody tells you how much effort parenting takes. You think the hard part is when they're babies. But that's easy, compared to keeping teenagers safe and on track."

"I'd like to give both ends of the process a try… with you."

"Oh, Dixon." She leaned into him for a second. "I don't know what's going to happen."

"I do." They reached the Volvo and he turned her toward him. "I'm gonna get this house fixed up—come hell, high water, or L. T. LaRue and his courthouse cronies. Next year, you'll be a free woman. And sometime after that, you'll realize you love me enough to put up with me for the rest of your life. Simple."

Staring up into his handsome, generous face, she wanted to believe. "I hope you're right."

"Take it to the bank." He bent his head, and she parted her lips in anticipation of a kiss.

But Sal's and Kelsey's voices came from too nearby to make the risk worth it. Dixon straightened up again. "Next time," he promised with a smile. "Oh, and I'll bring Trace home when he's finished. Don't worry about going out again."

"It will be good to stay home," she commented to Kelsey several minutes later as she turned the car onto the street at the gates of Magnolia Cottage. "I think a night spent dozing in front of a video sounds pretty wonderful."

"Mmm." The girl didn't say anything else for a minute. "So you and Mr. Bell are dating?"

"Not exactly."

"The message was pretty clear. He's expecting us to move in with him."

"Not anytime in the remotely near future."

"But eventually."

"I really don't know."

"You didn't think you should tell us you had a boyfriend?"

"I don't have a boyfriend."

"That's what it sounded like to me."

As if the scene at Jessica's party hadn't been enough for one day. Kate tightened her hands on the steering wheel. "Listen to me, Kelsey. I like Dixon very much. But I am legally married to your dad until next spring sometime. And I take that—that commitment seriously. I don't plan to date anybody until the divorce is final. I'm working with Dixon, and he's a friend, and that's all we will be to each other until I'm not married anymore. What happens after that is more than I can predict. And if you're smart, you won't worry about it."

Her daughter turned to look at her. "You don't kiss him?"

Kate wanted to swear. But she wouldn't lie. "I have kissed him, yes."

"But you're just friends."

"Torture me if you want to. I make mistakes, like everyone else. But I am trying to do what's right, and what's best for you and Trace. Surely, after all these years, I can expect you to believe that."

Kelsey slumped farther into the car seat.

"I...I'm surprised, is all. I had no idea you and he were more than just old classmates."

Neither did I, Kate thought. *Neither did I.*

A WORKING LUNCH, Dixon suggested when he asked Kate to meet him and Miss Daisy on Sunday. And he meant it.

Then Miss Daisy backed out on him. "LuAnne Taylor has invited me to have lunch with her, dear. I'm sure you'll do just fine without me."

"You're blowing my cover," he protested. "We could have at least pretended to talk about the house."

"You still can." She put a hand on his shoulder and he bent down so she could kiss his cheek. "I'm sure whatever Kate thinks will be just perfect."

And so he sat alone at the table when Kate came into the restaurant. A family-owned and -oriented Italian restaurant, nice but not especially romantic. Completely nonthreatening.

He got to his feet as she came close and pulled out a chair across the table from his. "It's great to see you. You look wonderful, as always."

She gave him a warm smile. "And you're sweet, as always." Then she noticed the two place settings. "Miss Daisy's not coming?"

Dixon explained and watched Kate's smile

fade. "I can't put the moves on you here, though. There're too many kids around."

"That's not…" She shook her head and sighed. "This is ridiculous. I should be able to have Sunday lunch with whomever I want." Picking up the menu, she hid behind it. "What shall we eat?"

Eventually, Kate relaxed and they did talk about the house, about paint and stain and light fixtures, about styles for the new bathroom and cabinets for the kitchen. And about bugs and frogs and weeds in gardens, from Kelsey's protest yesterday all the way back to the Garden of Eden.

They were laughing at some nonsense they'd come up with together when a family of three walked by their table. The woman glanced back over her shoulder, stopped and whirled around. "Hello again, Kate LaRue. I swear, I don't see you for weeks on end, and then we're together two days in a row." She backtracked and leaned down to bestow a hug. "Wasn't yesterday just fascinating?" Then she glanced at Dixon. "And it's been a long, long time, but I'm pretty sure I'd know you anywhere." He'd gotten out of his chair, and before he knew what was happening, he received his own hug. "Hello, Dixon Bell. Welcome home."

He gave Kate a signal for help. Who was this person?

"You remember Candy Lawrence, Dixon. She

was a year behind us in school. She married Reese Scot from our class."

The guy looked more familiar, though his balding head didn't help much with the memories. "Sure. Good to see you both again."

"This is our son, Bo." Candy pulled a kid about Trace's age into the circle. "He and Kate's Trace are good friends." Dixon extended his hand and got a sullen shake in return.

"Candy was at the party yesterday," Kate said. "Reese is a member of the city council. He owns the local TV station and a couple of radio stations, as well."

Dixon nodded at the other man. "Sounds like you did well for yourself."

The other man puffed up like a turkey gobbler. "I'm just thankful for my family and the opportunities that come my way."

"You and Kate were quite the topic of conversation at the tea party yesterday." Candy put a hand on his arm and batted her false eyelashes at him. "I certainly can see why she'd be defending you."

"Do I need defending?"

Reese put his hands in his pockets and rocked from heels to toes and back again. "Well, a lot of folks in town support L. T. LaRue's plan to build low-income housing on that property. And they're not quite understanding why you would come back after so many years gone just to get in the way."

"Low-income housing? I heard half-million-dollar condos."

"No, no. That was an early idea. But L.T. met with the mayor and some of the council and we... The idea of building a new housing project for the deserving people of New Skye just seemed like the right thing to do."

"So now I'm standing in the way of community service."

"You said it, I didn't." Reese put his hand at Candy's waist. "Come on, darling, our table is waiting."

She gave Dixon's arm a squeeze. "Y'all be good now."

He sat down in a state of shock and stared across at Kate. "I thought you said you had a nice time yesterday."

"I lied."

"That, I believe." He glanced at his barely touched lasagna and couldn't face it, settling for a long gulp of tea instead. "He's changed tactics."

"And put you on the defensive."

"One family's comfort against the needs of many."

"L.T. is a smart man."

Dixon nodded. "I guess so." He thought about his grandmother, about the family he hoped to make with Kate and bring up in the house that belonged to him. "But he let you go. That automatically means I'm smarter." He grinned as Kate's eyes widened with surprised delight.

"And I will win."

TRACE WASN'T A BIG FAN of the beach. Sand, sunscreen, salty water and hot sun, with nothing to do except ride his boogie board or sit and watch the crowds walk by. Girls in bikinis were okay to look at, but they didn't seem to come along as often as the fat old guys wearing white socks and black sneakers.

The day wasn't going too badly, though. It was just the three of them—Dad, Kelsey and himself. The Bimbo had stayed back in New Skye. No arguments, no lectures, no pouts from Kelsey. When things went this smoothly, Trace could almost wish his dad would move back home.

Almost. Because he knew enough now to realize that things wouldn't be like this if his dad came back. There would be the same hassles, the same fights, the same non-fights when Kate froze up and his dad stomped out.

And now Dixon Bell was in the picture. Whatever Kate might say—and Kelsey had told him what she said in the car last night—Trace had seen them together. They made Sal and Kelsey look like…like study partners. The feelings between Dixon and Kate were totally obvious.

"Trace? Son?" His dad scrubbed his knuckles over Trace's head in the way he hated. "While you were zoning out on gorgeous girls, your sister and I decided to get cleaned up and go for an early dinner on the way home. Coming with us?"

The questions started as they waited for their drinks in the restaurant. "So, Kate says you two are doing some yard work for a friend of hers. Getting paid for it, too."

Trace looked at Kelsey, but she was playing with her napkin. "Yes, sir."

"One of the neighbors?"

"Uh, no, sir."

"Sounds like it might be an older house, if the brush is so overgrown. On The Hill somewhere?"

Which would mean, Trace thought, it was one of the neighbors, so his dad knew that wasn't the case. "No, sir. Sorta on the edge of town." Kelsey kicked him under the table.

"Ah." The drinks arrived, and the server took their order. When she was gone, their dad picked up where he left off. "So this is some older lady, I guess, who needs the help?"

Trace grabbed at the option with relief. It was, after all, true. "Yes, sir." Then he caught Kelsey staring at him with horror in her face.

"Y'all are working for Miss Daisy Crawford,

I take it?" His dad's voice was smooth as glass, which was a warning all by itself.

And there was no way to avoid this answer. "Y-yes, sir. And her grandson, Mr. Bell." Might as well get the worst over with.

"Been over there a lot, have you?"

The server set their salads in front of them. Trace realized he'd completely lost his appetite. "Just twice."

"And I guess he's spent a lot of time at our house."

Kelsey looked up from spearing lettuce. "No, sir. Just to pick Trace up or drop him off. Oh, and that day he took Kate to lunch. He was there when we got home."

Trace felt his face heat up and knew his dad could see the flush. "That so, Trace?"

He tried a shrug. "Maybe one or two other times. Kate is working with him and Miss Daisy on the house."

"Right. The house on land I need so I can build housing for the decent people of this town. Here I am, committed to public service, and you two are doing everything in your power to shoot me down. What kind of kid deliberately sabotages his father's best intentions? Have you no respect for me, for the business I've built, for the good I'm trying to do in our community?"

The lecture continued in spurts during the two-hour drive home, with long, injured silences in between. Trace sat in the back seat of the SUV and tried to tune out his dad's voice. But the one time he fell asleep, a loud voice quickly woke him up again. "Are you listening to me, boy?"

They got back to New Skye just before dark. Kate opened the front door as if she'd been waiting to see them pull into the driveway. Their dad sat at the wheel of the car as Trace and Kelsey got out. When Kelsey said a timid "Good night. Thanks for the trip," he just shook his head in disgust. Almost before they'd set foot in the grass, he backed out of the driveway and roared off down the street.

Kate was smiling as they reached the porch. "Welcome back. How was the beach?"

"Great," Trace muttered, easing past his stepmother without meeting her eyes. "Just great."

ONCE SET IN MOTION, the plan couldn't be called back without an excellent, usually life-threatening, reason. As long as he kept Kelsey out of the equation, Sal couldn't think of even the smallest excuse for hesitating. Trace LaRue and his dad deserved everything they were going to get.

Since this was a matter of personal honor, he went along. LaRue Construction had six projects going in different parts of town. He and Ricky had scouted each site, deciding to hit the one farthest from the shopping areas and police action, and scheduled the job for late Sunday night, when most people would be in bed or getting ready for work the next morning.

Sal laid down the rules. As little noise as possible. No gang marks anywhere—he didn't want to answer for this particular stunt if he didn't have to. When he called a halt, there would be no arguments. The job ended then and there. His brothers all nodded in agreement. Then he turned them loose.

These were high-end houses, like the ones his mother cleaned. Four of them, in various stages of construction, and all with For Sale signs in front, meaning they belonged to L. T. LaRue alone. Sal liked that aspect of the job. He didn't require vengeance from anybody else.

Breaking boards and pipes really wasn't much fun, so they ignored the two buildings just beginning to be framed. The other two had walls, inside and out. Orange spray paint on gray wallboard. Smashed doors and windows. Insulation ripped out of the attic and off the sides of the houses. Sticks and rocks dropped into plumbing pipes. Just ordinary good times.

Before leaving, they tipped all the portable johns in the neighborhood. The smell followed them as they left the scene.

Sal didn't take the brothers home with him, as

he once would've. They hung out at Ricky's for a couple of hours, reliving the high points of the night. Somehow, he wasn't finding it as funny as the others. He had scored his point against L. T. LaRue, and against his son.

For a reason he didn't want to think about, the thrill of victory just wasn't coming through.

Over the protests of the rest, he was the first to leave. He drove by Kelsey's house and saw that all the lights were off. Tomorrow he would come to her house during his lunch break at work and spend at least a few minutes holding her hand, if that was all he could have. He needed her special kind of warmth around him right now. He was feeling really cold.

When he got home, his house was quiet and dark, too, except for the kitchen light. He found his mother at the table, drinking milk.

"Salvadore, you've been gone all day. Have you had anything to eat?"

"I ate." He sat down across from her and propped his head in his hands. "Why are you still up?"

"Too excited to sleep, I think."

"Excited about what?"

"Mr. Bell called your papa tonight. He starts work again tomorrow morning."

Sal sat back in his chair. "That's a surprise. Was Papa here to get the news? Was he sober?"

She got up from the table and went to wash out her glass. "He knows."

"And he's sleeping it off so he'll have a prayer of getting there early enough tomorrow?"

"Why must you be so cruel?"

He let his head drop back and closed his eyes. "I don't know, Mama. I'm sorry. I don't want to hurt you." *And how would she feel,* a voice in his head whispered, *if she knew where you've been tonight? What you've done?*

"I know you don't, son." Consuela came to him and put her arms around his shoulders, cradling his head against her. "Your papa hasn't always treated you right. I understand. But love is patient. Love never gives up." She kissed the top of his head. "Sleep well. I'll see you early tomorrow morning."

"You, too, Mama."

He listened to her walk down the hall, stopping to check on the children in their beds as she went, then the squeak of the door to the room she shared with his father. Now the house was silent, still.

But inside his head, Sal heard the protest of his conscience, loud and clear. *One side or the other. If you don't choose, someone will choose for you. And the people you love will bear the burden of your fear.*

CHAPTER TWELVE

THE PHONE RANG Monday morning as Kate was finishing her solitary breakfast. Trace and Kelsey were sleeping late in celebration of the end of summer school.

"Good morning, Katherine Ann."

"Hi, Mama. How was your weekend?"

"Distressing." Frances Bowdrey's voice was unusually crisp. "Your father and I need to talk to you. We'll expect you for lunch about twelve-thirty."

"What's wrong?" She knew, of course. The tale of Kellie Tate's birthday party had no doubt spread like wildfire and across every telephone line in town.

"We'll discuss it at lunch. Twelve-thirty and don't be late—your father can't take off the entire afternoon."

"Yes, ma'am." What she really wanted to say was "Sorry, can't make it. Better things to do." But the rules said that you didn't talk back to your parents, even when you were thirty-one years old, even when they were being rude and completely unreasonable.

So Kate settled for slamming the phone back into its cradle.

She wrestled with a strong urge to call Dixon, just to vent her frustration. What right did she have, though, to make that kind of demand on him? He would listen, empathize, probably give her good advice. They would be brought closer together, more in tune with each other than ever.

In other words, her dilemma over Dixon Bell would only get worse.

Did she love him? Without question. Was she in love with him? Desperately. Did she want a relationship with him? In every conceivable way, she wanted to be with this man.

But was she prepared to defy her parents, her children, her neighbors and friends, her community, not to mention her obnoxious almost-ex-husband, for that relationship?

Kate couldn't say that she was. And because she was a coward, seeing Dixon so often, letting their feelings for each other deepen, was just leading him on and torturing herself. Not seeing him made time stand still and took the sun out of her sky.

She left for lunch at her parents' house in a very bad mood.

John and Frances Bowdrey still lived in the

house where she and Mary Rose had grown up, one of the older homes on The Hill—not the largest, but always noticed by visitors for its elegant Colonial Revival proportions and the beautifully landscaped yard. Kate had learned her love of gardening from her mother and had absorbed everything she was offered about the attention to detail that went into keeping house properly.

She parked on the street so she wouldn't block her father in the driveway if he needed to leave before she did, and went to the front entrance, as would be expected. Her mother opened the door and offered a cool smile, then a cool hug. "Come in, dear. You look very nice."

"Thanks." She'd dressed carefully, in a pink linen sheath she knew her mother liked, with her hair in a French twist that her father always complimented. If this interview was going to proceed as she expected, the fewer targets she offered, the better.

"I thought we'd eat in the dining room," Frances said, leading the way. "The garden looks so nice this time of year."

"Your hydrangeas are gorgeous." Kate walked to the picture window. "Can I help you with anything?"

"I have the plates all made. I'll just set them out."

Her father's footstep sounded on the hardwood floor. "Kate, dear."

She turned to give him a kiss and a hug. "Hi, Daddy. How are you?"

"Well, as always. But I'd be better if you weren't set on stirring up trouble in this town."

"Now, John, let's eat first." His wife came in with a pitcher of tea. "There's no sense ruining lunch with discord."

Kate sat in her usual chair and took a couple of deep breaths. She picked up her fork, put it down again. "If Daddy doesn't have much time, maybe we should go ahead and get to the point. What trouble is this I'm stirring up?"

Her father took a deliberate bite of his chicken salad, a sip of tea. Then he cleared his throat. "You've been expressing some opposition to L.T.'s plan for the Crawford property."

"Not to mention cooperating with Dixon Bell in working on that house," her mother said.

"As a member of the city council, I find it an embarrassment—a great embarrassment—that my daughter would speak out against a project that would be so beneficial to the people of our community."

"And do you have any idea what people are saying about you, a married woman, working so closely with an unattached man?" her mother said.

"I'm sure Miss Daisy herself is appalled. She has very high standards."

Kate looked from one parent to the other. "Anything else?"

Giving her mother an invitation to continue was a mistake. "After all, it's not as if you are a professional designer, with the kinds of contacts and training one needs to actually dress a house properly. We have some excellent people working in this community who would be glad to help Daisy Crawford redecorate."

"I thought the point was that you want to tear down the house altogether."

John Bowdrey cleared his throat again, but Frances wasn't listening. "He's even hired that man L.T. had to dismiss all those years ago because he couldn't stay sober to come to work. What kind of—of mess have you gotten yourself into?"

"As you say yourself," her father, the lawyer, said, "the real issue is the disposition of the property. I'm not sure that L.T.'s plans include destroying the house. It is, after all, an historic building. But the Magnolia Cottage land is the heart of his plan, and he can't proceed without it. Which means Dixon Bell is denying the city a vital redevelopment effort."

Kate pushed her plate away—she wouldn't be

eating a bite of her food. "Dixon Bell is protecting his home. When did that become anti-American?"

"There are people who need that housing."

"L.T.'s original plan called for luxury condos."

"But the plan has changed."

"My belief is that he's figured out he can make more money cheating the government than a hundred or so private citizens."

Her father slapped his hands down on the table, so hard that the silverware and glasses jumped. "That accusation is uncalled for. Do I need to remind you that I have business dealings with the man?"

"Do I need to remind you that I was married to him? That I listened to him gloat over slick deals for ten years? I have no illusions about L.T.'s honesty. Frankly, Daddy, I doubt you do, either."

"Katherine Ann LaRue, are you accusing your father of dishonesty?"

Kate pressed a hand to her throat, choosing her words carefully. "I think Daddy doesn't know everything L.T. does that makes him money."

"So I'm not a criminal, just stupid?"

"No. I think it would take a great deal of intelligent strategy to avoid knowing about L.T.'s fraud and deceit."

Stunned silence greeted her statement. Finally, without another word, her father left the table. The front door slammed behind him, and the engine of his Cadillac roared as he backed down the driveway toward the street.

"Are you sleeping with Dixon Bell?"

Kate looked at her mother. "That's none of your business."

"I am simply trying to find some explanation for your rude, undutiful and, frankly, unbelievable behavior. If you're in love with the man, that would be some excuse."

"Then let me make you feel better. Yes, I am in love with Dixon."

"You're a married woman."

"Please, Mama, you have to wake up at some point and realize that it's over. L.T. left me for another woman—one he's living and sleeping with, remember. Our marriage died the day he walked out. We're just waiting for the funeral."

"If you would be more accommodating—"

"He might come home?" Kate got to her feet. "Thank you for the warning. I don't want him in my home. If he had more money than—than God—"

"Kate!"

"And left his sweet young thing and crawled across town on his knees, begging me to take him back…" She thought about it. "I believe I'd kick him in the teeth and shut the door in his face."

"But the children…"

"L.T. wins points when he spends money. Talk

to them sometime, ask how they'd feel about living with him again." Dredging up the last drops of her sense of duty, she rounded the table, put an arm around her mother's shoulders and kissed her cheek. A real kiss. "Take care, Mama. I'll talk to you later this week."

She made it to the car just before her trembling knees gave way completely.

DIXON HADN'T TOLD Miss Daisy or Kate that the injunction hearing was scheduled for Monday afternoon. Neither of them needed to be involved in what would essentially be a mock trial. L.T. wanted all his bases covered so he could put up a good front. Dixon didn't expect any kind of unbiased opinion from the judge, or anybody else.

While the old courthouse was preserved as an historic monument, the actual court system operated inside the town hall, built since he'd been gone. The courtrooms were modern and functional, with nice cherry paneling behind the judge's desk to add formality and make an impression.

"Judge Archibald Gillespie," the bailiff announced.

The man who tottered out from his chambers was the least formidable magistrate Dixon had ever encountered. Short, thin to the point of disappearing inside the black robe, he had a tuft of wispy gray hair above each ear and thick glasses magnifying his bleary gray eyes.

He settled himself in his chair, then peered at the nearly empty room. "What's this?"

"An injunction hearing, Your Honor," Jimmy Hyde said loudly. "Mr. Bell here wants to renovate his property. The city of New Skye thinks he should be restrained, due to the possible acquisition of said property by right of eminent domain for the purpose of building a public housing project." Beside him at the table, L. T. LaRue sat with his hands folded and an expression of earnest good intentions on his face.

Dixon wanted to slam his fist deep into that smug face. Flexing his fingers, he took a breath and settled back in his chair.

The judge said "Hmmph" and began to read the papers before him. During the next twenty minutes he made various sounds, some of which were words, most of which were coughs, growls, gargles, sniffs and other less polite noises. Finally, he looked up again. "So?"

Dixon took that as his cue. "Your Honor." He pitched his voice to reach the old man without sounding loud. "The property we're talking about has been in my family for close to two hundred years. My grandmother raised me in that house. She's in her eighties now—"

"She wouldn't thank you for saying that out loud," the judge cackled.

So he knew Miss Daisy. Dixon grinned. "No, sir, she wouldn't. I'd like the house to be comfortable and safe for her, and for the family I'd like to raise one day, myself." He was aware of LaRue shifting his position at the table. "While I know the city has needs, I'm not convinced that seizing my family's rightful possession is the way to meet those needs."

"Hmmph," Gillespie said again. "Wait here. I'll be back." He needed the bailiff's help to get out of his chair and down from the podium without falling.

Dixon ground his teeth at the prospect of being trapped in this windowless room with Jimmy Hyde and L. T. LaRue for more than five minutes. The mayor hadn't attended the hearing—he obviously recognized the need to retain some semblance of objectivity.

L.T. strolled over and propped a hip on the table Dixon sat behind. "So you want to raise a family in that derelict house of yours. How sweet." He smiled, looking very sharklike. "With my wife, I suppose."

Anger crowded the breath out of his throat, but Dixon refused to surrender. "No. I don't marry other men's wives." L.T. lowered his eyebrows, obviously confused. That allowed Dixon the chance and the breath to laugh. "When Kate and I are together, she won't be your wife in any sense of the word."

LaRue's face turned beet red. He stood up, told Dixon what he could do in language highly inappropriate to the halls of justice and went back to his seat. Nobody said a word until Judge Gillespie reappeared ten minutes later.

"Well," he said in his quavery voice, "I think this injunction is a bunch of nonsense. You can't stop a man from painting his walls unless you own those walls. Whoever signed off on this injunction oughta be kicked off the bench." He squinted at the page. "Judge Harnett. That explains a lot." Another cackle. "I'm revoking the injunction. You want this land," Gillespie said, looking directly at L.T., "you find a legal way to get it. Don't bother me with this garbage again." Three slams of the gavel against the desk, and Dixon could finally relax.

Jimmy Hyde said a word to L.T. and walked out without glancing in Dixon's direction. But L.T. had more to say. "This ain't over. I will get that land." He thumped a fist on the table. "And I'll tell you what else. My site got torn up last night. Funny thing it should be the one closest to your side of town. So I'm thinking maybe this wasn't just some random stupidity. Maybe the punks had an assignment from somebody to mess up my work. Maybe they were even paid to mess with me." His grin was gleeful and mean at the same time. "The cops are working on it. We'll let you know what they find out."

Dixon gave L.T. plenty of time to clear the building before leaving himself. The vandalism worried him. Given what else was going on, how likely was it that this was a random event? Trace had been involved with some property crimes in the spring, according to Kate. Was he striking back at his dad directly now?

There were two other people who would have cause to resent, even attack, L. T. LaRue. With a new job under way, Mano Torres didn't seem like a good suspect for causing trouble.

But then there was Sal, the young man with an attitude and access to any number of willing hooligans from Los Lobos, the gang of which, Pete Mitchell said, he was the leader. The young man dating Kate's daughter while feuding with her son.

Did Trace know something the rest of them didn't? What would L.T. do to Kelsey and to Kate if he discovered that Sal had wrecked his construction site?

What would Dixon have to do to protect the kids and the woman he loved from a stupid man's rage?

KATE WAS IN THE KITCHEN with Miss Daisy when they heard Dixon's diesel truck pull up to the garage. "There he is." The older woman got up to get a glass and pour some tea. "Now we'll find out where he went so dressed up this afternoon."

"Hey, Miss Daisy." He came in and gave his grandmother a kiss on the cheek. When he saw Kate, his tired smile widened into a grin. "What a great surprise. I didn't see your car in the driveway." Before she knew what he was doing, he came close enough to bend over and give her a kiss. "I'm really glad to see you."

She could feel herself blushing. "I—I didn't park in the driveway. It's so hot, I looked for some shade under the trees."

"Excellent idea. 'Blistering' doesn't cover this weather." Dixon took the tea Miss Daisy offered and downed half the glass in one swallow. "Thanks. I almost feel human again."

He looked a good deal more than merely human. His light tan suit and pale-blue dress shirt somehow conjured an image of the quintessential Southern gentleman. He'd taken off his tie and opened the button at his collar. Kate watched the brown column of his throat in fascination as he took another long draw on his tea.

Warmth washed over her. She reached for her own glass and took a healthy gulp.

"So sit down and tell us where you've been." Miss Daisy refilled everyone's drinks. "Your workmen didn't linger once you'd gone."

"I told them to take the afternoon off. I didn't like leaving you alone in the house with them, even though I'm sure they're perfectly good men."

"Once you'd gone to…" his grandmother prompted.

Dixon ran a fingertip around the rim of his glass. "Court."

"Did you get a parking ticket?"

"Uh, no."

Kate sat up straighter. "Today was the hearing on the injunction, wasn't it?"

He met her gaze with his own, wary but not apologetic. "Yes."

"Dixon Crawford Bell. You didn't tell us? Didn't take us with you?" Miss Daisy went from funny to furious in a moment. "Would you care to explain yourself?"

"I didn't think either of you needed to be exposed to what might have been a very unpleasant situation."

"You were thinking of us?"

"Yes, ma'am. Trying to, anyway."

Kate went to put her glass by the sink. She'd never been angry with Dixon before. The feeling was…strange. "Thank you for the drink, Miss Daisy. I'll call when I get some more fabric samples."

"I'll wait to hear from you, dear."

"You're leaving?" Dixon stood up and came to

put a hand on her arm. "I just got back. You don't even know how the hearing went."

"I assumed that if I didn't deserve to know it was happening, I didn't deserve to know how things turned out." She looked down at his hand. "Excuse me."

"Kate, that's stupid." He didn't let go. "Give me credit for trying to spare you some discomfort. Would you have wanted to sit in that courtroom with LaRue glaring at you? I was trying to keep my problems from complicating your life."

"Oh, really?" She could scarcely believe the rage rushing through her. Good girls didn't get this mad. "Well, let me set you straight on that issue. You've already complicated my life. My children are anxious, my friends are laughing at me, and my parents are furious because I'm siding with you against their expressed wishes. If that's not complicated, I don't know what is. Now, please, let me get by." With her free hand, she pushed at his chest.

Dixon immediately released her. "Sorry. I—" Shoving his fists into his pants pockets, he stepped back. Way back. "Of course you need to leave."

"Thank you." Without looking at him or at Miss Daisy, she picked up her purse and slipped out the kitchen door. Once in the Volvo, she turned on the engine and the air-conditioning and then simply sat there, trying to get her breathing back to normal.

She understood that Dixon had only wanted to protect her. But what it meant, actually, was that he didn't think she was strong enough to face controversy, even conflict, at his side. There didn't seem to be much hope for their relationship if he didn't believe she could support him through any crisis.

When she thought she had calmed down enough, Kate put the car in gear, automatically turning on the radio. She wanted a vacation from thinking, if only for a few minutes.

As luck would have it, the first song after the string of commercials was "My Dream." "Me lovin' you, that's all I would ask... You're the dream I won't let slip away."

She turned the radio off again. Dixon loved her like that. Was that the only way he loved her? As a dream, as a fragile doll to be protected at all costs? Some women would be happy to have that kind of worship from a man, free of responsibility and shared troubles. Kate thought she might have been one of them, not so long ago. She'd been a trophy wife for L.T., a symbol of what he could achieve and a demonstration of how much money he could earn, a caretaker for his house and children. Not a real and integral part of his world.

Dixon's homecoming had changed her life in

many ways. She didn't want to be an ornament. She wanted to be a partner. And he would have to understand her new goals. Or else...

There was no "or else." He would simply have to adjust.

Because she wouldn't let him go.

WHAT a fool he was.

He wanted—needed—to punch something. He noticed the crumbling plaster of the kitchen wall. Perfect. He could take the whole room out with his bare hands....

"That didn't go well."

He'd forgotten Miss Daisy was still in the kitchen. "No, it didn't." He relaxed his hands. His grandmother wouldn't appreciate having a wall punched out in her presence.

"You gave Kate a vested interest in seeing the house taken care of, but you don't want her involved in the problems associated with that process."

"Thanks, Miss Daisy. I did figure that part out."

She gave a delicate sniff. "As for myself, I've only lived at Magnolia Cottage my whole life long. I'd think that would be reason enough to be included in the process of keeping it safe."

Being lectured was not improving his temper. "Yes, ma'am. I understand. It won't happen again. I'll make sure you and Kate both have ample opportunity to witness what a jerk L. T. LaRue can be, how close he drives me to losing my temper, and how many people in this town whom you call friends would love to see you kicked out of your home so they can make some extra money. Yes, ma'am. I'll make sure you both have ringside seats."

That was as much as he could say without raising his voice and, no doubt, scaring his grandmother half to death. Dixon stalked out of the kitchen, went across the backyard and walked straight ahead into the underbrush, along the path Kelsey had cleared on Saturday, heading toward the creek at the back of the property. If he was lucky, he'd run into a mean ol' snake, maybe even an alligator.

He'd be the one to strike first.

L.T. SPENT THE AFTERNOON putting the rest of his plan into motion. He checked with his friend at the Public Housing Authority, made sure his ducks were in a row there. He called the zoning board, got that paperwork started. And he called Curtis Tate to be sure his petition was on the agenda of the city council meeting in two weeks.

"No problem," Curtis assured him. "Think that'll take care of the problem?"

"With the zoning changed and the PHA behind me on eminent domain, all we'll need is the city council's approval. So if you can deliver the council, it's in the bag."

"Shouldn't be too much of a problem. Me and Reese Scot will vote for you, of course. I'll make sure of Reverend Brinkman and Robin Burke. John Bowdrey'll be on our side. That's a majority, even if all the others vote with Bell."

"Well, you work on them, too. I don't want this to fall through."

"Don't worry, L.T. It'll all go just like we want."

Ending the call, L.T. got out of his SUV and stood staring at the two houses those reprobate punks had ruined last night. It would cost thousands, maybe even tens of thousands, to set things right, dollars he didn't have. Not until he got his hands on Magnolia Cottage, anyway.

He didn't want to be distracted by tracking down who did this, either. He had too much else to worry about.

But he wouldn't let it slide. The delinquents who dared mess with his work would be found and they would pay. If they didn't have the money, L.T. figured, he'd just take the cost right out of their hides.

By Friday, Dixon, Mano and Mickey had removed the plaster from all the walls in the entry hall and upstairs hallway. The electrician Dixon had expected couldn't seem to make time in his schedule for a consultation about new phone lines and wiring. Adam DeVries was surprised.

"He's always b-been a g-good man. Of course, he does work for LaRue s-sometimes."

"Which probably means L.T. paid him not to show up. Got any other recommendations?"

Adam gave him a couple of names, but they had too much work, it seemed, to take on more right now.

Dixon gritted his teeth and bought a book on electrical wiring. At least he would know what he was talking about when he hired some unknown to do the work.

He and Miss Daisy were on good terms again, which meant they avoided talking about the injunction hearing. Or the notice of a motion to rezone the property for multifamily public housing, the notice from the housing authority about eminent domain and the proposal to condemn the property and seize it for public use. Or the city council hearing scheduled to discuss the issue.

Kate didn't know about any of those problems because he hadn't talked to her since she left on Monday afternoon. He could have called, but she was the one who'd severed communication. Logic dictated that she be the one to restore the connection.

Logic...hurt feelings and more temper than he wanted to admit to. He'd given everything he had, these weeks since he'd come home. He'd waited thirteen years for her. Couldn't she be the one to compromise this time?

But she didn't contact him, and every day he worked like a devil from dawn until long past dark and fell into his bed too exhausted to think about why. He couldn't remember what had happened to his policy of moderation in all things. Something—someone—in New Skye, North Carolina, seemed to push him toward extremes.

Waking up Friday night in the dark was difficult...and painful, because he felt as if he was coughing his lungs out. He opened his eyes, but couldn't see for the tears pouring down his cheeks. Then the smell reached him. Smoke.

The house must be on fire.

He rolled out of bed, pulling his T-shirt off to hold over his mouth, and dropped to his hands and knees, hoping for better air. The door was opposite his bed, so he found it easily enough with his eyes closed.

Out in the hallway, the smoke was worse. Miss Daisy's door was farther along, toward the back of the house. Dixon crawled across the floor until he reached the opposite wall, then turned left and felt for the doorway. He sobbed with relief at finding the door shut. Maybe the smoke hadn't penetrated her room.

Wrong. "Miss Daisy!" He coughed, creeping

toward the right wall where her bed would be. "Wake up, Miss Daisy. Come on." Twelve feet seemed endless—was he in the wrong room? Had he missed her door? Eyes and mouth and throat and lungs all burned. He was afraid he was losing touch with reality. If he passed out, they would both die.

He found the bed by running headfirst into the post, which gave him a different pain to think about. Climbing the bedspread, he felt for Daisy's foot. "Come on, sweetheart. Wake up!"

She didn't stir. Dixon heaved himself to his feet, slid his arms underneath his grandmother's thin body and drew her up against his chest. Turning, he shuffled to where he thought the door would be. But he had to stop with his shoulder against the frame and carefully remember how to turn to reach the stairs. Left? Right? He had to guess correctly. Now.

He turned to the left and immediately realized that he'd made the right choice. His knees were weakening underneath him, and he leaned into the wall for support. But the wall was only lath for plaster, and some of it broken at that. Not much support. And he couldn't see the bottom of the stairs. When he was a kid, he'd known how many steps there were. Fifteen? Eighteen?

Dixon started counting. "One, two...seven... eleven..."

As he went down, the air cleared. He could see through the windows. The source of the fire must be on the second floor. "Eighteen." He'd come to the bottom step. Breathing a little easier, he got to the front door, turned the dead bolt and stumbled out onto the porch. Those loose bricks on the steps nearly sent him sprawling. Finally he knelt in the weedy—but mown—grass and eased Miss Daisy down.

"Come on, sweetheart. Can you wake up for me? Please, Miss Daisy. Breathe. It's nice fresh air, cool." He slapped her cheeks gently. "Come on, Grandma. Open your eyes."

She coughed harshly. "Don't call me that."

Dixon grinned. "Then open your eyes."

Her lashes fluttered, then lifted. "What's happened?"

"A fire somewhere upstairs. Mostly smoke, I think. I've gotta fetch my cell phone from the truck, call the fire department. Will you be all right here for a minute?"

"Yes, I—" All at once, she clutched at him with shaking hands. "Dixon, the cats. They're inside." She struggled to sit up, intent on getting to her feet. "We have to get the cats."

"I will. I promise." He held her arms, prevented her from standing up. "But you have to guarantee you'll stay right here. I'll get the phone. You call

911. And Kate. Call Kate. Don't move from here while I'm gone. Promise?"

"I promise. Hurry, Dixon. Hurry."

He sprinted to the truck, which he'd fortunately left unlocked, jerked the phone off the console and went back to Miss Daisy. "Kate's number is autodial," he told her, panting.

Then he turned and ran into the house.

CHAPTER THIRTEEN

WHEN KATE ARRIVED at Magnolia Cottage, police cars and fire-trucks blocked the driveway. For a second, she doubted they would let her through.

Then she saw Cromartie written across one firefighter's back. Tim Cromartie had graduated in the same class with her. She ran toward him and grabbed his thick coat sleeve. "Can you take me closer, Tim? Miss Daisy asked me to come."

Tim lifted his mask and blinked. "Oh, hey there, Kate. Sure—I heard her telling the captain she'd called you. Come on."

He led her to an ambulance where Miss Daisy sat on a cot, wrapped in a blanket, with an oxygen mask over her mouth and nose, and Audrey, the white Persian, in her lap. Clark, the silky black cat, dozed in the arms of an EMT. Cary, silver and sleek, peeked out from underneath the blanket pooling at Miss Daisy's feet.

"They haven't found Marlon yet," Miss Daisy said in a trembling voice. "And he's so fat. I'm afraid he won't survive."

Kate sat down on the cot and put an arm around

her friend, careful not to disturb any tubing. "Don't think that way. The firefighters will find him."

"It's Dixon who knows where to look, though. Marlon likes to curl up in out-of-the-way places. He might be in the linen closet, or the pantry, or the basement…"

"Dixon's still in the house?" The idea sent fear burning through her. "Have you seen him?"

"He found these three," Miss Daisy assured her. "He's only been gone a little while this time."

"And is the fire out?"

"Such as it was." The EMT holding Clark shifted the cat against her shoulder. "Insulation and damp cloths and green wood dropped between the walls, along with a cigarette. Made a lot of smoke, but would have taken a long time to burn the place down."

"You mean the fire was deliberately set?"

She shrugged. "Hard to tell. Somebody cleaning up could've just dumped all that trash inside the wall, figuring nobody would notice. Cigarette was at the bottom. Construction crews do that kinda stuff all the time."

"Not if they're careful, they don't." Black-faced, red-eyed, Dixon stood at the entrance to the rear of the ambulance, holding an armful of calico fur. "I found him at the back of the basement, sound asleep. Didn't like being woken up, either, but I figured we should bring him out."

"Oh, my dear, thank you!" Kate eased Audrey into her own lap as Dixon climbed into the ambulance. Daisy held out her arms and swept the fat feline into an embrace. "Now you let these nice young people look after you. Clark can sit on Kate's other side."

The EMT put the black cat down, but Dixon was backing out again. "I'm okay." A fit of horrible coughing gave the lie to that bit of bravado. "Honest."

"Come on, Mr. Bell." The EMT grabbed him by the arm. "We got a place for you to sit right here. Let's get you cleaned up, get you breathing a little better. Nothing else you can do in there tonight. The guys'll ventilate the house with fans, get the smoke out. You can come back tomorrow."

Dixon suddenly stopped resisting. He slumped onto the bench, propped his elbows on his thighs and hung his hands between his knees, then let his head drop forward. "Whatever you say."

His lethargy was almost as alarming as having him still in the house. "We were going to paint anyway," Kate said gently. "If you had to have a fire, now was the best time."

"Right." His chuckle turned into a cough. "Good way to look at it." He allowed the EMT to put an oxygen mask over his face and straightened up without protest when asked. Then, as Kate watched, he closed his eyes and leaned his head wearily back against the wall. She'd never seem him appear so...so defeated.

She didn't know how much time passed before Captain Mabry came to the ambulance. "Miz Crawford, you ought to go find yourself a bed and get some rest, if these folks here are ready to let you go. You, too, Mr. Bell."

Dixon opened his eyes and pulled off the mask. "You didn't find anything else?"

"No, sir. We're gonna hang around, keep checking for hot spots, get the smoke out as much as we possibly can before y'all come back. But you don't have to be here. And the police will leave a car once we're gone, just to keep an eye on the property. So you go on, get some rest. You know Miss Daisy needs it." He gave Kate a wink, sure that particular argument would work as none other could. "I'll talk to you and the arson investigator tomorrow."

Kate returned his smile. "How are Gena and Laura doing at college? Did they come home for the summer?" Kate had been a regular baby-sitter for the Mabry twins when she was in her teens.

"Just fine, thank you for asking. Yes, they're home, which lets their mother and me rest a lot easier, for a couple of months, at least."

Miss Daisy looked at Dixon. "Where are we

going to go that will take all the cats? I suppose LuAnne Taylor would let us stay, but she has that dog—Fuzzy, I think his name is."

Kate stood up. "You're coming to my house, of course. All of you, and no arguments. Trace and Kelsey have begged for a pet for years. Now they can enjoy four at one time."

Neither Dixon nor his grandmother appeared inclined to argue. Between the three of them, they gathered up the cats and got them to the Volvo, settling Miss Daisy in the back seat with all four. Dixon shut the door and looked blearily at Kate. "I think I'd better bring my truck so I'll have transportation tomorrow and won't have to inconvenience you."

She wasn't going to argue with him tonight. "Do you feel okay to drive?"

He passed a hand over his face. "I can make it ten minutes across town."

She kept him in her rearview mirror as they drove, which meant going very slowly. Obviously, he wasn't as unaffected as he wanted to believe. They reached Kate's house soon enough, though. Trace and Kelsey were both up, since she'd had to wake them to tell them she was leaving and why. Between them all, they made a huge fuss over Miss Daisy, getting her into a quick shower, a clean gown of Kate's, and then the guest bed with honeyed tea and the cats surrounding her.

Once Dixon had seen his grandmother settled, he allowed Kate to persuade him to take his own shower. Trace's sweatpants and T-shirt weren't too bad a fit, and Dixon came down to the kitchen after thirty minutes or so looking more like himself.

"I checked on Miss Daisy. She's asleep, with Clark and Marlon curled up beside her. Kelsey's got Cary and I think Trace convinced Audrey they belong together." He leaned his hips against the edge of the counter and took the tall glass of iced tea Kate offered. "So, for the rest of the night…" He squinted at the clock. "All three hours of it…I guess we'll be okay." Lifting the glass, he drained it to the bottom. "That feels good. Thanks." His voice sounded as if it flowed over ground glass, which was probably how his throat felt.

Kate poured him another. "I wish I had something to help you get to sleep. Warm milk? Um… buttered toast? What would make you relax?"

He downed the second glass of tea. "Honestly?"

"Of course."

"Could I hold you for a minute?"

"Oh, Dixon." She'd been afraid to offer him comfort, after Monday. Been afraid to call, afraid of what she'd done to their relationship. "Please." He set the glass down on the counter and she moved into his arms.

Dixon hadn't been sure she would come to

him. He managed not to clutch at her, as he was tempted to do, but simply welcomed her, accepted her against him. And then he sighed. She felt so good. So right. After going through hell the last couple of hours, he needed Kate in his arms as he needed his next breath.

She stirred in his arms, looked up at him, and he thought she would step away. Instead, her hands glided over his shoulders. As she gazed up at him, she cupped his face in her palms, and then pulled his head down, close enough for a kiss.

"Commiserating?" he murmured over her cheek.

Kate shook her head. "Craving," she whispered. "You."

Resistance was impossible. He set his mouth over hers. She tasted sweet, like a ripe and tangy melon, and as refreshing as water from a Rocky Mountain stream.

"Dixon?" She looked up at him, heavy-eyed.

"Shh," he whispered. "Everything's okay."

Kate closed her eyes, then let her head drop forward to rest against his shoulder. "You're right." She sighed. "Thank you." They stayed that way for a long time, in silence.

An argument followed, of course, when he found out she wanted him to sleep in her bed. "I'll be just fine on the couch. Get me a blanket and you won't be able to tell me from a felled log."

She crossed her arms over her chest and shook

her head. "Kelsey might want to come downstairs in her pajamas before you're awake. Miss Daisy is upstairs and might need you. I can sleep with Kelsey—she's got a big bed. You can shut the door to my room and get a decent rest. I'm not taking no for an answer."

He hated it, but he gave in. And his reward for selfishness was to lie down on the softest sheets he'd ever known, with Kate's rose and spice scent surrounding him. The pillow still had a dent from where she'd been sleeping earlier, and he put his head just there, willing to pretend she was right next to him. As he hoped one day she would be.

He heard the door across the hall shut and a squeak that must mean Kate had climbed in with Kelsey. Against his better judgment, Dixon found himself relaxed and ready for sleep.

In the absolute quiet, he realized the radio was on. And the song was "My Dream." He tucked the pillow a little closer under his cheek and closed his eyes.

I really should tell her about that tune, he thought drowsily. *She might be glad to know. Have to do that someday soon. Maybe when she finally says she loves me.*

If she ever did.

TRACE RUBBED HIS HAND over his face as he opened his bedroom door and stepped out into the hallway. When his eyes cleared, he saw Dixon Bell doing pretty much the same thing. Only he was coming out of Kate's room.

Dixon looked at him and grinned. "'Morning. I guess they're playing without us today—I couldn't believe it when the clock said nine. At least the teams'll be even."

"What are you doing in there?" were the only words Trace could come up with.

The other man glanced back over his shoulder. "Sleeping." He looked at Trace again and his grin had disappeared. "By myself. Kate went in with Kelsey." He started down the stairs. "Not that it's any of your business."

Which wasn't true, Dixon reflected as he went toward the kitchen. Trace had a right to be concerned about Kate because he depended on her. The kid had gone through a bad time this year. Only a jerk would deliberately make things worse.

If the shoe fits, wear it.

Kate and Miss Daisy were at the kitchen table with toast and juice. They stopped talking when he came in. "How are you?" his grandmother asked. "That smoke lingers, doesn't it?"

He coughed to prove he was okay and went into an uncontrollable hacking spell. "Yeah," he said when he could breathe again. "I guess it does."

Kate had already poured him a glass of tea.

"What else can I get you? Juice? Eggs and bacon and toast?"

Dixon downed the tea and then shook his head. "My throat doesn't feel much like swallowing. I'll stick to liquids." She refilled his glass and he gave her a smile, watching with pleasure as she blushed. Her shirt was blue and she wore jeans that fit just right. He wondered for a moment if she'd come into her room to change while he was still sleeping.

Which led his thoughts back to Trace. "I think you might need to talk with Trace. He was coming out of his room just as I came out of yours. I'm not sure he was reassured by my honest face."

"Probably not." Kate sighed. "Thanks for letting me know. I will make sure he understands."

"Meanwhile, I'm going back to the house." He set his glass near the sink, feeling like dirt because he'd obviously made things more difficult for Kate.

Miss Daisy stood up. "I'll go with you."

Kate turned and said the same thing he did, at the same time. "No, you will not."

She looked at them in surprise. "And why not?"

"Because it's horribly hot already this morning." Kate put an arm around Daisy and sat her down again. "The house electricity is off, so there's no air-conditioning."

Dixon nodded. "Because you inhaled a roomful

of smoke last night and you don't need to make it harder on yourself just to breathe."

"Because the cats would be distressed if you left, and they don't want to go back to a smoky, hot house when they can be cool and comfortable here."

The cats, of course, were the deciding argument. "You're such a sweet girl." Daisy leaned over and kissed Kate's cheek. "But we can't stay here forever."

"You can stay for quite some time. I probably should've suggested you come over to begin with. You wouldn't have had to deal with plaster dust."

Dixon drew a deep breath. She loved his grandmother, at least. "So that's settled. I'll give y'all a call when I know what's going on." He gave Daisy a kiss and a pat on the shoulder. "Have a good day."

Kate followed him to the front door. "Why do I have the feeling you're not planning to come back?"

Suddenly weary, he let his shoulders slump for a second, but then straightened up and faced her. "Sure, I'll be back. Can't go a day without seeing Miss Daisy's sweet face." He touched a finger to her cheek. "And yours."

"But…?"

He couldn't discuss this with her now. He didn't have enough control. "No buts. You'll probably

see me long before you really want to." Before she
could stop him, he got the door open and crossed
the porch. "Thanks for taking care of Miss Daisy
for me."

Shaking his head, Dixon climbed into the truck.
Talk about miserable behavior...his seemed to be
going from bad to worse. Next thing he knew,
he'd be yelling at anybody who crossed his path,
starting brawls in bars, resisting arrest. Maybe
he'd even kill somebody.

Just like his dad did.

THE TORRES FAMILY didn't eat out much. There
were so many of them, to begin with, and money
was usually tight.

But Saturday morning, after a full workweek,
Mano decided they would make the effort and
have lunch at Charlie's Diner.

Sal was not impressed with the idea. "Why
not go to Pedro's? He's a friend, he won't mind
if a couple of drinks get spilled or the children
get too loud." Los Lobos had done some graffiti
on the Carolina Diner walls last spring. Not the
worst of it, by a long shot—Trace LaRue and his
friends had put up some really nasty stuff and
made it look like Los Lobos. Just another reason
to hate the kid.

Riding high on his own generosity, though,
Mano waved away his son's suggestion. "Char-

lie and Abby Brannon are good people. They'll
be nice to the children and your mama. No tacos
today. We'll eat good American food."

And get dissed by good American bigots, Sal
thought. There would be trouble, he could feel
it. So he didn't have a choice but to go along and
try to make the day special for Consuela and his
brothers and sisters. And head off disaster, if he
could.

They arrived in the middle of the lunch rush
and had to wait for a table. Sal took the children
across the street to the school and they played tag
while Mano and Consuela stood inside. Thirty
minutes seemed like a long delay for the diner, especially when Sal noticed several different groups
of people leaving during that time. But he refused
to believe Abby Brannon would deliberately snub
them. A table for nine just took a while to arrange.

Finally, Mano stepped outside and motioned
them to come in. By the time Sal got the children collected, calmed down and safely across the
street, their parents were seated at a set of tables
arranged in a line down the middle of the dining
room. Getting everybody settled caused a major
commotion. Sal's cheeks burned as he noticed
the glances thrown their way by other customers.
Some of them smiled. Most were annoyed. And
a few were really angry.

Miss Abby managed to take their orders with-

out getting flustered or confused, even when
Christina and Maria changed their minds. The
drinks arrived soon enough to prevent complaints
about being thirsty, along with cheese dip and
crackers. Satisfied, the children behaved nicely
enough. Sal started to relax. Then his little brother
Alex pulled at his shirtsleeve. "I have to go to the
bathroom."

Business taken care of, Sal and Alex came back
down the hallway that ran alongside the kitchen.
They reached the dining room just as the bell
on the door jingled and two men came in. The
first was Mickey, the guy working with Mano on
the Bell house. Mano saw him and lifted a hand.
Strangely, Mickey barely nodded before going to
an empty booth as far across the room as possible.
Mano shrugged and reached for another cracker
to spread with cheese.

The second man was L. T. LaRue. He glanced
around as he followed Mickey, saw the big table
in the middle of the room and stopped cold. Then
he turned back to the booth, jerked his head and
said something that sent Mickey out of the diner
as fast as he could go.

"Come on, Sal, let's sit down." Alex grabbed
his arm and pulled. At the same moment, Sal
watched L. T. LaRue walk toward their table.
"She's gonna bring our food, Sal. Let's go."

They arrived at their chairs just as LaRue

reached the table. "Well, Torres," he said, looking only at Mano. "Seems like life is pretty good for you these days." He didn't have the courtesy to acknowledge Consuela with so much as a nod.

Mano got to his feet. "I have a good job, yes. With a good man."

"So you thought you'd bring all your little rugrats out to show off, I guess."

Consuela gasped. The children were staring at this man who seemed nice enough, yet had said something...they weren't sure what...that caused their father's face to turn red.

For once Mano had himself under control. "Vamoose," he told LaRue, sitting back in his chair. "Get lost."

L.T. didn't intend to be dismissed. He looked again at the long row of kids on either side of the table. Girls...little boys. And at the end, a face he'd seen before. His memory jerked, stumbled, then picked up the ball. "You? You're Mano Torres's spawn?"

The delinquent stood up. "Salvadore Torres," he said with an arrogant shrug.

Mano Torres was back on his feet. "What is this? What are you talking about?" He glanced at his son. "You know this man?"

"I had the pleasure of beating him to a pulp a few months ago." L.T. smiled, until he thought of the reason. "He had his filthy hands all over my daughter. Boy needed to be taught a lesson, I'm sure you'll agree."

Mano and Consuela both turned to look at their son. "This girl you're seeing…is LaRue's daughter?" Mano's voice shook. His fists had clenched.

Sal Torres gave them back stare for stare. "Yes. Kelsey LaRue."

The meaning of that sank in, and L.T. turned on the kid. "What d'you mean, 'seeing'? I told you to get out and stay out. Leave my girl alone. Do you tell me you've been there since?"

Another insolent shrug. "Kelsey's mother doesn't mind."

L.T. balled his fists. She would mind before this day was over. "I told you before, boy, and I'm telling you now. You stay away from my daughter. If I find out you've so much as said hello—and I will find out—I'm gonna hunt you down and kick you around like the dog you are." He turned on his heel, intending to leave.

And found Mano Torres right in front of him. "You touch my son, you will answer to me."

Before he could respond with a punch the way he wanted to, a big hand bearing a Semper Fi tattoo clamped down on his shoulder. The other hand grabbed Torres, and L.T. realized that Charlie Brannon stood beside them.

"Excuse me, gentlemen, but this is my place and I'm not having any brawls. Mr. LaRue, you're welcome to sit down in that booth back there, cool off with a drink. Mr. Torres, your lunch is waiting to be served. Why don't you two just go to your separate corners before things get out of hand?" There was real power in the old man's grip as he managed to shove them apart while letting them go.

Muttering under his breath, L.T. stepped past Brannon and Torres and got out of the diner. Bad enough that Torres had seen him with Mickey, though what had happened between them would probably keep the idiot from remembering that detail.

But he couldn't believe Kelsey was still seeing that kid, against his express orders. Kate had no business ignoring what he said when it came to his children—she wasn't even their real mother. If she thought she could get away with this kind of crap, she'd better think again.

And he would help her with that process.

HALF OF SATURDAY afternoon had passed, and Dixon hadn't come back or called. Kate didn't know what that meant. Miss Daisy and her cats had retired to the guest room for a nap. Trace and Kelsey were watching a movie, and Kate was thinking that maybe a nap would make her feel less drained, less hopeless. At least she could stop thinking for a little while.

Just as she started up the stairs, a sudden squeal of brakes and the slam of a car door drew her back to the window. L.T. was striding across the front lawn. She'd barely gotten turned around when he flung the door open so hard the pictures on either side fell off the wall. Again.

"I want to talk to you." He stalked into the family room and punched off the movie. "All of you." Taking Kelsey's arm, he pulled her up out of the recliner and into the great room. "What do you think you're doing, seeing that kid behind my back?" He let go and she stumbled backward a step, but recovered and straightened up to confront him.

"I care about him. And Kate said I could see him."

"'Kate said I could see him,'" L.T. mimicked in an ugly voice. His face was ugly, too, as he turned on Kate. "You knew how I would feel about this. You lied to me."

Strangely enough, now that the confrontation had come, she felt rather calm. "You didn't ask, L.T. You just assumed we would follow your orders. And since you didn't bring it up, I saw no reason to mention the subject."

"The kid's a delinquent. Do you want her hanging out with a gang? They're probably the ones who tore up my houses last weekend."

"Do you know that for a fact?" She'd read about

the vandalism on his work site in the newspaper, but the article said the police had no suspects. Sal did have connections to a gang, however. And the idea that he'd been responsible had occurred to her. But she wouldn't say so to L.T.

"Makes a lot of sense, doesn't it? His dad's had a grudge against me ever since I had to fire him."

"There are a lot of people in this town who have a grudge against you."

"Yeah, your boyfriend's one of them. And ol' Mano's working for him. I'd say there's a pretty strong link between Bell and Torres and my ruined houses."

"Dixon Bell wouldn't stoop to vandalism. He'll deal with you face-to-face."

"I'll believe it when I see it."

"So open your eyes." Dixon spoke from the entry hall, where he stood with Sal at his shoulder. "And say what's on your mind."

L.T. turned. "What's he doing here?" He nodded at Sal.

"He thought I should know you were heading over to harass Kate and the kids. Given what a foul temper you've got, we were both a little worried you'd be taking it out on somebody smaller than you. As usual."

"This is family business. The two of you don't belong."

Kate couldn't let that comment pass unchallenged. "You're the one who doesn't belong, L.T. By your own choice."

He swung back to her, his hand raised. "Listen—"

Dixon snaked an arm around L.T.'s throat from behind. "Enough." Dragging the man backward, he strode to the front door. Kate followed, brushing past Trace and Sal, and reached the porch in time to see Dixon launch L.T. down the steps and into the grass.

"Get out and stay out," Dixon said. "You've bothered these folks long enough."

L.T. got to his hands and knees, and then to his feet. Kate held her breath, hoping he would simply leave.

Instead, he charged.

Dixon met him at the bottom of the steps. The two men clashed like freight trains moving in the opposite direction on the same track. Grunting and sweating, they grappled for purchase on clothes, on flesh. When they finally fell, they rolled over and over across the lawn, locked together in rage.

"What are you going to do?" Kelsey stood shaking beside Kate. "How will you stop it?"

"I don't know." She thought about the garden hose, but was afraid water wouldn't work. She didn't have a gun.

Sal started past her. "I will."

She caught his arm. "No, you will not. Neither you nor Trace is big enough to get between them." She held him and looked straight into his dark eyes. "Did your gang vandalize those houses?"

He didn't flinch, but regret altered his face. "Yes, ma'am."

She released his arm. "Go home, Sal. Don't come back. And don't call."

"Kate!" Kelsey stepped forward. "You can't do this."

"Yes, I can." She looked at the boy. "Go." And he went, without a glance at Kelsey, giving wide berth to the men still grappling on the lawn.

Neighbors had come out of the houses on either side and across the street. A couple of the men started forward, then were pulled back by their wives. Dixon had L.T. on his back now, and knelt above him, arm drawn back to deliver a brutal punch. L.T. hadn't given in by any means—he had a dirty grip between the other man's legs and sneered up at him.

"Who do you think can deliver the most pain the fastest?"

"I think it's worth the risk," Dixon said calmly. "I've been wanting to beat your face in for weeks now. For years." He drew his arm back another inch. Then his face twisted as L.T. dug in his fingers.

Neither of them had seen Kate approach. She

kicked as hard as she could at L.T.'s shoulder, surprising him into loosening his grip. Then she grabbed Dixon's hand with both of hers, using all her strength against him. "Stop it. Stop it now. Trace has gone to call the police. If you don't want them out here arresting you, you'll both be gone within three minutes."

Dixon stared at her for a blank moment, almost as if he didn't remember who she was. Then his face changed and he pushed himself away from L.T. From her. Stumbling to his feet, he walked stiffly across the grass, climbed into his truck and drove away.

L.T. got to his feet. He looked at Kate and opened his mouth to say something just as a siren sounded in the distance.

"If you're here," she told him, "I will swear out a complaint. Count on it."

He hesitated, with a glance at Trace and Kelsey on the porch, then lurched through the crowd of neighbors to his SUV, gunned the engine and headed down the street just as the police cars arrived.

A police officer approached Kate. "We got a report of a disturbance at this address." He looked down at the bruised and battered grass. "Are you all right, ma'am?"

"Yes. There was an argument." Kate tried for a smile. "But it's over. Everything is over."

CHAPTER FOURTEEN

THERE WAS, of course, hell to pay when Kate got inside the house with Trace and Kelsey. Both of them started talking at once.

"Hush," she told them harshly. "Don't say another word until we're in the kitchen." They managed to obey, but as soon as the door swung shut, they were on her again.

"You just let him leave, when you know he's the one who vandalized those houses? How can you do that?"

"How can you tell him never to call me? I can't believe you would be that mean."

Kate let their protests swirl around her as she poured herself an iced tea, carried it to the table and sat down. Her hands were shaking so badly she had to use both to hold the glass steady when she took a sip. And still the kids pummeled her with words.

"You should've let the cops take them both away. I can't believe we were there on our own front porch watching them slug it out in the front yard, with everybody in the neighborhood standing by."

"You've known he was in a gang all along, so why do you have to get all bent out of shape about it now? Maybe he wasn't even there. Maybe some of the other guys decided to wreck those houses. Just because Sal knew about it doesn't mean he helped them."

Trace turned on his sister. "Oh, sure. Like he doesn't have a grudge against our dad for firing his."

"What are you talking about?"

"Sal's dad worked for LaRue Construction. Dad fired him a few years ago and he hasn't had steady work since. I'm sure the whole family has it in for anybody named LaRue."

"Sal knows this?" Kelsey sat down in the chair next to Kate's.

"He sure does. I told him."

"When?"

"Couple of weeks ago."

"Just about the time he stopped looking for me at school?" She stood up again and punched her brother in the shoulder. "You…you jerk. You couldn't think of any other way to do it, so you broke the news and broke us up." Shoving him to the side, she ran out of the kitchen and up the stairs.

Kate was dealing with the same shock. "Trace,

you're saying Sal didn't know about your dad firing his until you told him?"

"He sure acted like he didn't know."

"And why did you do that?"

"Because he's a pain. What difference does it make, anyway?"

"How can you be so shortsighted? Sal's gang destroyed your dad's houses because Sal blames him for the trouble his family has had these last few years. That makes you responsible for the vandalism."

"No way. I didn't order them to tear up those houses."

"You gave them a reason to do so."

"Torres's dad was the one who couldn't handle the work."

"Mr. Torres does very good work indeed. Your dad didn't want to pay him for the quality he produced. So where does the fault lie, Trace? I'd say squarely on LaRue shoulders—your dad's and yours."

He stared at her for a minute, his jaw hanging slightly loose, as if he wanted to say something but couldn't think what it was. And then he, too, left the kitchen and ran up the stairs with the heavy, pounding footsteps a teenage boy can produce.

Kate sat for a little while in the relative peace and quiet of her empty kitchen, trying to think about what had happened this afternoon, unable to see past the moment and assess the possible outcomes. She was still sitting, head propped on her hands, when Miss Daisy and her feline followers came into the room.

"Well," the older woman said brightly, "that was a lovely nap. Did I miss anything exciting?"

DIXON CALLED Adam DeVries from his cell phone. "Sorry we didn't make it to the court this morning."

"N-no problem. I heard you h-had some real t-trouble last night."

"Yeah. Mostly smoke damage. Kate pointed out that we were going to paint anyway, so it's no big deal."

"G-good way to l-look at it."

"I guess so. Listen, I wondered if there was any possibility that you could take over the work on this renovation project."

"I t-thought you w-w-wanted to do the w-work yourself."

"I did. But the time that'll take is more than I have."

"Why the s-sudden limit? What's g-g-going on?"

"I don't think I'll be staying in town after all. So I'd like to get the house fixed up for Miss Daisy to be comfortable in before I leave."

"W-what about K-Kate?" DeVries might stutter, but he got to the point pretty fast.

"Things don't seem to be working out." That was as much as he could safely say.

"I'm s-sorry to hear th-that. I thought you m-made a good p-pair."

"Me, too. Anyway, can you give my proposal some thought? I'll be willing to pay more to get this job done fast."

"Y-you must have m-me c-confused with L. T. LaRue. I'll l-l-look at the sch-schedule and s-see what I can w-work out."

"Thanks, Adam."

"Sure. But, you know…I c-can't help f-feeling you're wrong about you and K-Kate. You're just what she n-needs. And I know you always l-liked her. You might w-want to reconsider."

"I will. Talk to you later."

He'd reconsider, all right. Probably every day for the rest of his life he would think about the heaven he'd held between his hands and then let slip away, simply because he couldn't control his temper.

Sure, LaRue was asking for a beating, deserved it. But there were ways to defeat somebody like that without using violence. The fact that he'd succumbed to the worst part of his nature just proved that he wasn't good enough for Kate Bowdrey. And if he hadn't managed to be good enough in thirteen years of isolation, what chance was there that another few months would do the trick?

Of course, if he left town he'd be ducking out on Miss Daisy. And she would probably need him more and more as she got older. That was a responsibility he really couldn't abandon.

So maybe he would stay in town and not see Kate. Shouldn't be impossible to manage. She could stay on her side and he would stay on his. Simple.

What he couldn't do was put his heart and soul, not to mention sweat, into this house when Kate wouldn't be living there with him. He'd get DeVries to do the work and keep it for Miss Daisy to live in while she was alive. And when she was gone, he would sell the place and take himself back to Colorado. Buy a spread, raise horses, write songs and turn into a crazy recluse.

Not the life he'd always wanted. Then again, hadn't he known that life was just a dream? "Me lovin' you, it's only a dream. And dreams are for fools…."

THE HOUSE WAS VERY QUIET when Sal got home late Saturday afternoon. He found his mother in the kitchen. "Where are the children?"

She didn't look up from her mixing bowl. "Felicia took them to the library."

"And Papa?"

"He went to the grocery store. He should be back soon." A car door slammed outside the house. "There he is now."

Perfect timing. Sal sat down at the table and braced himself.

Mano came into the kitchen and set the sack he carried on the counter. He glanced at Sal, then looked back at his wife. "They didn't have the kind of sauce you wrote down. I got a different brand."

Clicking her tongue, she looked into the bag and pulled out a jar of enchilada sauce. "This will be okay. Thank you." She smiled and touched his arm for a moment, then went back to the mixing bowl.

"What's going on?" Sal got to his feet. "This scene of domestic bliss is driving me crazy. Where's the yelling? When do I get to hear about how I betrayed the family by dating a girl whose dad fired mine and brought misery to the house? Do I get kicked out, or just ordered never to see her again? Because I can save you the trouble— her mother already told me to get lost."

His dad pulled a beer out of the refrigerator, popped the top and took a long swig. "It sounds to me like you know everything already. I'll save my breath."

Consuela gave him a reproving look. "You can do better than that."

Mano sighed. "Says you." He pulled out a chair and sat down, motioning for Sal to do the same. When Sal hesitated, he rolled his eyes. "Sit. We got stuff to talk about."

Sal sat. And waited for Mano to finish the beer. "So?"

"So...we should've told you I got fired by LaRue. That was probably all it would've taken to keep you away from his daughter."

"Why didn't you?"

"You were twelve. What difference did it make to you? And I wasn't exactly thinking straight at the time." Mano shook his head. "Haven't been for years. Anyway, you didn't know. Can't blame you for that."

"I found out. A couple of weeks ago."

Mano tensed, on the edge of exploding in his usual style. Then he sank back in the chair. "How?"

"Trace LaRue thought it would be funny if I knew."

"Like father, like son. But you were still seeing her."

"It's been harder." Harder to see her, torture not to. "I didn't know what to say. But I didn't tell her, either."

"Now it's all out in the open. Are you still gonna date her?"

"I told you—her mother told me not to come

around or call." He might as spill the rest. "Los Lobos did the number on LaRue's houses last weekend. I'm definitely not welcome there anymore."

"Salvadore." His mother turned to gaze at him, her hands finally still. "You planned that? You participated?"

"Yes, Mama."

Instantly, there were tears on her cheeks. She faced away from him, but he could hear her whispered prayer.

Mano propped his arms on the table. "How'd Mrs. LaRue find out you were involved?"

"She asked me. I didn't lie to her."

"She gonna call the police?"

"I don't know."

"Well, she hasn't yet, or they'd be here by now. What are you gonna do?"

Good question. Sal could only shrug. "I'll finish school, if they let me. Then I'll get a job."

"And Los Lobos?"

"You don't just quit."

"No, you don't. So what," his dad asked again, "are you gonna do?"

Sal propped his elbows on the table and pressed the heels of his hands against his eyes. "I don't know. I honestly don't know."

Through the open windows they could hear the voices of the children as they came along the street, returning from the library. The chance to talk was almost gone.

Mano stood up and put a hand on Sal's shoulder. "We'll figure out something," he said quietly. "I got a little respect left with some people in the neighborhood. If you want out, I'll see what I can do."

"Thanks." Sal turned his head, but his dad had already gone to the front porch to open the door for the children. The weight of his hand seemed to linger, along with a kind of warmth.

It was, Sal realized, the first time in five years his father had touched him with love.

DIXON FINALLY RETURNED to Kate's house about ten-thirty Saturday night, after the kids and Miss Daisy had gone upstairs. "Your grandmother wanted to know when you got here," Kate told him as she shut the front door. "We were worried about you."

Seeing him didn't do much to relieve the concern. He still wore the grass-stained shirt and slacks he'd fought in. In addition to a black eye, there were bruises on his face, arms and hands. Walking stiffly, he headed for the kitchen. "I'll look in on her when I go upstairs. Do you have some ice?"

She wrapped a damp towel around ice cubes and handed it to Dixon as he sat at the table. Then she took out a glass for more ice. "I seem to be pouring a lot of tea these days. Would you rather have something else? Plain water? Milk? Soda?"

He shook his head, then stopped quickly with a hiss of breath. "Tea's great. You make the best I've tasted in a long, long time. If you have some aspirin to go with it, that's all I could ask."

The words echoed in her head as she fetched the aspirin. "All I could ask..." Then she remembered the complete line of the song. "Me lovin' you, that's all I would ask. You're the dream I can't let slip away."

But she felt her own dream slipping away tonight.

She handed Dixon the bottle, only to watch him fumble as he tried to make his swollen knuckles bend. "How many do you want?" she asked, taking the bottle back.

"Let's see what three will do."

Kate turned off the overhead light, leaving the kitchen illuminated by indirect lighting under the cabinets. The atmosphere was similar to last night's. Only the mood was completely different.

"I'd like to apologize," Dixon said finally. "I had no business instigating a brawl in your front yard. There's no excuse for such behavior. I really am sorry to have embarrassed you that way in front of your neighbors. And your children."

"Don't worry about it." She reached for his

hand, but when she covered his fingers with her own, he didn't respond. "L.T. deserved everything he got and more. I wasn't sorry to see you punch him. I stopped you because…" Kate thought back. "Because I didn't want you to hurt him badly. He would have made so much trouble if you had."

Dixon nodded. "Yeah. He's the kind of coward who would sue over a fistfight. Still, my behavior was unacceptable." He made it sound like a Supreme Court judgment—unassailable, irrevocable.

"It's over. Let's move on. You have work to do on the house and we need to think about the city council hearing and how to persuade them to save Magnolia Cottage. Miss Daisy and I were talking this afternoon, and—"

"I've been doing some thinking."

She stopped in surprise, because Dixon rarely interrupted someone else.

"I've decided to let Adam DeVries finish up the renovation. He thinks he can find the time. I'm sure he'll be glad to work with you as far as the details go. In fact, that's probably a good contact for you, if you're interested in expanding this talent of yours into a moneymaking enterprise. Maybe he would like to hire you as a consultant for his clients on that end of the job."

"But—"

"Anyway, I'm gonna hand the job over to him.

I still have to preserve the house, of course, or else there's no point. I can't believe L.T. can buy off the whole council, though I suppose I could be wrong about that."

"I'm confused."

He ignored her. "So then Miss Dixie will have a comfortable house to live in for as long as she needs it, or as long as she chooses. I figure I'll stick around to take care of her. And then I'll probably head west again. These small spaces don't feel so good anymore."

Kate gripped his wrist, and because there was a bruise there, he winced. "What are you trying to say?"

"I guess…I'm trying to say I was mistaken about coming home. About living here. It's not gonna work for me. So I'll settle Miss Daisy and take care of her and then…" He shrugged. "And then I'll go back to my wandering ways. I didn't realize I'd feel quite so tied down in New Skye."

"I don't believe you."

"That's your choice." Getting to his feet, he took his glass to the sink. "I know I told you I love you." He spoke with his back to her. "I wasn't lying, and that hasn't changed. But the marrying part just won't work." His shoulders lifted on a deep breath. "I thought I had become somebody different, somebody you could live with. But I haven't. And I don't think I can."

"I don't want someone different. I want you as you are."

"No, you don't. You want the cool, controlled guy I was trying to be. But what you'd be getting is the dirty fighter, the hotheaded moron who jerked a man out of your house this afternoon and nearly throttled him."

"Dixon, everybody loses their temper. Especially around L.T."

"But when I lose my temper, people get hurt. Like when I worked as a bouncer in a bar in Nashville and put a drunk in the hospital. Or in Amarillo, when I spent a night in jail until the other guy woke up out of a concussion and said he'd started the fight. I've lived with what happens when a man gets angry. I can't do that to you, and Trace and Kelsey. This afternoon was just the final proof."

"What do you mean, you've lived with what happens when a man gets angry?"

"I was three years old when my folks died. There's not a lot I remember about them, except that the last time I saw them, my dad was storming around, angry over something. My mom was doing her own yelling, and there was a lot of anger in the air. But they had to go somewhere, so they stomped out to the car, still snarling at each other. Next thing I knew, they were dead. My dad wasn't paying attention, I guess, took a curve too fast, and went off the road into a telephone pole." One shoulder lifted. "The lesson's fairly clear."

"The lesson that you should pay attention to your driving? Yes, it is." Kate got to her feet and went to stand behind him, laying her hands and then her cheek on his back. "But he could just as easily have been laughing, Dixon. Or sad. Or simply absentminded. Even more important is the fact that you aren't your dad. His accident doesn't have to—won't—happen to you."

"That's what this afternoon was about, Kate. I lost control, like he did. I stopped thinking about anything but getting back at L.T. for all the trouble he's caused me. For the ten years of hell he's put you through. If I'd been behind the wheel, I could just as easily have killed a pedestrian I didn't even see because I was too busy wanting to smash L.T.'s face in."

He stepped away from her touch and crossed to the kitchen door before turning around. "I guess I'm behaving in the most ungentlemanly way possible by rescinding my marriage proposal. I hope you'll forgive me, because I mean it for the best."

She didn't have an answer for him. His feelings went back decades—how could she argue with such intense, entrenched distrust?

And so Dixon left the kitchen. She heard his steps on the stairs, heavier and slower than his usual light tread. He continued down the hall to the guest room, where she heard the door open and shut again almost immediately. Miss Daisy was no doubt asleep.

And then came the distinctive creak of her own bedroom door, the slight rattle of the springs as he sat on the bed. She visualized him taking off the dirty shirt and slacks, pulling on the clean T-shirt and sweatpants she'd left for him. Then the springs again as he stretched out.

Would he go to sleep right away? Or would he lie there thinking about what he had just done?

She spent the sleepless night in one of the recliners in the family room. Somehow she knew that Dixon was awake, as well.

MISS DAISY AND THE CATS stayed with Kate, but Dixon moved back to Magnolia Cottage on Sunday morning after a quick, quiet breakfast. He had never imagined himself turning his back on this woman and walking out of her life, but that's what he was doing. He felt all hollow inside, like somebody had carved out his heart and his guts. Not a pleasant sensation.

When he got home, he heard chopping and tearing noises coming from the yard. Following the sounds, he came upon Sal clearing brush in the same place where he'd been working for weeks now.

Too exhausted, after a sleepless night, to lend

a hand, Dixon leaned against a pine tree. "Pretty hot to be making that much effort."

Sal barely slowed down. "Feels good."

"How'd things go at home? Your parents yell a lot?" Sal had explained about the scene at the restaurant as they drove to Kate's yesterday.

"No. They…understood." He shook his head as if he didn't. "I guess having a job with you really makes a difference to my dad. He's not so furious with everybody and everything these days."

Dixon made a mental note to get Mano a job with Adam DeVries. Seemed like everywhere he turned, there were people depending on him, so he couldn't just cut loose and run.

Even Sal was counting on the money he made clearing brush. "Did Mrs. LaRue say anything about me?"

"Like what?"

Finally, the boy stopped working. He leaned on the handle of the shovel, staring at Dixon as if gauging what his reaction might be. "She asked me yesterday if Los Lobos had vandalized those LaRue houses. I told her yes."

"You planned it?"

"Yes."

"Pretty stupid." Dixon thought for a minute. "Though he deserves it. And a lot more."

"You gave him the 'more' yesterday."

"Yeah. That was stupid, too." He didn't want to

think about it. "So you're wondering if she called the police."

"She could."

"I imagine if she was going to, she would have done it before now. I guess this'll just be a secret everybody knows but L.T."

The sturdy shoulders relaxed a bit. "I won't be involved in that kind of job again."

"I hope not." Good intentions, however, didn't always hold. "I'm going inside. Stop by for a drink and your pay before you leave."

"Yes, sir."

The house reeked of smoke. They'd have to do a lot of cleaning before they could even get back to work. He figured he might as well keep busy until DeVries took over. It wasn't as if he had anything else meaningful to accomplish.

There was still no electricity, so inside was as hot as outside. He was washing down the bathroom walls, wet to the skin from a combination of sweat and shower spray, when he heard car doors close outside. Trace and Kelsey were standing in the driveway when Dixon reached the front porch.

"We figured you still needed to get the yard cleaned up." Trace didn't quite meet his eyes. "So Kate dropped us off. She'll be back about six, if that's okay."

"Sure." He couldn't figure this out. Had he not been clear enough last night? "Sal's working in the same spot. You're welcome to attack where you'd like."

Trace picked up his tools and headed for the opposite side of the house from Sal. Kelsey stood for a minute, chewing her lip, gazing longingly toward the noise in the brush. Then she shook her head and gave him a wobbly smile. "I'll go into the backyard. It's nice and shady."

"Good idea." Dixon watched her march after her brother. Love was tough on teenagers.

Adults didn't have such an easy time, either.

TRACE ACTUALLY ENJOYED hacking away at the underbrush, in a dirty kind of way. Using his muscles, muttering under his breath pretty much nonstop with nobody to hear and get upset about it, destroying the intruders in what had once been a nice garden…there were worse ways to spend a Sunday afternoon.

"Help." At first he wasn't sure he'd heard the word, until it came again, louder. "Help. Help!"

"Kelsey?" He ran to the edge of the grass near the house, looking around for his sister. "Where are you? What's wrong?" If that jerk had finally slipped his leash…

Torres came running from the other side of the house. "Where is she?"

"Kelsey?"

"I'm…in the back by…the…creek."

They headed toward the backyard together. Trace had never been farther than the brick deck, but he could see the weeds Kelsey had pulled lying in a pile at the edge of the lawn. With Torres following, he ran down the path she had cleared.

"Stop!" She sounded as if she wanted to yell and couldn't. "Snakes."

"Oh, man." Trace halted in his tracks, nearly fell forward when Torres braced a hand on his shoulder to keep from running into him. "Go get a couple of hoes," he told Sal. "Shovels. Something sharp. Hurry."

As Torres ran back, Trace started forward again, carefully. "What kind of snakes, Kelse?"

"How should I know?" She took a breath and he could hear it shudder. "Brown. Pointed heads. Nasty."

Cottonmouths, he would bet. "How many?"

"A whole—" another shuddering breath "—nest of them."

As she finished, he came around a turn and saw her. She stood in the tall grass and weeds by the creek. About a foot away was a flat-topped rock in a patch of sunshine. Draped over and under the rock was a coil of coppery reptiles.

"They're mostly asleep," he said softly. "Can you back away? Slowly?"

"No." She'd chosen today to wear shorts, of

course, because it was going to be so hot, and low sneakers. No leg protection at all.

"Why not?"

"Because there's one right by my foot."

"Oh, man," he said again.

Behind him, Torres came down the path. He handed forward a hoe. "Where...? I see. The rock."

"The real problem is in the grass next to her foot. If we startle the snake, it'll strike."

"Yeah." After a minute, he put a hand on Trace's shoulder. "Have you ever watched that guy on TV, the one who captures crocodiles and talks to snakes and lizards?"

"Yeah. So?"

"He gets the snakes to coil around a stick without striking. Maybe we could do that long enough to get Kelsey away, at least."

Trace looked into Sal's dark eyes. "Are you crazy?"

"You got a better idea? We go in there slashing, you already said what'll happen."

"And what's your plan?"

"See if you can coax the snake to crawl up the handle of the hoe. I'll come around behind Kelsey—if you distract the snake, I can get her out of the way."

"This is stupid. I'm gonna end up bit."

Torres flashed a white smile. "We'll drive you to the hospital."

"Thanks." Trace switched the position of the hoe. "Here goes." He eased forward, gave the snake a nudge. The triangular head came up quickly, forked tongue flicking in and out.

Kelsey squeaked. "Shh, *querida,*" Torres said, quietly coming up behind her. "You'll be okay."

Trace extended the handle toward the snake, trying to visualize the TV exploits he'd seen. He stroked the tip of the wood along the reptile's throat and was surprised to see the animal extend itself along the handle. In his direction.

But at least it seemed to have forgotten Kelsey. In another minute, half the snake's body was curved along the hoe.

"Now," he said through gritted, chattering teeth.

In a flash, Torres had swung Kelsey up into his arms and was running away. The snake turned at the movement and dropped back into a full coil–strike position but aimed, for at least a second, away from Trace.

That was all he asked for. He threw the hoe on top of the snake and scrambled at full speed back the way he'd come. Ahead of him, Sal crashed through the grass, bushes, weeds, whatever was in the way. Neither of them cared about anything at that moment except leaving the creek and its residents as far behind as humanly possible.

CHAPTER FIFTEEN

WHEN KATE RETURNED to Dixon's house, she heard no sounds of work in progress, saw no sign of human activity in the drowsy afternoon heat. She'd asked Trace and Kelsey to keep track of the time and wait for her on the front porch, hoping she could minimize the length of her contact with Dixon. With no one in sight, however, she resigned herself to a walk around the side of the house, thinking the troops might have taken another marathon water break.

The scene on the terrace looked more like disaster relief. Kelsey huddled on the glider next to Sal, with his arm around her shoulders and her face buried against his chest. Trace sat in the chair nearest his sister, his worried face turned in her direction. Dixon was just coming out of the house with a pitcher of iced tea and a plate of cookies.

"Hey, you're right on time." He set the tray down on the table. "I'm glad I brought out extra glasses." His tone was casual enough, even friendly. She thought his face looked ravaged, far older than his years. The bruises were the least of his injuries.

Then again, she was feeling wounded today, herself. She walked over to put a hand on Trace's shoulder. This close, she could see that he was pale and shaken. "What's wrong?"

Dixon started pouring drinks. "Kelsey ran into a nest of cottonmouth snakes down by the creek. Sal and Trace very neatly rescued her, but everybody's a little spooked."

"Did someone get bitten?"

"Nope. Well, maybe the hoe Trace says he left down there." Dixon grinned. "Everybody's okay. But I really am sorry." He crouched in front of Kelsey and held up a glass of tea while he looked into her face. "I didn't even think there might be snakes down there. I'll clean all that out by myself so you won't have to worry about it anymore. Okay?"

She shuddered, but smiled a little. "Okay." Taking the glass, she sat up enough to drink it, though Sal kept a protective arm around her.

Kate suddenly remembered her instructions for Sal to stay away from Kelsey. Judging from their faces, Sal and Kelsey did, too. Awkwardly, he pulled his arm back and got to his feet. "I—I guess I'll be going." Then he glanced at Trace. "Good work, man." Slowly, he extended his right hand. "It took both of us."

Trace stood up, hesitated, then gripped Sal's palm with his own. "Yeah, we did all right." He grinned. "Now we just have to figure out how to keep her out of trouble."

Kelsey bounced up. "Don't talk about me as if I'm a—a little girl. Anybody could've run into those snakes."

The boys looked at her with a sort of masculine tolerance, then realized they still had their hands clasped. They both let go quickly and stepped back. Without another word, Sal vanished around the side of the house.

"I didn't see his car." Kate looked at Dixon. "How will he get home?"

"His dad brought him. He may walk—he does sometimes. I've offered to drive him, but..."

"Sal doesn't take handouts." Kelsey carefully wiped her fingers under her eyes. "He's got a lot of pride."

"Which can be good, or not." Dixon turned back to the pitcher and glasses. "Can I pour you a drink, Kate?"

"N-no, thanks." There seemed to be a wire stretching inside her, and she was afraid that if she stayed much longer it would snap. "I think we need to go. Miss Daisy said she would fix supper." But she couldn't just leave it there. She took one step closer to Dixon. "You're welcome to join us. I know she wants to see you."

He took a step back. "Thanks, but I'm too filthy to go anywhere tonight. Tell her I'll stop by tomorrow sometime, when I'm presentable. She can call me on my cell phone if it's important."

"If that's what you want." Kate started to follow her children as they headed around the house toward the driveway, but then she turned to face Dixon again. "You won't be able to cut yourself off, you know. You're too generous and too caring a man. You will be involved. If not with me, then with your grandmother, with the other people you won't be able to stop looking out for. Your passions run deep—anger, yes, but also love and kindness and sincere concern. Denying them won't change who you really are."

She managed to walk away without looking back...until she got to the corner of the house. Then a glance showed her Dixon sitting on one of the lounge chairs, hunched over with his elbows on his knees and his hands covering his face. Kate longed to go to him, to comfort and console and convince him.

Instead, she ran across the grass toward her car.

BETWEEN SATURDAY'S EXCITEMENT, the work he'd done for Dixon, and then rescuing Kelsey from a snake attack, Trace was pretty much trashed when they got home Sunday night. The smell of pot roast followed him up the stairs to his room—

he only hoped he'd be able to stay awake long enough to eat.

A shower loosened up all his muscles. Clean, soft clothes tempted him to climb between the sheets and send the world away, even though his stomach was signaling for food. Before he could make the decision, there was a knock on the door.

"Can I talk to you?" Kate sounded as tired as he felt.

He opened the door and stepped back to let her in. "Something wrong?"

"Not exactly." She sat on his computer chair, so he dropped onto the end of the bed. "But I need to make sure you understand…" Her voice trailed off.

Since Trace was too tired to keep prompting her with questions, he just waited and, after a few seconds, she went on. "I want you to understand about Dixon and…and me."

He looked down at his hands hanging between his knees. "It's your business. You don't have to explain anything."

"No, I don't." When he glanced at her in surprise, he found her smiling gently. "But I love you, and I have to be sure you know that whatever happens with Dixon, nothing will change. For us, I mean—you and Kelsey and me. We're together, no matter what."

Trace swallowed hard and sat for a minute, still

staring at his hands. Then he got up and went to the window, keeping his back to Kate. Blinking hard. "You're gonna get married? To Dixon?"

"I honestly don't know. Not for at least a year, and probably longer."

"You could…live together." He had to force out the last words.

"We won't, though. You and I have talked about that. I think it's a bad idea, no matter what the situation."

"Yeah. But…" No way could he say what he was thinking. Not to Kate.

"Some people do before they get married," she said. Evidently, Kate didn't need to be told what was on his mind. "But until the divorce goes through, I'm married to your dad. I won't betray the promises I made to him. And, contrary to what we see on TV these days, two adults can love each other and yet wait to be together until the time is right. That's something I hope you and Kelsey will remember."

Trace cleared his throat. "Uh, yeah." He searched for a way to change the subject. "But… after…Dixon will want…" What?

"Dixon cares about you and Kelsey. If—*if*— we get married, then he'll become part of our family. We'll all have to make adjustments, and we'll all probably make mistakes. But we'll be together, Trace." He hadn't heard her get up, but she was there behind him, with her hand on his shoulder. "Never be afraid that I'll walk away from you and your sister. As long as I'm able, I'll be your mom, loving you and caring for you in any way I can." She chuckled softly. "You'll probably want me gone a long, long time before I'm ready to let go."

But he didn't feel like laughing. A big, tight ball had just melted inside of him and he was having a hard time breathing. He really needed to be by himself.

Kate seemed to understand that, too. She patted his shoulder and stepped back. "I didn't mean to talk so much. Just know that I'll always be here for you, no matter who else comes into my life. I think Dixon is a very special man, and I know he really likes you, or I wouldn't let him in the house. So…" His door squeaked open. "Miss Daisy's got dinner ready, but you come down whenever you feel like it. I think we'll just take things easy tonight. Okay?"

"Sure," he croaked out. Then the door shut and he could relax. But that had its own drawbacks, and he flung himself facedown on the bed, crying like a baby for reasons he wasn't sure he could name.

The next time he opened his eyes, the Monday-morning sun streamed through his windows, announcing a new and better day.

No ONE COULD SAY Dixon didn't learn his lesson. When he called Miss Daisy on Monday, he told her that the city council hearing on condemning Magnolia Cottage and rezoning the land had been scheduled for the next Monday night.

"That gives us a week," Miss Daisy said. "We have seven days to turn the tide in our favor."

"It's a pretty strong tide." Kate couldn't believe what they were up against. "L.T. has the mayor and at least four council members firmly on his side. That leaves four members who might be un-committed. The mayor votes if there's a tie. How can we win?"

"We'll have to persuade one of the members on L.T.'s side. Who do we have the best chance with?"

"Reese Scot carries L.T.'s advertising on his stations. Roy Calhoun, the banker, wants the money he's lent L.T. paid back. I don't believe they would vote against their own self-interest. Reverend Brinkman sincerely believes we need a public housing project built in New Skye and thinks tearing down an old plantation house to do it is true justice. I can't see any of them chang-ing their minds." She sighed. "Which leaves my father."

"Have you talked to him?"

"Just that once. He has money invested in L.T.'s

company, too. I'd like to think he's objective, but I doubt it."

"Well, then, we'll have to attack where he can be hurt."

"Which is?"

"The ballot box."

And so began the phone calls—to every member of the historical society, to the members of the women's club, to Miss Daisy's book club and the members of their churches. They stressed the importance of Magnolia Cottage as an historic site in the community, talked about preservation and grants for restoration, about civic history and pride. Trace made flyers on his computer announcing a meeting at the historical society building on Saturday, which they posted all over town.

Amazingly, the crowd was standing room only. Kate had invited her father to view the kind of support the people in his district would offer him for conserving Magnolia Cottage. He stood at the back of the room, listening to LuAnne Taylor talk about the history of the town and the part Crawfords and Bells had played in that history. Miss Daisy explained the background of the house itself and a man from the Museum of North Carolina History up in Raleigh—one of Miss Daisy's former Sunday-school students—contrasted their house with others in the area. No private home within a hundred-mile radius could claim the size and craftsmanship and provenance of Magnolia Cottage.

A petition circulated during the talks, and the signatures filled twice as many pages as they'd hoped for. If only half the people who promised to attend the city council meeting actually showed up, there would be no room left for the council members themselves.

"What do you think, Daddy?" Kate joined him in the back corner where he had leaned a shoulder against the wall. "I'd say a hefty percentage of your constituents would like to see Magnolia Cottage preserved."

John Bowdrey straightened up. "What the public thinks it wants and what is best for the community as a whole are not necessarily the same."

"You would support a move that goes against the wishes of the people who vote for you?" She didn't know whether to interpret his disdain for the voters as independence of conscience or personal greed. "They elected you to represent them in city government."

"And I do, to the best of my ability." He put a hand on her shoulder for a second. "I'll think about it, Kate. That's as much as I can promise right now. There's your mother, by the door—I'd better collect her so we can get home and change clothes before dinner at the club."

Kate didn't hold out much hope that her dad's thinking spell would change his opinion, unless Frances had caught the preservation fever and tried to influence him. But he'd given Kate no chance to ask her mother what she thought. Another bad sign.

The phone rang that night and Kate answered warily, expecting a rant from L.T. once he'd heard about the meeting.

But her expectations were wrong. "Hey, Kate." Dixon's voice had regained some of its smoothness after the irritating effects of smoke. "I hear you and Miss Daisy had yourselves quite an event this afternoon."

"There are a lot of people in this town who want to see Magnolia Cottage stay right where it is for another couple of centuries."

"That's good to know. I'm hoping the city council will listen."

"My father was at the meeting today. He's a reasonable man, even if he does do business with L.T. I've got to believe he'll see the value in preserving such an important part of the town's past."

"Well, we can cross our fingers and say a few extra prayers. Speaking of which, is Miss Daisy around? I wanted to ask her about church tomorrow."

Kate fetched his grandmother to the phone and then went into the great room and sat down facing the window, prey to a sudden and overwhelming desperation. From the moment she'd first seen him during that thunderstorm, Dixon had been an irreplaceable part of her life. Just when she'd realized they truly could have a future together, he'd taken that choice away from her. Was she going to let him go? Was there nothing she could do to change his mind?

Miss Daisy came in from the kitchen. "Sitting in the dark, my dear? Are you watching the lightning bugs?" She eased down into the armchair. "Dixon will pick me up tomorrow at nine for church."

"That's good. He really cares about you, Miss Daisy."

"I know he does. And it's good to have him to depend on. But Dixon needs more in his life than just one old woman."

"I—"

"So whatever is standing between you needs to be dealt with and put away."

Kate went to stand by the window. "Dixon erected the barrier. I don't know how to break it down again."

"Do you remember that Christmas-morning feeling? How excited you were to know that Santa had left presents under the tree, and yet you were terrified to go down and see what they were?"

"Oh, yes."

"Actually getting what we want is often frightening. When it comes to relationships, perhaps even more so for men than for women. We expect relationships to work. Men don't."

"You think Dixon is afraid?"

Miss Daisy got to her feet. "I think it's possible that, at the moment when he's about to get everything he's ever wanted, he has convinced himself he doesn't deserve it. Then, if things don't work out, he'll have somewhere to place the blame." She walked to the entry-hall doorway. "Good night, Kate, dear."

"Thank you, Miss Daisy."

The older woman's words of wisdom didn't tell her how to convince Dixon they could build a future together.

But at least she could take comfort from the knowledge that his grandmother believed in her. With Miss Daisy on her side, Kate had to think the odds were in her favor—on this vote, at least.

DIXON HAD JUST FINISHED talking with Adam DeVries on Monday morning when his cell phone rang again.

"Mr. Dixon? It's Sal Torres."

"Hey, Sal. What's going on?"

"I just remembered something I thought you should know about. Saturday, L. T. LaRue wasn't at the diner by himself. He came in with another guy."

"Somebody important?"

"Not exactly. It was Miguel—Mickey. The one who works for you. When Kelsey's dad saw us, he told Mickey to leave. I got the feeling he didn't want them to be seen together."

"No kidding?" Dixon thanked Sal for the information and ended the connection. Mickey had been seen talking with L.T. Now, what would a guy working on *his* house have to say to the man who wanted to tear the place down?

He thought about it all morning while the four of them nailed wallboard over the frame they'd built for Miss Daisy's new closet. About eleven they took a much-needed break. Mano, Mickey and Danny went to sit on the front porch, facing west and still shaded from the sun. Dixon made himself a sandwich, sat at the kitchen table and waited.

A few minutes before noon, the workmen climbed to the second floor and returned to the task at hand. Once the hammering began again, Dixon left the house by the kitchen door and went around to the front porch. There, beside one of the columns, in the flower bed Kate hadn't weeded, he found the soup can he'd provided for use as an ashtray. Not until Sal's call this morning had he realized that Mickey was the only one of the workmen who smoked. So, which of them would have had the opportunity to stuff a lighted cigarette between the walls?

He put the can in his truck, to be taken to the arson investigator if necessary. Then he joined the others upstairs. They almost had the closet walled in.

"Looks good," he commented.

Mickey was holding a piece of wallboard in place, ready for Mano to start nailing. "Come on, man. This thing ain't getting no lighter while I stand here."

"Hold your pants up." Mano was almost ready. "Gotta get this nail gun loaded."

"Hey, Mickey," Dixon said, loud enough to be heard over the sounds of work. "How much were you paid to sabotage this job?"

Mickey jerked his head around, his mouth and eyes round with surprise. His hands instinctively loosened; he let go of the wallboard, which dropped directly onto his feet. Howling in pain, he bent over to grab his toes, then sat on the floor, fumbling at his boots and sobbing in anguish.

Before he could get the laces untied, Dixon grabbed him by the shirtfront and jerked him up again. "I asked you a question. How much did you get paid to ruin my house? To nearly murder me and my grandmother in our beds?"

Mickey squeezed his eyes shut as his whole

body shook and tears of pain streaked his cheeks. "F-f-five…five thousand."

"By whom?"

He swallowed hard. "LaRue."

Hearing what he knew to be true, Dixon tightened his fists around the man's shirt. Rage rushed through him, billowing in a red fog before his eyes. His muscles tensed and he bent his elbows, preparing to shove the focus of his fury up against the nearest wall. Or maybe out the window. Or both.

Your passions run deep—anger, yes, but also love and kindness and sincere concern. Denying them won't change who you really are. From deep inside him, he heard Kate's voice as if she were in the room with them.

As quickly as it had come, the red haze receded. Dixon dragged in a deep breath, then loosened his grip, though he didn't let go. "Listen up, Mickey, my friend. You see those two guys over there?" He turned so they both could view Mano and Danny across the room. "You see them?"

Mickey gulped and nodded.

"Well, they just heard you admit to setting that fire. You're the only one here who smokes, and I've got the butts to prove it. My advice for you is to stay as far away from this house—and me— as you can get. Because if any other little 'accidents' happen around here—like the chandelier, which I'm sure you planned real carefully—I'll be talking to the cops about who had the opportunity and the five-thousand-dollar motive to set that fire. Understand?" The man in his hold nodded frantically. "Good." Dixon pushed him away. "Now, get out."

The three of them remaining in the room listened without saying anything as Mickey hobbled down the stairs and out the front door. The engine of his van fired up, an explosion of sound in the afternoon quiet. Spraying gravel, he sped down the driveway, turned the corner with a screech of brakes and, finally, was gone.

"Whew." Dixon backed up to lean against the wall. "What some folks won't do for a little cash." Mickey might have a family he needed to take care of, just like Mano. Hungry kids would tend to make a man's sense of right and wrong a good deal more flexible.

"We didn't know about it, Mr. Dixon." Mano came to stand in front of him. "I swear, I didn't know he was crooked when I asked him to work here."

"I believe you. LaRue has more people in this town on his payroll than we can begin to imagine. We just have to keep fighting. Speaking of which, are you guys busy tonight?"

Mano and Danny looked at each other and

shrugged. "I guess not," Mano said. "You want us to work?"

"Not exactly." Dixon straightened up. "I want you to come to a meeting."

THE CROWD ATTENDING the city council meeting overflowed the old courthouse, trailing down the steps and onto the grassy lawn circling the building. Signs for both sides were on display—red, white and blue placards proclaiming LaRue Cares About Us and Public Housing Has a Heart versus Magnolia Cottage—Our Past in the Present and Historic New Skye Lives On. As Kate followed Miss Daisy up the steps, there were a number of good wishes sent their way. "We're behind you, Mrs. Crawford." Even, "You go, Daisy." Miss Daisy smiled and nodded to everyone who spoke.

But the other perspective was there, too. "Got that great big house all to herself—rich woman thinks she's better than us."

Kate turned back, but Miss Daisy simply held her hand tighter and drew her up the steps into the courthouse rotunda. "Ignore bad behavior," she said when they could talk face-to-face. "Reward good behavior."

Although the court offices had been moved to a different building, the city council still held open meetings at the courthouse, in an oak-paneled chamber hung with portraits of past mayors of New Skye. Twelve-foot windows framed by maroon velvet drapes looked out on the newly renovated Main Street. At the front of the room, council members would sit in high-backed maroon upholstered chairs behind carved tables. All these relics of New Skye's past had been saved by other people who'd hoped to retain the town's connection with its history. Kate could only hope they would be equally successful tonight.

Dixon had managed to save two seats for them against the pressures of the crowd. Miss Daisy sat next to him, with Kate on her other side. Trace and Kelsey had come along of their own accord, but they had to stand at the back of the room against the wall. On the other side of the aisle, L.T. sat with his arms crossed, looking cool and confident. He must know the odds favored him going in.

Dixon caught the direction of Kate's gaze. "Don't worry," he said, grinning. "L.T. bluffs well. But he'll be the one sweating at the end of the night."

"I hope so."

"Of course he will." Miss Daisy sat with her back straight, looking around with her usual fierce interest. "Right makes might."

At that moment, the council entered through a door in the back corner. Mayor Tate stepped to the speaker's stand in the center and adjusted the microphone while the other members found their chairs. The four members Kate thought would vote for L.T. sat on one side, with her father closest to the center, while the undecided four sat together on the other side. She wondered if the arrangement had occurred by accident or design.

"Ahem." Mayor Tate banged his gavel several times. "Settle down, folks. I call this meeting of the New Skye City Council to order." He examined his papers. "The purpose of this meeting is to discuss a Public Housing Authority proposal to condemn and seize, by right of eminent domain, the property known as Magnolia Cottage for the purpose of building a public housing project for low-income residents of our fair city. First we will hear from the head of the Public Housing Authority, Mr. Jake Tower."

The stereotypical bureaucrat, Jake Tower was short and round and flushed with the heat. He came to the speaker's microphone facing the council table, placed a thick sheaf of papers on the stand, then put on his wire-rimmed glasses.

"Mr. Mayor—" he began, but the mike was too high to catch his voice, forcing him to stop and adjust the arm. "Mr. Mayor, members of the council, I thank you for allowing me the time to address this issue. The Public Housing Authority has been in dialogue with the council for several years now about the need for more public housing to serve the New Skye community. The proposed parcel of land meets all the requirements for government use.

"Moreover, though the contract bidding would, naturally, be open to any builder interested in the project, LaRue Construction, Incorporated, has already submitted a proposal that falls well within our budgetary guidelines while meeting all the relevant code requirements and government specifications.

"In short, I believe the interests of the community and its citizens would be well served by a public housing project developed on the land known as Magnolia Cottage, a former plantation house—a former residence of slave owners. I highly recommended that the right of eminent domain be exercised in this case so that we can proceed with rezoning and eventual construction on that site."

As soon as Tower stopped speaking, a murmur rose from the crowd, rising quickly to a roar. Mayor Tate got to his feet and banged the gavel again. "If y'all can't be quiet, I'll clear this room of every spectator so we can conduct our meeting in decent order. Now…" He consulted his agenda again. "I believe there are citizens from the community who wish to speak in favor of the public housing project."

Dixon had to admire L.T.'s strategy. He didn't

plead his own case—he let others do it for him. A mother with two toddlers clinging to her legs, a baby on her hip and another on the way. A disabled veteran in a wheelchair, followed by a single mother with an adolescent son who would never be able to take care of himself or live on his own. Last, but far from least, an elderly couple surviving on social security checks who had lost two sons in Iraq. All of them made eloquent arguments for a public housing project without needing to say a word. The words they spoke only added weight to L.T.'s argument.

The meeting room was perfectly quiet as the older couple went back to their seats. Curtis Tate let the silence stretch, impressing them all with the emotional impact. Finally, he stood up. "Thank y'all very much for your willingness to come here tonight and testify for what you believe in." He cleared his throat. "Now we will hear from the other side in this dispute, beginning with the owner of the property in question, Mr. Dixon Bell."

More political tactics. Instead of taking a break and coming back with the opposing view, the mayor was forcing Dixon to state his case directly against the persuasive force of the previous speakers.

So be it. He got to his feet and went to the microphone, adjusting the arm to his height. "Mr.

Mayor and council members, thank you for the opportunity to speak. Yes, I do own Magnolia Cottage and the land around it. My family has held the deed to the property since 1832. And, yes, Magnolia Cottage was once a thriving plantation, growing tobacco and food crops and using slaves for labor. I can't change the past. I can only learn from it, and hope to improve the future.

"Today, the fields that were once part of Magnolia Cottage provide space for a tool and die factory that employs two thousand people from New Skye and surrounding areas. A major highway runs across former Magnolia Cottage land, providing access to downtown New Skye from the interstate. There are fifteen individual private businesses along that highway, as well as a new development being built by L. T. LaRue, with house prices running from one hundred fifty to three hundred thousand dollars."

He got a murmur of surprise from most of the audience with that piece of news. "I sincerely believe New Skye needs more public housing for low-income families. But I do not believe that goal can only be achieved by destroying my home, the house my grandmother has lived in all her life. In the last week I've surveyed some of the farm property for sale around this town. I found three parcels that would be equal in size, in convenience and accessibility to what's left of

LYNNETTE KENT347

Magnolia Cottage. Yes, that land would have to be purchased, as opposed to being confiscated from me without adequate payment. But any one of those sites would be perfectly suited to the project the council and the housing authority have in mind.

"I think one issue needs to be made clear here tonight. This is not a case of public service versus personal greed. This is a conflict between government power and individual rights. The council is proposing to take my property simply because it's possible, because it's convenient. Perhaps because someone stands to gain financially by using Magnolia Cottage land for their own purposes." Dixon didn't glance at L.T. But he knew others had.

"I don't believe that's what this country is all about. Some of my ancestors fought a war against that kind of tyranny. Many of you can claim the same. Will we let the government abuse us in such a fashion? If they take my property, what will protect you when they decide they want yours, too?"

He bowed his head for a second, gathering his thoughts for the last push. As he spoke this time, he met and held the gaze of each council member in turn. "I will not allow my land and my house to be seized and condemned. Not without a fight. I will pursue this case all the way to the Supreme Court of the United States, if necessary, before I give up my rights. The city will be tied up in litigation for so many years that we'll never get the public housing we so desperately need. And that would be a real shame."

Dixon let the words echo for a moment, then picked up his single sheet of notes and went back to his seat. Again the room was completely silent.

Finally, the mayor came to the microphone. "We'll take a break now. The meeting will reconvene in fifteen minutes." A couple of gavel blows, and the room exploded with noise.

Miss Daisy reached over and took Dixon's hand. "Thank you." She had tears in her eyes. Miss Daisy never cried. "Thank you so much."

Dixon blinked hard. He didn't usually cry, either. "You're most welcome. I love you."

All around him, people were talking excitedly about what he'd said, what they'd said, weighing the pros and cons and trying to pick a winner. There was only one other opinion, besides his grandmother's, that Dixon cared about. He looked at Kate, lifted an eyebrow in question.

She smiled at him, her hazel eyes shining with pride and...love? "That was magnificent. You couldn't have said it better." Glancing around, she shook her head at all the noise, the crush of people. "Is there somewhere we can get away for a few minutes? I need to talk to you."

His heart did a belly flop. "Talk about what?"

Kate stood up and nodded for him to follow

her. They threaded their way out into the rotunda, where an empty window nook gave them a semblance of privacy.

Then she turned to him and looked up into his face with a serious expression on her own. "Listen carefully," Kate told him. "Because I have a plan."

CHAPTER SIXTEEN

BECAUSE OF THE LATENESS of the hour, when the council members took their seats again, the crowd had diminished and could fit inside the chamber, though it was still standing room only. Trace and Kelsey had found seats near Kate's. She saw, looking around, that Sal and his father were here with one of the other men working on the house—Danny or Mickey, she wasn't sure which. Jessica and Jimmy Hyde were sitting with Candy Scot. Reese, of course, was on the council. The four of them had avoided meeting her eyes throughout the evening.

Pete and Mary Rose came over. "We couldn't get near you before," her sister said as she leaned over for a hug. "But we heard everything. What do you think?"

"I think it's not over." Kate smiled at Pete as he and Dixon shook hands. "Thanks for being here."

"Politics in this town is not for sissies," Pete told Dixon. "You need all the help you can get."

"I'm figuring that out."

Curtis Tate banged his gavel and called for

quiet. "Now we have some speakers in support of Mr. Bell's position. Miss LuAnne Taylor is first, I believe."

Much of what Miss Taylor said was a combination of Saturday's comments. Her brother, Judge Taylor, spoke after her and backed up Dixon's position with solid legal points. The other speakers were equally persuasive, but none of them carried the emotional impact of L.T.'s witnesses. It would be hard to win against such obvious need.

"And finally," the mayor said, looking at his list, "we have Mrs. L. T. LaRue." He gave her the proper title, she knew, so that no one would be confused about exactly who she was. She had thus been established as a traitor, not to be believed.

"Thank you, Mr. Mayor." She'd made notes, but she didn't think she'd need them. "I'm speaking as a citizen of New Skye, as a friend of Mrs. Crawford and Mr. Bell, and, yes, as one who has an interest in preserving and restoring Magnolia Cottage. I have a great deal of sympathy and concern for the people we heard speak on behalf of the housing project. As a community, we have ignored this situation too long, and we should seek a quick and sufficient remedy.

"But not," she continued over some audible gasps, "with the Magnolia Cottage property. We shouldn't sacrifice our past for expediency or for personal gain." She allowed herself a glance at

L.T. "That land and the house standing on it represent the history of New Skye, for better and for worse. Yes, Magnolia Cottage was a plantation house, and that plantation used slaves as its labor force. We need to remember, precisely so that something so dishonorable will never happen again. Building on that land will not erase the wrongs done there. Like the Holocaust Museum in Washington, we need a place to document and recall the mistakes of our ancestors so that the future can be free of their shadow.

"I, therefore, have a plan to propose. First, I suggest that Mr. LaRue locate his project on another tract of land, aided by monetary donations from some of New Skye's most affluent citizens. Including, of course, Mr. Dixon Bell."

Some of New Skye's most affluent citizens, L.T. and several council members among them, started shaking their heads. Kate swallowed hard and moved on.

"Second, I would propose that Mrs. Crawford be allowed to reside with her family in Magnolia Cottage for the remainder of her life." She turned and smiled at Miss Daisy. "I'm expecting to celebrate her hundredth birthday in a couple of decades or so."

"Thirty more years, at least," Miss Daisy said strongly.

"In the meantime, Magnolia Cottage could

be restored to its original antebellum condition. There are grants that would help in this process available from historic organizations interested in preserving landmarks, as well as what Mr. Bell is personally prepared to contribute. The house can be registered with the National Trust. The grounds can be improved and restored...all with the idea that at a future date, the entire property, house and land, will be donated to the city of New Skye for use as a public museum of history and a community park."

She had their attention, Kate was glad to see. Especially her father's. "The details would have to be worked out, of course. But I would imagine a trust fund could be established to provide for maintenance of the building and the grounds. Thus, Magnolia Cottage could be a public property, maintaining a direct connection with our past."

Shaking, now that she was finished, she eased her way across the aisle to her seat. When she reached Dixon, she had the urge to collapse into his lap and hide her face against his shoulder. But she gritted her teeth and moved on to her own chair.

Mayor Tate sat silent, staring straight ahead with his eyebrows drawn over his eyes, for a long moment. No one else in the room made a sound. Finally, he stirred.

"Mr. Bell."

"Yes, sir." Dixon got to his feet.

"Did you know about this…plan…of Mrs. LaRue's?"

"Yes, sir, I did."

"And what is your opinion?"

Dixon moved to the microphone. "The plan has my support, and that of my grandmother. I had anticipated living the rest of my life in Magnolia Cottage, but—" he looked down for a second at his hands resting on the speaker's stand "—you never know how life's going to turn out. I am quite willing to abide by Mrs. LaRue's suggestion that we donate Magnolia Cottage to the city as a museum and park. When my grandmother no longer has need of the house, of course."

"What about donating to the purchase of another property?"

"I think all of us in the city who have more than we need ought to support this cause. I'll be first in line with my checkbook."

"Well." Curtis Tate sounded tired. "The city council will now retire into closed session to discuss the matter. If we can come to a conclusion within a reasonable time—" he looked at his watch "—say, by midnight, then we will come back and announce the decision. If not, we'll postpone our deliberation for further discussion."

"They can't keep us hanging," Mary Rose said

as she and Pete sat down in the row behind Kate. "Surely it's not hard to see who has the best idea. Y'all are brilliant, coming up with the museum plan."

"Kate gets all the credit," Dixon said. "It's her brainchild from start to finish."

"Let's just hope they see the sense of it." Kate was afraid to be more optimistic. "Otherwise…"

"Otherwise, they'll have a fight on their hands," Dixon promised. "And by the time I'm finished, they'll wish they'd never heard of L. T. LaRue."

The next minutes dragged like hours. No matter how many times Kate glanced at the clock, its hands never seemed to move. Miss Daisy went to get a drink of water with LuAnne Taylor and the judge. Trace yawned, put his arms on his knees and his head on his arms, and fell asleep. Kelsey had been perfectly quiet all night, but Kate noticed now that her hands were twisting and turning in her lap. Figuring out the source of her agitation required little thought—Sal stood across the room, and in the few moments Kate watched, he had glanced at Kelsey several times.

She put her hand over her daughter's. "Go talk to him. Stay in this room, but find yourselves a place to sit."

Kelsey's eyes filled with tears. "His dad will yell at him."

"I'll talk to him." Dixon stretched to his feet. "I

doubt he'll make much of a fuss." He went to sit by Mano Torres and the other man, and though Sal's father frowned at first, in another moment he shrugged and gave his son a nod of agreement, if not outright approval. Like two magnets of opposite charge, Sal and Kelsey immediately connected in the center of the room and sat down with their heads close together. The rest of the world had ceased to exist for them. L.T. watched from his seat across the aisle and was obviously upset, but he couldn't afford to make a scene—not to mention come across as the bigot he was—in front of his friends and supporters.

"Are they having problems?" Mary Rose had been living with Kate and the children last spring when Kelsey and Sal first became involved.

"Sal's father and L.T. just found out that they've been dating. Neither one was happy about it." She couldn't tell her sister about the vandalism because she couldn't ask Mary Rose to keep a secret from her new husband. And as a state trooper, Pete might feel compelled to report what he knew. "So Sal hasn't been around for a while. They've missed each other."

"I can imagine. What about you and Dixon? Are things any better there?" Mary Rose glanced in his direction. "I have to say, he's not looking very well."

"He's staying in the house, working all day

with no air-conditioning. I don't think he's eating enough. And, no, things haven't changed." Under her breath, she added, "Yet."

Midnight came...and went. Five minutes past, then ten, then fifteen. The tension was unbearable, the fatigue even more so. Kate thought she might fall asleep. Or simply pass out. Dixon returned to sit beside her, his face becoming more strained with every minute. Only Miss Daisy remained calm.

"The longer it takes them, the better for our side," she assured them all.

At 12:27, the door to the council chamber opened and the members returned to the room. Try as she might, Kate couldn't read their faces. Not even her father's. She had no way to prepare for what would be announced.

The faithful remaining few filled in the first three rows of the meeting-room chairs and sat down quietly without the aid of the gavel. When the mayor stood, he had nothing to do to get their attention but clear his throat.

"Ahem." He looked down at the paper in his hand and hesitated—the first hint Kate got that he might not like what he had to say. Instinctively, she reached for Dixon's hand. His fingers closed tight around hers.

"Ahem." Curtis drew a deep breath. "After much discussion and debate, the city council announces that by a vote of five to four…" He shook his head, quite clearly reluctant, and Kate started to smile. "By a vote of five to four the proposal to seize and rezone the Magnolia Cottage property for the construction of public housing has been… denied. The council will further consider the plan to create a museum and park from the property at a later date. Session adjourned."

The explosion of joy was instantaneous and tremendous. Everyone hugged everyone else, there were kisses all around. In the midst of the frenzy, Dixon swept Kate up against him.

"Thank you." His kiss was more than grateful, more than apology, more than reconciliation. "I love you so much. Thank you."

He set her down again when someone else claimed his attention, though she could barely stand on her shaky knees. A hand fell on her shoulder and she turned to find her father there. "Well, Kate, you got what you wanted."

"You voted with us, didn't you?" He nodded and smiled. "Thank you, Daddy." She gave him the hug he deserved. "This is so wonderful."

"I was powerfully persuaded by Mr. Bell's argument. And by yours." Her father reached out and stroked her hair back from her face. "You would have made a fine lawyer, Katherine Ann. I find myself quite sorry that L.T. denied you the chance." He shook his head. "Now, I'll go home and tell your mother, and perhaps she'll stop nagging me. I've heard about nothing else but this meeting since Saturday afternoon."

Kate watched him leave, unable to stop smiling even if she wanted to…until L.T. stepped in front of her.

"The Bowdreys always get what they want in this town. That's why I thought it would be good being married to you."

She didn't have the patience for this tonight. "Oh, why don't you shut up, L.T.? I am so tired of hearing you whine."

When she turned her back on him, his hand on her shoulder jerked her around again. "You listen to me—"

Like an ax, Dixon's hand chopped through the air in front of Kate. Groaning, L.T. dropped his arm.

"You listen to me." Dixon put himself between Kate and L.T. and the rest of the crowd, blocking their view and their ability to hear what he said. "If you threaten Kate or your children or my grandmother or me ever again—no matter how slightly—it'll be the last time. Because if you do, I'll go to the police with the evidence I have about exactly who started the fire at my house. I'll take along the two witnesses standing right over there." He nodded to Mano Torres and Danny. "Both of them heard the arsonist confess that he'd been paid to do it. By you. You've been seen meeting with the guy in public, LaRue. This is not a rap you can beat. So you'd better be on your best behavior. Otherwise, you're gonna be building with Tinkertoys in the state prison. Got it?"

L.T. stepped back, glanced once at Kate, and then left the room. His supporters had already deserted his sinking ship, which left the meeting room in the possession of the victors for an impromptu and heartfelt celebration.

"What a day," Miss Daisy commented later as they walked carefully down the steep courthouse steps, finally headed for home. "I'm quite ready for a good night's sleep. At least we don't have eviction hanging over our heads for a change."

Dixon walked them to the Volvo and opened the front passenger door. "Things will settle down now, I'm sure. I don't know exactly when the house'll be ready for you to come back, but I think you're safe where you are." He looked at Kate across the roof of the car, a question in his eyes.

She smiled at him. "Of course. For as long as it takes."

"So you just relax," he told his grandmother as he tucked her into the seat. "I'll check in with you tomorrow."

Trace had dropped down into the seat behind

Miss Daisy. "Basketball next weekend," Dixon asked.

He got a yawn as an answer. "Sure."

Kelsey and Sal had lingered behind. Kate gestured for them to hurry up. "Come on, Kelsey. We need to get home. Tell Sal we'll talk about things tomorrow. Though I don't know what I'm going to do," she said more quietly to Dixon. "He's the leader of a gang. I don't think I can pretend anymore that it doesn't matter. Not after—" She stopped, realizing she hadn't told Dixon about the vandalism.

"I know. He told me."

"Ah. Well, if you have any insights, pass them along. I could use some help." Kelsey came running up and got into the car. "That's it, then." Once more, she met his gaze across the roof. "I'll see you…later."

"Sure." He watched her get into the car and start the engine, then turned to walk toward his truck, shoulders bent, steps heavy and a little slow. Not the walk of a man who had just won a major victory.

But then, Kate didn't feel that she'd won, either. *Not yet.*

L.T. WENT TO HIS OFFICE. There wasn't any sense going home to tell Melanie that he'd lost the fight, because Melanie wasn't there anymore. She'd taken off to visit her sister in Atlanta, so the note said, and wasn't sure when she'd be back. Given that she'd taken every stitch of clothing she owned with her, L.T. didn't expect to see her again, period.

He would miss her. She was a sweet girl. But he didn't mind not having to explain the mess his life had become. Dixon Bell knew he'd hired Mickey to screw up the work. L.T. hadn't specified arson in his instructions, but that wouldn't matter to the cops. And he really didn't want to end up in jail.

He'd thought the kids would come over to his side if he gave them more time, spent more money. That hadn't happened. He'd lost there, too. Lost all the way around. This was the point where some guys pulled the pistol out of their desk and blew their own brains out. The idea held a certain appeal.

Whatever he was, though, L. T. LaRue was not a quitter. There was still money to be made in this town. He could still use his plan to pad the government contract for public housing. He'd just have to use a different piece of land. And Kate had suggested he could do that at Dixon Bell's expense. Now, *there* was an idea that appealed to him. Play on Bell's guilt and sympathy and milk him for more than the actual value of the land. Certainly worth a try.

DIXON SAT alone in the dark, watching the fireflies dance in the trees, listening to Evan Carter's latest album. He'd written several of the songs, though the hot one right now was that first release. Still going strong, he'd heard from his agent. Royalties were looking real good.

He would probably need them, along with some of his investment money. L.T. would try to cheat him on the public housing project—push him to take on the biggest share of the liability, inflate the price of the land and somehow attempt to pocket the excess. Dixon didn't think he had the energy left for another big fight. Maybe he'd get a lawyer to deal with this one.

Out in front of the house a car door shut, loud in the quiet night. Heart pounding, Dixon got to his feet. There couldn't be too many people who'd choose to visit at two in the morning. DeVries, maybe, coming to celebrate? Or…

She came around the corner of the house, wearing something white that made her look ethereal, unreal. "Kate?" He had to clear his throat and say it again to be heard. "Kate?"

"Hi. I should have called to warn you, I guess, but I thought you might have left your cell phone in the truck." Her words blended with the summer night's breeze, soft and seductive. He remembered that he still hadn't written that song about a woman's voice. He'd been too torn up recently to write more than his name.

Like the figment of his imagination he half feared she might be, Kate glided across the terrace, getting nearer with every silent step. "I'll go away again if you want me to. Just say the word."

"I—no. Here, have a seat." He pulled up a wrought-iron chair. "Would you like a drink? I've got water in the house." He turned toward the door.

"No, don't." She caught him by the hand. "I'm not thirsty. Really. Sit down."

Because he couldn't think, he followed orders and sat down again on the lounge chair. "What are you doing here?"

Her face was pale in the night, her eyes and hair dark. She smiled. "I came to see you. No, actually, that's not true. I came to do this."

She kissed him. Desperately, thoroughly, until neither of them could think. The garden was quiet for a long time.

"I need you so much," she whispered at last, her head on his shoulder. "You made me depend on you, count on your friendship and advice. I need your laugh and the twinkle in your eyes."

He smiled as his right hand stroked along her arm, her shoulder, the sweet curve of her throat to cup her face.

"You can't send me away," she continued. "I

won't let you. You taught me to love you. Please let me."

Both his arms were around her now.

"I love you," he whispered conversationally. "Did I mention that?"

She snuggled against him. "Not recently enough. I love you, too, in case you didn't catch what I said."

"Oh, I caught it." His deep breath was a little shaky at the memory.

"Good."

As if on cue—and with all the magic this night held, Dixon wouldn't be surprised to know a fairy had arranged it—the Evan Carter album started over with "My Dream," the first cut.

He sat there trying to think of how to explain, and realized Kate was humming the tune. "You like that song?"

"What woman wouldn't? It's such a beautiful idea—that a man could love a woman with tenderness and strength and courage." She reached up to touch his lips with her finger. "The way you love me."

"Ah." Deep breath. "I wrote it. For you."

Kate went absolutely still in his arms. "What did you say?"

"It's my song. And I wrote it thinking about you."

"But—" She sat up straighter, out of his hold,

and stared at him from the end of the lounge chair. "It's Evan Carter singing."

"Yeah. I'm not good enough to hold the spotlight. I let those other guys take over with the audience. I just give them the words and tune." He stared at her anxiously, trying to gauge her reaction. "Do you mind very much? I make pretty good money doing it."

Kate wasn't sure what she thought. Her mind whirled, her heart was taking leaps and somersaults inside her chest, her hands and knees shook with excitement, with fear. All along, she'd been in love with the man in that song. And now here he was and he wanted her—could she live up to those expectations? Was she the person to inspire such a gracious, generous love?

She gazed at Dixon, noting his tousled hair, his wide, worried eyes, the firm, delicious mouth. She loved him with all of herself. If she wasn't enough now, then…she would just have to become more. And that would be possible, with *him*.

Kneeling on the chair, she took his hands in hers. "Will you marry me?" He opened his mouth, but she rushed on. "I know I'm not free until next spring, and I probably should wait even longer, just for decency's sake. Is there a period of mourning for divorce? It can't be a year. I couldn't possibly wait another year. But I have to ask you to wait until then because of the kids. I would like them to think that marriage is special." Kate drew a deep breath. "If it's too much, I'll understand. I just hope—"

She had to stop because Dixon had put his hand over her mouth. "Yes," he said, grinning at her. "Yes, I'll marry you. Yes, I'll wait a year or more to be with you, because it's important to abide by your beliefs and standards. Yes. Yes. Yes."

They kissed again, to celebrate their future.

CHAPTER SEVENTEEN

THE DIVORCE WAS FINAL in May but they waited until the third weekend in September to have their wedding. The church was filled with gold and white chrysanthemums as well as most of the inhabitants of New Skye.

"This dress is so cool." Kelsey twirled in front of the floor-length mirror in the bride's room, watching the layers of leaf-green chiffon float around her. "I think I'll wear this to the prom next year."

"That's a first." Mary Rose was holding Kate's flowers as her sister put on her hat. "No one ever wants to wear a bridesmaid's dress in public after the wedding. But they are lovely, Kate. Thanks for choosing something even a pregnant lady can look good in."

Kate smiled and kissed her sister's cheek. "You are only three months along and barely showing. Does the hat look right?"

"Perfect."

"Well, then." Kate hesitated, feeling the butterflies in her stomach take flight. "Kelsey, run and tell them I'll be there in just a moment."

Her sister came close and put cool fingers on her cheek. "Are you okay?"

"Yes." She looked around for a chair and sank onto it. "I just need a minute. All at once..." Tears burned her eyes. "Oh, Mary Rose, I'm so afraid."

"Afraid?" Mary Rose knelt beside her. "Honey, this is Dixon waiting for you. There's nothing to be afraid of."

"What if—" The words couldn't be said.

Mary Rose got to her feet and drew Kate to stand, too. "This man has gone through hell to be with you. He only wants to make you happy. What do *you* want?"

"I want him to have everything he wants."

"Sounds like the perfect recipe to me. Just give, Kate. You're so good at that. This doubt you have about yourself...I'd kill L.T. if I didn't think it was more punishment for him to stay alive. Be yourself. You and Dixon between you can create all the joy you'll ever need."

"Kate?" Kelsey stuck her head in the door. "Are you coming?"

She didn't really have a choice. Not if she loved Dixon Bell. "Yes. I'm right behind you." Then she turned back to Mary Rose. "Is my face all right?"

"Fine."

"Do you know how much I love you?"

"Almost as much as I love you. Now let's go."

EVEN AFTER A year of restoration work, Magnolia Cottage was in no shape to host a wedding reception. Miss Daisy and the cats were staying at LuAnne Taylor's house until the interior of Magnolia Cottage was completed and Miss Taylor, generous to a fault, insisted Miss Daisy ask her grandson to celebrate his marriage in the Taylor garden. The day of the wedding turned out to be an absolutely perfect September afternoon.

Dixon managed to mingle with all the assorted guests, but rarely let Kate completely out of his sight. He couldn't quite believe she was his wife, this exquisite woman in a soft-gold suit with a small hat of the same color perched on her curls. Around Christmastime last year she'd asked him if he would mind if she cut her hair. Since it was her hair, he hadn't ventured an opinion one way or the other. But the shorter length freed her curls to bounce around her face, made her look less fragile, happier, somehow. He was delighted. More important, so was Kate.

"She's not going to disappear." Pete Mitchell handed him a glass of punch. "I've got the place surrounded by troopers."

"Thanks. Sometimes good luck is hard to believe, you know?"

"I do." He put an arm around his wife as she joined them. "Feeling okay?"

"Perfect. I can't believe Evan Carter is a friend of yours, Dixon. He's got to be the biggest star in country music today. And he's going to sing at your wedding?"

"That's what it looks like." Evan had joined the band on the stage built under Miss Taylor's oak trees. "I think I'll claim my wife for this dance."

Kate turned from her parents when he took her by the hand, and came willingly into his arms. "Can we leave now?" she sighed, resting her head on his shoulder. "I've talked to everybody twice."

"Soon." The violin player started in on "My Dream." "It's about time we danced this waltz together."

The song was a sweet interval, over too quickly. Someone asked to cut in, and another someone swept Kate to the other side of the garden. Dixon waited as long as he could bear before deciding the rest of the party would have to get along without them.

He pulled Kelsey away from Sal, drawing her back into the shaded allée along the side of the Taylor house. "Send Kate over here, please. And Miss Daisy. Don't say anything to anybody else."

"You're leaving? Don't you want us to throw bird seed?"

"You and Trace and Sal can throw seed. Let's just keep it secret."

Kate, his grandmother, and the kids joined him in another minute. "What's wrong?"

"Not a thing." Dixon took her hand. "Let's go."

"But—" Kate cast a glance behind them. "You're right. Let's go." She turned to Miss Daisy. "Thank you so much for everything. You've made this day just perfect."

"Thank you, dear, for making my grandson a happy man." Miss Daisy returned Kate's hug, then stepped back and dabbed her eyes with a lace handkerchief. "Now, you two run on. The children and I will see you when you get back."

Dixon bent and kissed her cheek. "I love you."

She laid her hand along his jawline. "You're everything a man should be, son." Dropping her hand to his shoulder, she gave him a little shove. "Now go, before they catch you!"

With only a few handfuls of bird seed showering them, they ran down Miss Taylor's front walk and jumped into the limousine just as the rest of the crowd came around the corners of the house. They could hear the rain of seed on the roof as a few of the younger men caught up before the limo reached full speed.

"An excellent idea, getting away." Laughing, Kate pulled off her hat and combed her fingers through her hair. "My smile feels permanently stretched."

"Did you get anything to eat or drink?"

"Not a crumb or a drop, except that bite of cake you fed me."

"Well, I think we have some provisions in here." He opened the refrigerator and took out flower-sprigged baskets in which all kinds of delectable food were cradled by damask napkins. "This all looks terrific."

Kate nodded, bit into some kind of little tart and chewed for a second, her eyes closed in pleasure. "Mmm...crab. Cass Stuart is the best caterer in the state, if you ask me."

They had an hour's drive to get through. This was an important night, though. The beginning of the rest of their lives.

And so they ate the hors d'oeuvres they'd missed at the reception, and talked. About Sal's graduation from high school and his new job at one of the garages in town. About his divorce from Los Lobos and his adoration of Kelsey. The next problem would be convincing her to go away to college while Sal stayed at home. But tonight wasn't the night to worry too much about that.

They talked over Trace's improvement in school, his performance on the basketball team last winter and his place on the varsity football team this fall. Miss Daisy was busy researching

Magnolia Cottage history and planned to write a book for the future museum to offer. Dixon's horses were happy and healthy at Phoebe Moss's farm, though Cristal still had manners to learn when it came to taking a saddle and rider. Magnolia Cottage would be livable before Christmas, and they'd already agreed to look for another old house they could restore when the time approached to leave this one. All the good things in their lives had finally come together.

They reached the Moseby House Inn just after dark. Kate stepped out of the limo and looked around in amazement. "Oh, Dixon, how wonderful. I'd hoped this was what you had planned."

Following her out into the cool night air, Dixon breathed a sigh of relief. They'd been here a few times to eat, but he'd kept his wedding-night plans a secret from absolutely everyone, including Kate. No cute surprises, no bawdy jokes waiting for them in their room. He wanted this honeymoon to be perfect.

And he wasn't disappointed. The staff noted their arrival without any fuss and got the bags put away while they were still admiring the entry hall. Like guests in a private home, he and his wife—his wife!—were escorted upstairs and left alone with a gentle wish for a good night.

I hope so, Dixon thought. *I hope so.*

"Look at this desk, and the table…and the fabrics are gorgeous." Kate walked across the room, admiring the eighteenth-century furniture, both reproductions and antique pieces. "I love this room. The flowers are fabulous, aren't they?" She looked at the card, which he'd signed with just his name, then smiled at him. "Thank you. They're perfect. You know how much I love yellow roses."

"You're most welcome." Somebody or something had wrapped a vise around his throat. He had no idea what to do next. "Would you like some dinner? I made late reservations."

She was gazing out the window overlooking the garden, but at that she turned to look at him. "Are you hungry?"

"Are you?"

His voice must have given something away, because she smiled and moved toward him. "Dinner can wait." Her arms came around his neck. "I love you, Dixon Bell. And you love me."

"I do, indeed. For now…" He folded her close to him. "And for always."

Just before dawn, as night leaves the sky,
I reach for your hand, then open my eyes.
I still can't believe my dream has come true,
But your kiss drives the last doubt away.

Me lovin' you—it was only a dream
And dreams are for fools, so they say.
Me lovin' you—I have all I could ask.
You're the dream I won't let slip away.

* * * * *

HEARTWARMING INSPIRATIONAL ROMANCE

Contemporary,
inspirational romances
with Christian characters
facing the challenges
of life and love
in today's world.

**AVAILABLE IN REGULAR
AND LARGER-PRINT FORMATS.**

For exciting stories that reflect traditional values,
visit:
www.ReaderService.com

Love Inspired® SUSPENSE

RIVETING INSPIRATIONAL ROMANCE

Watch for our series of edge-
of-your-seat suspense novels.
These contemporary tales
of intrigue and romance
feature Christian characters
facing challenges to their faith...
and their lives!

AVAILABLE IN REGULAR
& LARGER-PRINT FORMATS

For exciting stories that reflect traditional values,
visit:
www.ReaderService.com